JGAN

Amy Cross is the author of more than 100 horror, paranormal, fantasy and thriller novels.

OTHER TITLES
BY AMY CROSS INCLUDE

The Dog

AMY CROSS

First published by Dark Season Books,
United Kingdom, 2017

ISBN: 9781521901939

Also available in e-book format.

www.amycross.com

CONTENTS

§

PART TWO

THE
DOG

AMY CROSS

PART ONE

AMY CROSS

CHAPTER ONE

IT STARTS SUDDENLY ONE MORNING, WITH no warning.

Dozing at the foot of Jon's bed, I'm not quite awake but not quite asleep either. I'm just waiting for him to stop snoring and wake up, so that we can go outside. Sunlight is already streaming through the window, and the air is alive with the scents of morning. Even though my eyes are barely open, my nose is already wet and twitching, picking up on all the different smells that fill the air. And the other sense, the weird human noise that constantly hums in the background, is all around us as usual.

And then suddenly the background buzz stops.

I open my eyes and raise my head.

Silence.

After a moment, I look over at the small black object that Jon always keeps next to the bed. Sometimes he speaks into it, too, and it always emits a faint crackling buzz that I don't think he can hear. Right now, however, that buzz has suddenly stopped. I look over toward the open door that leads into the kitchen, and I realize that the entire cabin seems to have fallen completely still. Silence, the kind of silence that never really happens around humans, is suddenly everywhere. With Jon still asleep, I figure it wouldn't be fair to disturb him, but still...

Rising from my warm patch on the blanket, I take a moment to stretch and then I jump down onto the floor. I glance back at Jon to check that he's still sleeping, before walking through to the hallway and then into the kitchen. Again, the background buzz – the buzz that usually crackles from all the plug sockets, and that fills the air even out here away from the city – is suddenly and inexplicably absent. It's as if someone somewhere hit a giant switch and turned the rest of the world off.

Even out here at the cabin, there's usually some trace of the buzz. In the city especially, humans seem to love surrounding themselves with objects that emit a faint electrical hum. They put these objects everywhere in their homes, they screw them to their walls, they carry them in their pockets, they seem to enjoy bathing in this vast, crackling field of electrical noise. Sometimes I think they don't even notice the sound, which wouldn't surprise me since their hearing never seems to be up to much. But for me, the buzz is much more noticeable. Whatever it is, it seems somehow artificial and constructed, as if it's something the humans have made.

And now it's gone.

Heading over to the glass door, I peer out through the panel and see the forest spreading out far beyond the cabin. In the distance, I can just about see the city down in the valley, and I can immediately tell that something is different. Even up here, miles from the city's sprawl, I can usually pick up on the buzz and din of all those people packed together so tight, but this morning the whole world seems so much quieter. And the electrical buzz has disappeared from the air all around us.

Something has changed.

Something big.

Behind me, a floorboard creaks.

"Hey, buddy," Jon says wearily as he comes through from the bedroom. "Need to go out?"

He pats my flank as he unlocks the door and slides it open. I immediately step out onto the porch and then I stop again at the top of the steps, sniffing the air in an attempt to work out exactly what is happening.

"Goddamn phone," Jon mutters.

Turning to look up at him, I see that he's frowning as he fiddles with the black device. He seems a little irritated by it, perhaps because it's no longer emitting that constant, droning buzz, but finally he shrugs and sets it on the table before glancing at me with a smile.

"Well, I guess we *did* come up here to get away from civilization for a few days," he says with a sigh, reaching down and briefly stroking my side before turning and heading back inside. "I'm gonna put a pot of coffee on, and then after breakfast how about you and I

7

go exploring down by the lake? Julie won't be here until later anyway."

Once he's in the kitchen, I sit at the top of the steps, not wanting to go too much further until I figure this out. My eyes are fixed on the distant city, and I can't shake the feeling that something must have happened down there. The wind is blowing in the wrong direction for me to pick up any scents that might help, but the whole city somehow seems to have been switched off. I think I should stick closer to Jon than usual today, just until I'm sure that everything is okay.

I don't like it when things change.

Still, as I glance back into the cabin and see Jon in the kitchen, it's clear that he's not concerned about anything. And if he's not concerned, then I guess there's nothing to worry about.

CHAPTER TWO

CRASHING INTO THE UNDERGROWTH, I push through lines of grass and bracken until finally I find the stick resting beneath a tree. Grabbing it between my teeth, I turn and force my way back out to the edge of the field and then I race after Jon, who has already made it down to the edge of the lake.

I pick up the pace a little, reveling in the strength of my legs and I pound across the grass. Sometimes I think I could run forever.

"Isn't it beautiful, Harry?" he asks, taking the stick from my mouth as soon as I reach him. "Wow, that's a lot of slobber. You want me to throw this in the lake? You wanna go for a swim?"

He smiles at me, before turning the other way.

"Don't worry. I wouldn't be that cruel. I know how much you hate getting wet. And I thought Jack Russells were supposed to be all-weather dogs."

With that, he throws the stick toward the other

treeline. I instinctively race off in that direction, desperate to fetch the stick so that Jon can throw it again. Again, I feel so powerful when I'm running, and my heart is pounding. Once I get to the edges of the forest, it takes just a few seconds for me to find the stick in the grass and carry it back, by which point Jon has already sat at the edge of the lake. I know that when he sits, he can't throw as far, so when I get back to him I simply set the stick down and then sit, panting as I look out across the calm, clear water.

My nose is twitching. There are so many smells right now.

"Julie's gonna love it up here," Jon says after a moment. "I know she's a city girl, but when she sees this place, she'll..."

His voice trails off, and after a moment he places a hand on the back of my neck and ruffles my fur.

"I sure hope she loves it, anyway," he continues. His heart just starting beating a little faster. "You wouldn't mind seeing more of Julie, would you? I mean, maybe even having her move in with us? You know she thinks you're the best dog in the world, right? And you'd still get to sleep at the foot of the bed, just like now."

I don't really understand most of what he's saying, but I know that Julie is the woman who has been spending more and more time with us over the past few months. Her scent has begun to get onto everything, not only the house but also Jon, and she's often allowed to sleep in the bed with us. At first I was a little concerned, just because she's new, but now I'm getting used to her presence and I can tell that she makes Jon relax a lot more. Turning, I look around in case there's any sign of her now, but I'm certain that there's not a single other human for miles in any direction. Whenever Jon and I come up here to the cabin, we're usually completely alone.

"In fact," he mutters, "I might even ask her to..."

His voice trails off, and when I turn back to him I see that he's absent-mindedly twisting a blade of grass around one of his fingers.

"Come on," he says suddenly, grabbing the stick and getting to his feet, "let's walk around the entire lake. I know that might sound crazy, but hell, there's nothing wrong with taking on a challenge, is there? You want to run, dog? Huh? You want to run your little legs off?"

It takes a long time for us to make our way around the lake's southern side. Jon throws the stick over and over again, and I keep running to fetch it so he can throw it again. These days are my favorite, when the sun is beating down and there's no-one around to disturb us. I don't mind when Julie is with us, either, but I have to admit that I prefer it when Jon and I are out here alone. Still, perhaps I have to get used to Julie's presence a little more, and I've noticed that Jon brought a few things up here to the cabin that hold her scent. I wouldn't be surprised if she shows up soon.

Reaching the crest of the hill, Jon throws the stick yet again. I race after it, but suddenly I stop as I see the city in the distance, far below us in the valley. This time, the wind has changed direction a little, and I'm picking up a different scent.

Blood.

I stand completely still, sniffing the air.

Ignoring the stick, I let my nose twitch furiously as I try to work out whether the blood is close, and whether I should be concerned. I quickly realize, however, that while the blood scent is very strong, it's coming from a long way away, from the heart of the city. Still, if I'm picking it up all the way out here, that must mean that it's very strong at its source, as if the whole city has suddenly started to stink of blood.

I tilt my head, but the smell is the same.

"You okay, buddy?" Jon says. "Something got your attention?"

I continue to stand completely still. The only part of my body that's moving is my nose as I try to get a better sense of the scent. Jon is still speaking, but his voice fades into the background for a moment as I focus entirely on my sense of smell. I've picked up the scent of blood many times in the past, of course, but it's always been from somewhere close, and from something small, whereas right now it seems as if there's a huge, overwhelming smell of blood rising up from the city and spreading this way, carried on the breeze. Lots of different types of blood, too. Lots of different people.

Suddenly Jon touches my flank.

"Harry?"

I turn and look up at him, but I can tell from his scent that he's not worried at all. In fact, he's smiling.

"What do you smell?" he asks, crouching next to me and looking toward the city. "Rabbits again? Do you want to hunt some rabbits?"

It's clear that he hasn't noticed the scent of

blood. I've learned over the years that Jon and other humans have a very poor sense of smell, and they only really notice things that are strong and close. Still, it's hard to believe that he hasn't noticed the overwhelming aroma of blood that's being blown this way. I suppose I should trust him, though. Jon is always right about these things, even if I don't really understand *how* he manages to be right.

"Come on," he says with a sigh, getting to his feet and setting off again, along the path that runs around the edge of the lake. "No rest for the wicked. We've got some serious walking to do. Hell, maybe we should run."

I hesitate for a moment, before turning and hurrying after him. He tosses the stick again, but this time I let it go. Until I'm absolutely certain that everything is okay, I want to stick much closer to Jon. Despite his sense of calm, I can't ignore the scent of blood in the air, and I can't relax.

"Come on!" he yells, as he starts running. "Keep up, slow-ass!"

I race after him, and suddenly everything seems okay again. So long as I'm out here with Jon, the rest of the world doesn't matter at all. And as we run down the hill and past the edge of the lake, I've already overtaken him.

This feels good.

We'll just play until the rest of the world goes back to normal.

CHAPTER THREE

"STILL NO PHONE SIGNAL," Jon mutters later as we sit on the dark porch at the end of the day. He's fiddling with the black device he usually keeps in his pocket, and he seems frustrated. "It can't be broken, I only got the damn thing a few months ago."

He reaches over and ruffles my neck.

"You're so lucky you guys don't have phones. Sometimes, Harry, I think dogs have the right idea of life."

It's dark and the only light comes from a set of candles on the table. Beyond the porch's edge and the steps that lead down to the grass, the fields and forest are just a wall of darkness, although I can hear plenty of activity out there. There might not be humans anywhere around for several miles, but there are rabbits and deer and hundreds of other animals. Nothing that I consider to be a threat, of course, but I still have to remain alert just in case anything unusual arrives in our territory. Right now, however, all I hear is a series of scratching sounds beyond the treeline, and it's clear that they're caused by nothing more menacing then a few rabbits.

The wind has changed again, so at least the scent of blood has faded.

"I wonder what's keeping Julie," Jon says with a sigh, getting to his feet. "She said she'd be here today. Then again, I guess something must have delayed her. I wish I could call and check, but she'll probably arrive tomorrow." He pats my head before turning and heading inside. "Just you and me for another night, buddy. I guess you get to stretch out on the bed again."

I can hear him pottering about inside. I'd usually go in and keep him company, but tonight I can't quite settle. The whole world just seems quieter somehow. After a moment, I get to my feet and wander along the porch, heading around the side of the cabin until I reach the top of the other set of steps. Sitting again, I look toward the distant skyline. For a moment, I can't quite work out what's different, but finally I realize that there's no light.

Usually, even though the city is partly hidden behind the trees, a vast haze of light is cast up into the night sky. Tonight, however, the sky is dark even directly above the city where there should be a glow, and the stars seem brighter than ever.

"It's dark out here, huh?" Jon says, as he comes through to join me again. He pauses for a moment, watching the horizon. "I guess there must be, like, a power outage or something. Looks like the whole goddamn city is out of juice."

We both stare at the horizon for a couple of minutes. For the first time, I can detect just a hint of concern in Jon's tone.

"I bet people are panicking like crazy," he continues, reaching down to ruffle the hair on the back of my head. "A little power outage and everyone goes nuts. Not like you and me up here, buddy. We've got it all figured out. Still, I guess that explains why Julie didn't make it up to join us tonight. She's probably had to stay at home until the power comes back on and..."

His voice trails off. Glancing up at him, I can see the worry in his eyes, but he quickly forces a smile.

"I guess we'll hear all about it tomorrow," he tells me, still stroking my fur. "I've gotta admit, it's kinda funny to think about everyone running around down there right now like headless chickens. I'm sure the lights'll come back on pretty soon."

We stay on the porch for a little while longer, both of us watching the dark horizon. But the lights don't come on, and they're still off when – a few hours later, after spending some time reading and playing guitar – Jon finally decides it's time for us to sleep.

Settling at the foot of his bed, curled tight, I figure everything will be back to normal tomorrow.

***

The bang is loud and sudden, and I immediately sit up at the end of the bed. The room is still dark, but as I look over toward the window I hear another bang in the distance, and then a third.

"What was that?" Jon asks groggily as he sits up. "Harry? Did you hear it?"

Staring at the dark window, I try to calm myself by focusing on the fact that the bang sounded distant, perhaps a couple of miles away. Still, I'm almost certain it was a gun, and every muscle in my body is tense as I wait in case there's any further sign of danger.

"Don't worry," Jon says, putting a hand on my shoulder, "it's just -"

Before he can finish, there are two more bangs in quick succession.

I immediately get to my feet, standing on the bed and snarling as I look toward the window.

"Hey, buddy," Jon says, climbing out from under the duvet and walking around the bed. He heads to the window and stops, looking out. "Did that sound to you like someone shooting a gun?" He pauses, and I can see his silhouette against the treeline and the starry night sky. "Why the hell would someone be firing a gun in the middle of the night, huh? It sounded pretty far off, but still..."

He pauses, before heading to the door and making his way out into the corridor. I immediately jump down off the bed and follow. The sound of the gun already had me worried, and now it's clear that Jon is concerned too, which makes things even worse. In fact, as he opens the back door and we both step out onto the cool, breezy porch, I can't help noticing that his heart seems to be beating much faster than usual.

"It wasn't *too* close," he says after a moment, as if he's trying to persuade himself that nothing's wrong.

"Sounded like it was coming from the main road, at least. Maybe even further."

Looking toward the trees, I realize that the forest seems quieter than usual. Even in the middle of the night, there should be the sound of animals out there, but right now I hear barely a scratch. It's as if the sense of alarm and concern is starting to spread, and all the rabbits and deer have moved on.

"I think the power's still off," Jon says finally. "Outages don't usually last this long, I wonder what the hell's going on down there. Probably goddamn panic."

He reaches down and pats the top of my head.

"Well, we *did* come out here to get away from civilization," he mutters. "I'm sure there's no reason to worry. Julie'll show up tomorrow and we can get all the gossip from her. Come on, buddy, let's get back to bed."

He heads inside, but I remain in place, watching the dark forest.

"Harry, come on," Jon calls out from the doorway, clapping his hands together.

I know I should go to him, but I want to sit here for the rest of the night, just to make sure that there are no more bangs, and that nothing approaches the cabin.

"Harry, get inside right now!" Jon says firmly, and I realize I have no choice.

Turning, I head inside and Jon quickly slides the door shut and locks it.

"There's no need to be worried," he explains, leading me back to the bedroom. "Everything's okay, you know. If some drunk asshole wants to fire his gun in the middle of the night, then let him. Let's not be typical city guys and get freaked out by every little sound."

Once we're back on the bed, he falls asleep fairly quickly, but I remain wide awake and alert. Curled at the foot of the bed, I keep my eyes trained on the window. It's hard to smell much of the outside world from here, but at least I can listen out for any hint of something getting closer. Instead of sleeping, I'm going to spend the rest of the night like this, guarding the cabin and making sure that everything's okay. I just hope that tomorrow, everything goes back to normal.

CHAPTER FOUR

"SO WE'LL LEAVE THIS NOTE HERE," Jon mutters, pinning a piece of paper to the cabin's front door. He's drawn squiggly lines all over the paper. "If Julie arrives while we're out for our morning hike, she'll read the note and she'll know to stay put and wait for us to come back."

He turns to me and smiles, but I can tell he's worried.

"We won't go too far this time," he continues. "I want to be back in a few hours, just to check whether she's here yet. And she will be."

He pauses, as if he's considering changing his mind and staying right here at the cabin, but finally he makes his way down the steps and claps his hands loudly.

"Come on, Harry! Let's stop worrying and go take a look around, yeah?"

***

I don't want to go into the forest, but that's where Jon leads me and I have no choice but to follow. After all, I have to stick close to him, and he doesn't seem to have noticed just how still and quiet the world seems right now.

"Picking up any fun scents?" he asks, tossing another stick into the distance.

I ignore the stick.

"Harry? Don't you don't feel like playing this morning?"

I keep my nose close to the ground. There *are* scents out here, but they all seem a little stale. Usually I love coming to the forest early in the morning, when I can pick up on the trails of all the animals that have been through during the night, but this time it seems that the forest stayed completely empty after the sun set. It's hard to believe that Jon hasn't noticed the change. I know he's not very good at picking up scents, but even *he* should surely have noticed by now that the forest around us is not only empty, but also completely quiet.

Sometimes I think humans can barely smell anything at all.

"Still no signal," he mutters, checking the black device he pulled from his pocket a moment ago. "That's over twenty-four hours now. I can't remember the last time phone coverage was out for *that* long."

He fiddles with the device some more.

"I wish there was some way of contacting Julie, just to find out what the hell's going on," he continues.

"I'm not worried, but I'd still like to know for sure." He turns to me. "Have you noticed anything weird, buddy? Anything tickling that super-strength nose of yours?"

Ahead, the forest-floor drops down a shallow incline, and I can see the light of a field in the distance. Glancing over my shoulder, I look back the way we just came, and I can't sake the feeling that the entire forest seems completely lifeless. There's no strong, *local* scent of blood, so it's not as if there was some kind of incident here. Nothing died in the forest. Instead, all the rabbits and mice and other animals simply seem to have cleared out, preferring to go somewhere else, perhaps further away from the city.

Maybe they smelled the blood too, as its scent drifted between the trees.

We stop at the edge of the forest. The lake is spread out in the distance, and the city is even further off. The wind is blowing the wrong way for me to pick up any strong scents, so I can't tell if the city still smells of blood, but I *can* tell that the whole world still seems strangely silent. I'd usually be able to hear a distant rumble from the roads, and an electrical buzz in the air, yet for the second day running there doesn't seem to be anything at all.

"Have you noticed any planes?" Jon says suddenly.

I turn to him and see that he's shielding his eyes from the sun as he looks up into the sky.

"Remember last time we were up here?" he continues. "Remember how I was bitching about planes going over, on their way to the airport?"

He pauses for a moment, before turning and looking the other way.

"I only just realized," he adds finally, "but I don't think I've seen or heard any sign of a plane since a couple of days ago. I would've thought the airport'd have its own generators, but I guess not."

He looks back toward the city.

"Hell, it's almost as if the power outage is still going on. What's going on down there? How can the city be out of power for this long?"

He takes the black device from his pocket and checks it again, although after a moment he lets out a faint sigh.

"This is going on for a little too long for my liking," he mutters, clearly concerned. "Harry, I'm not gonna start panicking, but if we don't hear from anyone by tomorrow morning, how about we take the car down to the main road? I know we were supposed to stay up here the whole time and get away from the crazy world, but I'd like to just make sure that nothing too bad has happened. Does that sound good to you?"

Again, he forces a smile, but again he seems more worried than he's letting on. His heart-rate is faster, his breathing is shallower, and his voice sounds more clipped.

"Maybe there's been a terrorist attack or something," he adds, "or... I don't know. Something."

He pauses.

"I'm sure it's nothing," he continues, patting me again before setting off across the field. "We'll be laughing about this tomorrow. Julie'll show up tonight, I guarantee it, and then she can fill us in on whatever's been going on. I'm sure it'll be hilarious." He glances back at me. "Come on, dude. Let's take the path back to the cabin. She's probably there already! I bet you a dog snack that Julie's on the porch, waiting for us!"

***

As the rest of the day passes, Jon becomes more and more concerned, even if he's trying to act normal. He checks the black device a lot, while muttering to himself, and he keeps mentioning Julie's name as if he expects her to suddenly show up. He spends a lot of time on the porch, too, watching the dirt-road that leads up here, as if he's waiting for her to arrive.

Usually we spend our afternoons exploring the area nearby, but this time Jon seems to want to stay close to the cabin.

"In her last messages," he says a little while later, as he taps at the black device in his hands, "Julie mentioned something about having to work a double shift at the hospital."

He runs his finger against the device. I don't know what it is, exactly, but that rectangular object really seems to absorb his attention sometimes.

"She said something about people getting sick," he adds. "I didn't really pay much attention at the time, and she didn't seem too worried, but..."

He pauses.

"So maybe that's it," he continues, turning to me and forcing another nervous smile. "Maybe there was some kind of incident and everyone's having to pull double or even triple shifts in the ER. Meanwhile, there also happens to be a major power outage, which is making everything ten times harder. Seems like quite a coincidence, but..."

His voice trails off, and finally he sets the black device aside and reaches over to rub the fur on top of my head.

"Don't worry," he tells me. "Everything's going to be okay. I promise. This isn't the end of the world. It just feels a little bit like it right now."

For the rest of the afternoon, however, he keeps checking the black device every few minutes. He reads for a while on the porch, then he plays guitar, then he reads again, and then he just sits and watches the trees. He talks to me a lot, too, although I only understand a few of the words. He mentions Julie several times, and I think he's a little more worried about her.

Finally the sun starts to dip in the sky, and the fields and forest become darker. While Jon plays his guitar, I sit at the top of the steps and look toward the horizon above the city. Again, the stars are much easier to spot than usual, and once night falls it becomes clear that there's still no light glow in the distance. It's as if the entire city has suddenly disappeared. Or rather, the city is still there, but all the people are gone.

"I guess she'll be here tomorrow, then," Jon mutters finally. "Probably bright and early."

I stay awake again all night. This time, Jon doesn't sleep much either. At least there are no more loud bangs in the distance. In fact, I don't hear anything.

CHAPTER FIVE

"OKAY," JON MUTTERS THE FOLLOWING MORNING, as he takes the old piece of paper from the door and pins a new one in its place, this time with a completely different set of squiggly lines. "Just in case Julie shows up while we're gone. Which she probably will. We'll only be a few hours, but..."

He pauses for a moment, clearly lost in thought. I can tell that he's really worried now, and he's not even trying to hide the fact that he thinks something is wrong. After a moment, he glances at me and forces a smile.

"Fancy a ride in the car, Harry?" he asks, leaning down and ruffling the fur on the side of my neck. "Remember that gas station we passed on the way up here last week? It can't be more than ten miles away. How about we go touch base with civilization and make sure the rest of the world didn't go up in flames, huh?"

***

As the car comes to a halt in the gas station's parking lot, I look out the window and immediately see that something seems different. I remember coming here a few times before, and there were always lots of other cars, and lots of other people too. This time, there are no other cars at all, and all the lights are off. The main road is empty, too, whereas usually there are always a few cars passing in either direction.

"Do you see any sign of anyone?" Jon asks as he switches the engine off. "Anyone at all?"

We sit in silence for a few minutes. Jon seems reluctant to get out of the car, maybe because he'd like to see at least some hint of movement first. He's much more cautious than usual, and it's clear he's starting to pick up on the fact that something is wrong. Maybe he's finally picking up on some of the signs that I first noticed a couple of days ago.

Finally he turns to me.

"I know I usually make you wait in the car, buddy, but do you want to come with me this time? It's not like there's any traffic to worry about."

He pauses before getting out of the car and then, to my surprise, he opens the door next to me and claps for me to jump down. Cautiously, I hop out and make my way across the tarmac, while carefully sniffing the air. There are tall trees all around, so it's difficult to really pick up any proper scents from afar, but the first thing I notice is that no-one seems to have been to this place for at least a day, maybe longer. In fact, there's no sign of recent human activity at all.

"I don't mind admitting," Jon mutters, stepping past me and heading toward the gas station's main building, "I don't like this too much. Stay close, buddy."

Not wanting to let him get too far away, I hurry after him and then keep pace. The building up ahead looks completely dark and empty, and after a moment I realize I'm picking up the scent of blood from close by. I immediately stop and let out a low, rumbling growl, to warn Jon.

"Harry?"

He stops and looks down at me.

"What is it, buddy?"

Keeping my eyes fixed on the door ahead, I maintain my growl. There's definitely blood somewhere on the other side of that door. Not a lot, but enough to make me really, really not want to go any closer.

"You're freaking me out, Harry," Jon says after a moment, leaning down and patting the back of my neck. "Come on, let's not overreact here, okay?"

He keeps walking, heading toward the door.

I bark to warn him, and he immediately stops and turns to me.

"Harry?"

I bark again, followed by another low growl. I don't know *exactly* what's wrong, but I know there's a strong scent of blood and I can tell it's coming from inside that building.

"What are you picking up?" Jon asks. He turns and looks toward the door. "Is someone in there?"

I bark again, before lowering my head a little and snarling to warn anyone who might be watching us from those dark windows. The scent is so strong, it's hard to believe that even Jon can't sense it now.

"Hell, Harry," he continues, "you really know how to put me at ease, don't you?"

He stares at me for a moment, before looking toward the building again.

"Are you saying we shouldn't go in there? Is that what it is?"

I continue to growl at the door as Jon hesitates, but finally he takes a couple more steps forward.

I bark again, and then again, to make him stop.

"Calm down!" he says, holding up a hand. "Harry, quiet!"

Ignoring him, I bark at the door.

"Harry!" Jon says firmly. "Quiet! I'll be fine, okay? I'm just going to take a look! Quiet!"

I know what that word means, but I also know that the sense of blood is getting stronger. The wind has changed direction a little, and now I can tell that whatever happened on the other side of that door, it caused human blood to get spilled about a day ago. The blood has definitely had time to start drying, but its scent is rich and strong, and I think there's a lot of it.

"You can wait out here if you want," Jon tells me, his voice tense with anticipation, "but I think I... I have to go take a look inside, okay?"

He pauses, before stepping closer to the door.

I bark again, desperately hoping that he'll stop.

"Harry -"

And again, louder this time.

"Harry, seriously..."

Realizing that he doesn't seem to understand, I hurry toward him and paw at his leg.

"Harry -"

I bark again, and then I growl as I stare at the door. A moment later, Jon reaches down and runs a hand across the back of my neck.

"Jesus, the hairs are standing up," he mutters. "Harry, are you picking up on something?"

Stepping past him, so that I can protect him if something comes out through the door, I snarl a little louder. The scent of blood is even stronger now, and although I can't hear anything moving inside, I still don't want to let Jon go any further.

"Hello?" he calls out. "Is anyone home?"

Still snarling, I watch the door, poised in case there's any hint of movement.

"I don't think there's anyone here, buddy," Jon continues. "Listen, I'm just gonna take a look inside, okay? You can stay out here, but I have to go in. I'll be careful, I promise. I mean, come on, it's just a gas station, right?"

He steps around me and onto the step outside the door.

I bark again.

"Harry!" he says firmly. "Quiet!"

I let out a whimper as Jon opens the door, and I immediately see that the area inside is dark and gloomy, with no lights at all. The scent of blood is so much stronger now that the door is open.

"Is anyone in here?" Jon calls out, leaning through the open doorway. "Hello? Anyone?"

He pauses, before turning to me with a faint smile.

"See, Harry? I get that you're worried, but I really don't think there's any need to freak out, okay? Obviously someone just headed out of here." He turns and looks back inside. "And left the door unlocked," he adds, with a little more uncertainty in his voice. "Which seems a little... odd."

I bark again, but he ignores me and steps inside.

Suddenly realizing that the door is starting to swing shut, I panic and hurry forward, slipping through the gap just in time. I hate the idea of getting close to the blood, but I have to stay with Jon.

As soon as I'm inside the building, the smell of stale blood hits me much harder. There's something else, too. Old meat, not quite rotten but still not good. My nose is quivering now, as I look along the aisle and see that Jon has made his way almost to the counter at the far end.

"Hello?" he calls out. "Is anyone here?"

Although I just want to get out of here, I cautiously make my way along the aisle. When I get to the far end, I see a cabinet high up on the counter, with a glass pane and some kind of meat on the other side, hanging from a metal pole. I've seen Jon eat meat like that before, and I know it's usually warm and cooked, but this time it seems to have been abandoned and left to go bad. Still, at least I know what was causing the smell of old meat, although the scent of blood seems to be coming from further back in the building, past the counter and through a door that has been left propped

31

open.

Jon still seems not to have noticed the blood. Sometimes I wonder how he survives with such a terrible sense of smell. Maybe that's one of the reasons so many humans seem to like keeping dogs in their pack. They need us.

I watch as Jon steps around the counter, and suddenly I realize he's making his way toward the open door at the back.

I bark to warn him, and he turns to me.

"What?" he asks.

I bark again, and now my whole body is trembling with fear.

"What the..." Jon stops and puts his hand on the door, running his fingers against a series of marks in the wood. "Are these bullet-holes?"

I step closer, while staring through the door and seeing the dark room ahead. I can't make out very much, but I can see a patch on the floor now and I'm certain we've found the blood.

"Maybe this place got robbed," Jon says cautiously, before peering through into the next room. "Hello? Is anyone here? Is anyone hurt?"

He pulls the black device from his pocket and glances at it, before putting it away again. Turning, he heads over to a white device on the wall and he pulls part of it away, listening to it for a moment before putting it back.

"Landlines are down too," he mutters, stepping back over toward the door.

I bark again.

"Easy, boy," he continues, "it's okay. There's no-one here now. I think something might have happened, though. Something bad."

He taps at the black device, and suddenly the front becomes very bright. Turning it toward the door, he lights the way as he steps forward into the darkness. I can tell his heart is pounding, and he seems scared, so I hurry after him and peer through into the next room, ready to fight in case anything tries to attack us.

"I was right," he says after a moment. "There's definitely no-one here now."

Reaching the patch of blood on the ground, I lean closer and take a sniff. It's human blood, that's for sure, and although it's not completely fresh, it's not old either. Just a day at most.

"What have you got there?" Jon asks, coming over to me and crouching down. "Hell, is that blood?"

I look up at him, hoping against hope that now he'll finally realize that we need to get out of here. There's no need for us to be here, or for us to start poking about in darkened rooms. We should simply go back to the cabin and wait for everything to go back to normal. When he doesn't say anything, and simply continues to stare in shock at the blood, I use my paw to nudge his knee, and I let out a faint whimper.

"It's okay," he replies, rubbing my head as he gets up. "Something definitely happened here, though. I think the place got robbed, and then..."

He steps back through into the first room, and I quickly follow.

"And then someone got hurt," he continues,

"and ran. Maybe that's what caused those gunshots we heard the other night. This gas station is open all-night, so obviously there was a robbery, but why has no-one been back since? Unless..."

He pauses, before glancing down at me again.

"Unless whoever got shot... Maybe they didn't make it very far, but still..."

I follow as he heads back over to the main door and pulls it open. Relieved to be back outside again, I hurry across the parking lot until we reach the edge of the main road, where Jon stops and looks both ways.

"Why are there no cars?" he asks, turning to look down at me. "We've been here at least ten minutes now, and this is usually a busy highway. So where the hell did everybody go?"

CHAPTER SIX

WITH THE CAR'S ENGINE STILL RUNNING, Jon continues to turn the little round dials next to the steering wheel, but the only noise that comes from the speakers is a kind of whirling static that hurts my ears.

"There's no radio," he mutters, finally cutting the engine and stopping the horrible noise. "Nobody's broadcasting anything. That seems weird. Hell, it's more than weird. This must be the first time the airwaves have been silent since... Hell, since radio was invented."

I'm sitting on the seat next to him, and after a moment he looks back over toward the gas station's main building. I can tell that he's worried, but I don't understand why we're still here. We should go back up to the cabin and make sure that we're safe. Everything will be okay if we just go back up there and wait. Whatever's going on here is none of our business.

"This isn't right," he says suddenly, climbing back out of the car. "I don't like it."

Although I don't want to follow, I jump down and head around to join him. I don't understand why we haven't left yet, but I trust Jon and I'm sure he's got his reasons. And while we're here, I have to stay close and be ready to defend him in case anything tries to attack us. After all, there's blood in the building, and blood means danger.

"We've been here for a while now," he says, stepping over toward the edge of the road again. "It's Saturday afternoon, we're not that far from the city. This road should be..."

His voice trails off as he stands in silence for a moment.

"Someone should have gone past by now," he continues. "I don't know what's going on, but whatever it is, someone should have driven past." He turns to me. "Unless there's something seriously, *seriously* wrong."

He turns and looks along the road again, but suddenly I realize I'm starting to pick up a new scent. Sniffing the air, I can tell that there's another person not that far from here. Jon doesn't seem to have noticed, but I turn and make my way back around the car, only to find myself staring at the vast pine forest that spreads away from the edge of the parking lot. I can't *see* anyone, and the scent is clearly coming from at least a mile off, but I swear someone is coming this way. Still sniffing, I realize the scent also seems slightly wrong somehow, although I can't quite work out what it is that I don't like.

I can't help letting out a faint snarl, however, followed by a bark to alert Jon.

"What is it?" he asks, coming over to join me. "There's nothing there, Harry."

I bark again. He must trust me enough to know that I wouldn't be doing this if I hadn't picked up some kind of scent.

"I don't see anything," he continues. "Is that the direction the guy from the gas station went? Or have you just found the scent of another rabbit?"

Hurrying forward, I start sniffing the ground as I realize I'm starting to pick up a faint trace of blood. By the time I get to the edge of the forest, I can see a couple of dark patches ahead, and I'm certain it's the same blood that we found inside. Whoever got hurt, they seem to have headed off in this direction.

"Is that blood?" Jon asks, as I stop and sniff another patch.

Looking at the forest again, I realize I can *definitely* smell someone. I might be wrong, the wind might be tricking me, but I feel as if whoever's out there, they're less than a mile away and they're coming this way.

"You really know how to freak me out," Jon says, reaching down and rubbing the fur on the back of my neck. "You know that, right?" He pauses. "Then again, I'm already pretty freaked out as things stand. Maybe we should head into the city, just to make sure that everything's okay. I don't want to cut our cabin week short, but we can come back up here as soon as we know there's nothing wrong."

He heads back over to the car and starts the engine, and suddenly I hear the tires starting to turn.

AMY CROSS

Filled with a sense of panic, I turn and see that he's starting to drive away. I start barking as I rush after him, but he stops again just a few meters ahead, next to one of the tall metal machines in the parking lot.

"Relax," he says as he switches the engine off and climbs out, taking a moment to pat the top of my head. "I just need to fill up the gas tank. You didn't think I was going anywhere without you, did you? Hell, if this really *is* the end of the world, I need my trust little Jack Russell more than ever."

I watch as he unhooks a piece from the nearest machine, and then he pulls out a long hose and attaches the section to the side of the car. He fiddles with the machine for a moment, muttering something under his breath, and then finally he steps back.

"Of course, electricity would be useful," he says with a sigh. "No electricity, no pump. No pump, no gas."

He pulls the hose out of the car and turns to me.

"Confession time, Harry. I was planning to fill her up on the way back to the city. I know I should have done it on the way to the cabin, but I didn't think it'd be a big deal. Still..."

He turns and looks back toward the main building.

"There's a load of gas right beneath our feet," he continues, "and I'm sure I'm smart enough to figure out a way to get some of it. Or maybe they even have some pre-filled gas cans kicking around somewhere. Don't worry, I'll figure something out."

With that, he turns and makes his way toward the building.

I bark a couple of times, warning him to stay close.

"I'll be fine," he calls back to me. "Seriously, Harry, just stay calm. We need a little more gas before we set off again. So just don't go anywhere, okay? Stay, boy. Stay!"

That's one of the words I know, and it means he wants me to not move from where I am. Still, I can't help taking a few steps after him, hoping to follow him back into the building so I can make absolutely certain that he's safe.

"No, stay!" he says firmly, turning back to me. He holds a finger up, which is his way of reinforcing the order. "Harry, stay!"

I let out a faint whimper, hoping he'll realize that this is a mistake.

"Harry, sit!"

I sit, but at the same time I whimper again.

"Harry, stay!"

He stares at me for a moment longer, as if he's waiting to make sure that I obey.

"Okay, good," he adds, turning and heading over to the door. He takes out the black rectangle and taps at the front again, and he's muttering something under his breath.

I whimper once more, but I'm powerless to stop Jon as he goes inside.

Now that I can't see him, I'm filled with panic. The blood scent is still inside, and it's clear that something really bad happened here at some point in the past few days. Jon's smart, and I know he's in charge, but at the same time I think he really doesn't understand all the warning signs. Finally, after a couple of minutes have passed, I start wondering whether it's okay to stand up again. I almost lift my butt, before figuring I should stay a little longer. The last thing I want is for Jon to come out and see me disobeying his orders.

After a few more minutes, however, I get to my feet and take a few cautious steps toward the building while letting out a series of low grumbles. I desperately want to bark, to get his attention and draw him out, but I doubt he'd be very happy about that.

Suddenly I hear a cracking sound nearby, and I turn to look over at the trees.

The wind keeps changing direction, so it's difficult to be certain, but I think there's still someone out there. I picked up their scent earlier, when they were further away, but – whoever they are – they're getting much closer now. I raise my nose slightly, hoping to get a better idea of the scent, and after a moment I realize that something definitely doesn't seem right.

I glance at the building again, hoping against hope that Jon is on his way out. There's no sign of him, however, so I turn and make my way cautiously past the car and over to the edge of the forest.

Stopping, I stare ahead at the trees.

The scent is stronger now, and easier to make out.

It's a human.

Sweaty and unwashed, but there's something else, something that's making the fur on the back of my neck stand up.

Death.

I lick my nose, hoping that a little extra moisture might help me to get a clearer idea of the scent.

I definitely smell death, but at the same time it seems different this time. The death scent seems somehow mixed with the human's sweat. I've picked up on the scent of death before, of course, but only when I've come across dead birds or rabbits in the forest. One thing I know for certain is that any creature that smells of death should actually *be* dead. In fact, it seems completely impossible that someone could smell this way and yet keep coming closer.

Nevertheless, the scent of death is coming closer. It's moving toward us through the forest.

Glancing over my shoulder, I see that Jon still isn't out of the building. I let out another whimper as I turn and look back toward the forest. I can't let it show, but I'm scared now.

I watch the gaps between the trees for a few more minutes, with the scent getting closer and closer, and finally I spot a hint of movement in the distance. It's not much, but I'm more and more certain that someone is coming this way. I let out a low snarl, and a moment later I hear a couple more cracking sounds, as if the person is stepping on old twigs. I can see the figure a little more clearly now, and from the scent I can tell it's a man. He's coming closer with each passing second, but he's not walking very fast. In fact, he seems to be stumbling slightly.

And his blood...

I can smell his blood, and it's the same as the

blood in the gas station's back room.

I snarl again.

He doesn't stop.

I look back toward the building again, but there's still no sign of Jon. Feeling as if I need to get him out here, I bark a couple of times and then I wait, but it's almost as if he's completely disappeared. I turn back and look into the forest, and now the staggering figure is even closer. He's coming straight toward me, and above the sound of his feet stomping through the undergrowth I can also hear a persistent, faint gurgling sound coming from his mouth. Humans don't usually growl, not like this, but something seems to be wrong with this man and finally I take a few steps back, keen to make sure I can get away if he comes too close.

I bark a couple of times, hoping to make him stop.

He doesn't even slow his pace. Instead he keeps stumbling this way, while steadying himself against the trees. Now I can see that he's hurt, with torn and bloodied clothes, and it's hard to believe that someone could still be walking when they're clearly so badly injured. Taking another cautious step back, I see something dark glistening around the man's stomach area, and I realize that there's a fresh scent in the air. I take a couple of deep sniffs, and it's almost as if part of the man's gut has burst through and is hanging outside, although I know that's not possible. Blood and meat and bone seem all mixed together, and I can even see a faint gap in the center of his chest, as if something blasted straight through.

And his unblinking eyes are fixed on me.

I hold my ground as he gets closer, and I start growling. The man stumbles a little, almost falling, but so far he's showing no sign of fear at all. He's still letting out that faint gurgle, and now he's close enough for me to see that his flesh seems much paler than it should, almost gray. I'd usually not be scared at all, not facing a human, but the stench of death and dried blood is almost overwhelming, and nothing seems to be slowing him down. I can't run, though. Even those this man's scent is terrifying, I refuse to show weakness. I have to make him fear me.

I bark as he reaches the edge of the parking lot, but he simply reaches out toward me.

I bark again and again, but he -

"Harry! Get out of the way!"

Turning, I see Jon running from the main building.

"Harry! Move!"

I turn back to the strange man and see that he's about to grab my collar. I don't want him to touch me, but at the same time I can't let him think that I'm weak, so I bark louder than ever, warning him away. He doesn't flinch, doesn't even seem to notice, so I bare my teeth, preparing to bite as he leans down. Scraps of loose, rotten flesh and meat are hanging down from his bones, fluttering in the breeze.

Suddenly a hand grabs my collar from behind and pulls me back.

"Get away from him!" Jon says firmly, leading me back toward the car.

I turn and look toward the man, and I start barking again.

"What the fuck is that thing?" Jon stammers, his voice filled with fear.

I bark again, but the man doesn't seem scared of anything. He's just lumbering slowly toward us and, as I continue to bark, I realize I'm not sensing any fear coming from him at all. It's almost as if he's somehow empty, as if he has no reaction to anything. I can even sense his heart beating in his chest.

"Stay back!" Jon shouts. "Don't come any closer!"

The man's gurgle gets louder as he lumbers toward us, and now I can see his chest more clearly. He looks hurt, as if something tore his ribs open and punched a hole just below his neck, and his intestines are partially hanging out. I've never seen anything – human or animal – keep moving when it's so bad injured, or when it reeks so strongly of death. I thought I understood what happens to living creatures when they're hurt, but this man seems to be defying all the usual rules. Something dead shouldn't be able to walk like this.

"Keep back from him, Harry," Jon says firmly, grabbing my collar and pulling me away from the man.

I let out a low, rumbling snarl, hoping to warn the man away, but it has no effect. If he tries to hurt Jon, though, I'm going to have to fight him, even though all my instincts are warning me to keep well away. Whatever else happens, I have to protect my master.

Suddenly Jon opens one of the car doors.

"Get in, Harry!" he says, lifting me inside and then slamming the door shut.

He runs around and gets in the other side, before starting the engine just as the strange men reaches the window next to me and places his pale, bloodless hands on the glass.

Suddenly the tires squeal as Jon reverses the car across the parking lot. In just a matter of seconds, we're safely away from the strange man, although Jon stops the car again once we're almost at the main building. With the engine still running, he sits and stares out at the figure, which has already started to lumber slowly toward us.

"What the fuck is wrong with him?" Jon says after a moment. "He looks like a..."

I feel safer now that we're in the car and not so close to the man, but for some reason Jon seems to want to stay here and watch him limping this way.

"He looks like a zombie," he says finally. "That shirt he's wearing has the gas station's logo, it looks like he's been shot straight through the chest. I think maybe he came from here."

I start snarling as the man comes closer.

"He's *not* a zombie, though," Jon continues. "He can't be. I mean, he's in a bad way and he looks hurt, but..."

His voice trails off for a moment.

"He's just hurt," he adds. "That's all. It looks like he's been shot in the chest, it's a miracle he's alive."

He pauses, before checking the black rectangle again.

"Still no signal."

Another pause, and then he opens the door.

"Stay here, Harry," he says firmly. "I'm just going to see if I can help this guy. If he can walk, he must be able to talk."

He climbs out of the car. I step across to the other seat, hoping to follow, but he quickly pushes the door shut. I can't believe Jon would actually go out there, and I watch in horror as he takes a couple of cautious steps toward the man, who's still only about halfway across the parking lot. I bark a couple of times, to warn Jon that he needs to stay back, but he simply keeps walking.

"Hey!" I hear him calling out. "Can you hear me?"

I bark again, filled with panic as Jon waits for the man to get closer.

"I want to help you!" he continues. "I don't think I have enough gas to get to a hospital. Can you help me with that, and then I'll take you?"

Still barking, I start furiously scratching my paw against the door, hoping to get out there so I can help Jon.

"My name's Jon! Can you tell me *your* name?"

The man is much closer now. Finally, I'm relieved to see Jon stepping back, and a moment later he opens the door and climbs back into the car. He pulls the door shut and reaches out to me, placing a hand on the back of my neck.

"What the hell do we do now?" he asks, watching as the man stumbles closer. "I don't want to overreact, buddy, but I don't like the look of this guy. He seems..."

His voice trails off, and for a moment he simply watches as the man finally reaches the car.

"It's okay, Harry," Jon says. "We just -"

Suddenly the man leans down and slams his hands against the window, while staring in at us with wild, reddened eyes. I start barking, but nothing seems to scare him off. Instead, he starts banging his hands against the glass as if he's trying to break through, and at the same time his mouth opens and he lets out a rattling, gasping growl.

"I want to help you!" Jon tells him, as the man continues to pound against the window. "Just hold on, okay? Just try to -"

He flinches as the man starts hitting the glass harder and harder.

"I know he's not a zombie," Jon mutters, "but he's doing a damn good -"

Before he can finish, there's a crunching sound and the man's left hand bends back, as if he's hitting the glass so hard that he's broken his wrist. The pale skin tears slightly, but no blood runs from the wound. All that's left on the window is a pale, yellowish smear of rotten flesh.

"What the hell is going on in his chest?" Jon asks, his voice filled with shock.

As I continue to bark, I see that something seems to be moving in the man's bloodied, exposed ribs. After a moment, I realize that there are maggots wriggling through his flesh. I've seen maggots before, but only on dead bodies, and this man looks and smells like he died a couple of days ago. The fact that he's walking about, however, means that he *can't* be dead. I genuinely don't understand what's happening here, but I know I don't want him getting any closer. I know the difference between life and death, but this man seems to be both at the same time.

Suddenly Jon grabs the steering wheel, and the car lurches forward. He drives us away from the man, over toward the edge of the parking lot and then out onto the main road, but then he stops again. We both look back and see that the man has already starting stumbling after us. For a moment we sit in silence, but I can tell that Jon's heart is pounding and I can sense his fear.

"We can't leave him," he says finally, "but I don't... Maybe I'm being paranoid, but I don't want that guy touching me. I swear, Harry, he looks like..."

He pauses, still watching the man.

"He looks like a zombie," he continues. "Did you see those maggots? How can a guy be walking about with maggots infesting a huge, open wound in his chest? I could actually see through the hole and out the other side!"

He checks the black rectangle again.

"Julie would know what to do. Damn it, where the hell is she?"

He turns to me.

"Hey, buddy, what do you think the odds are that she's up at the cabin right now?"

I don't know what he's saying, but he just mentioned Julie. I turn and look around, but there's no sign of her.

"I don't want to leave this guy here, stumbling around like this," he continues. "He must be in agony, but I don't know what I'm supposed to do. Maybe I should just go out there again and try to talk to him. If he's walking, he must still be conscious in there somehow. I mean, he can't just be..."

He reaches to open the door, but I bark and he stops.

"I know how you feel," he says, "but I can't just drive away. He needs help."

I bark again, before realizing that the scent is suddenly different. Whereas a moment ago I was picking up a strong stench of death and blood coming from the man, now the wind seems to have changed and I can smell the same scent coming from another direction. I turn and look out through the car's rear window, and I immediately see another figure stumbling toward us.

I start barking, louder than ever.

"Harry, what's wrong?" Jon asks, before turning just as the second figure bumps against the rear of the car. "What the hell, is that another one?"

The new figure is louder, snarling as it comes around to the door and bangs its fists against the glass. As I continue to bark, I see that this figure seems to be a woman, and she's just as discolored and strange-looking as the man. Her belly seems bloated somehow, but unlike the man she doesn't seem to have any bloody wounds.

"Okay, this is definitely getting too weird for me," Jon mutters, driving the car forward for a moment before stopping again. His hands are trembling. "We're getting the hell out of here."

Turning, I see that both figures are still coming toward us.

"What do we do?" Jon stammers. "These people actually look like -"

Before he can finish, the woman throws herself against the car's rear window. As she does so, her bloated stomach suddenly bursts, spraying the glass with a kind of yellowish liquid. Nothing seems to stop her, though, and she's already lumbering around to the window next to Jon, still trying to find a way to get into the car. Her burst belly has left flaps of skin hanging loose, with more of the yellowish liquid dribbling out.

"Okay, I'm not going out there again," Jon says, driving the car forward a little further. He stops again and looks back at the two figures, before hitting the pedal and moving the car even further along the road. This time, he doesn't stop. "We're going back to the cabin, buddy," he tells me, as his voice trembles with shock. "Julie'll be there now. She has to be. We'll go back, we'll talk to Julie, and we'll figure out what the hell is going on. It's not what it looks like, though. It can't be."

CHAPTER SEVEN

AS SOON AS JON opens the car door and lets me out, I sniff the air and realize that Julie isn't here. None of the scents have changed since we left the cabin a few hours earlier, although the car itself smells very different and I hurry around to the other side, where the woman's burst belly has left some kind of foul liquid all over the window.

"Julie?" Jon calls out, heading over to the cabin. "Damn it, her car isn't here."

Although I want to smell the liquid on the side of the car, so I can get a better idea of what it contains, feel as if I shouldn't get too close. Whatever was wrong with that woman, she's made the car smell diseased, and I'm certain that her body was starting to rot. The liquid has already started to dry in the afternoon sun, and after a moment I step back, feeling as if it might be dangerous. Somehow, it seems to smell of pure death.

"That's disgusting," Jon says as he comes over

to join me. "Don't lick it, buddy."

He grabs my collar and pulls me back a few paces, which I don't mind at all.

"I wanted to help them," he continues, stroking the back of my neck as he looks at the smears on the side of the car, "but... You saw what they were like. Those two people at the gas station, it's like they..."

His voice trails off.

"That stuff stinks," he adds finally, leaning a little closer to the car. "I mean, even *I* can smell it, so it must absolutely reek for you, huh?"

He opens the car door and takes out a bottle of water. After unscrewing the cap, he pours the water over the smear, but the stench remains.

"I really thought Julie would be here," he continues, taking a step back. "I don't like this, Harry. My phone's been out of signal for two days now, and it looks like there's still some kind of major power outage. And whatever happened at that gas station..."

He pauses.

"Why was no-one else on the road?" he asks. "Why had no-one else seen what was going on at the gas station? Why were those two people just left to wander about like that? I mean, it was like a scene from some kind of zombie movie, but..."

Looking up at him, I see that he seems lost in thought. Jon's usually pretty sure of himself, but right now it's clear that he doesn't know what's happening. He checks the black rectangle again, tapping at the screen as he mutters something under his breath.

"I took a couple of photos of the guy," he

continues, staring at the rectangle. "He sure as hell *looked* like a zombie. They both did, but they just can't be."

He stares for a moment longer, before turning and heading to the cabin. Determined to stay close, I follow him up the steps and through the door, and then I watch as he opens a cabinet in the far corner and takes out his rifle. For the next few minutes, he seems intent on checking that every part of the mechanism works properly. He rarely ever takes the rifle from the cabinet, but this time he sets it on the table and then grabs a rattling box.

"I'm probably overreacting," he tells me, "and Julie will probably show up any moment now and make fun of me for the rest of my life, but... For the first time in my life, I'm sure as hell glad that Daniel persuaded me to buy a gun. He said I should have it, just in case I ever ran across a bear up here, but now..."

He pauses, staring at the gun for a few seconds.

"I won't need it," he continues. "I won't. It's crazy. But I think I'll keep it out, just in case."

He comes over to me and pats the top of my head, before heading out to the porch. I follow, and we both sit at the top of the steps, looking out at the field and watching the distant trees. There's a light breeze now, causing the branches to sway and the leaves to rustle, but fortunately nothing seems to be moving counter to natural world now.

"Let's look at this logically," he says after a moment, "and try to stay calm. Don't worry, buddy, I'm kind of just talking to myself right now." He sighs.

"Julie was going to drive up and join us a couple of days ago, and she's not the kind of person who'd suddenly blow us off. Obviously the phones went on the fritz, and the power too, so I guess she had to stick around at the ER and help people. I mean, that's what Julie's like, she'd never leave her post if there was an emergency. So she's probably fine, she's probably working flat-out and getting no sleep, but she'll be okay. She's smart, she knows how to look after herself."

I wait for him to continue, but he says nothing for the next few minutes.

Finally I let out a faint whimper and place my paw on his leg.

Smiling, he turns to me.

"You were very brave back there, Harry. Good dog. Very good."

He pats my head again. Usually I'd feel better when he tells me I'm good, but this time I can tell he's still worried.

"I think we should stick it out for a couple more days," he says after a moment. "We don't actually have enough gas to go too far, not until that gas station is back up and running. So there's no point hitting the road. We have tons of food, I brought enough up for Julie so we can last a couple of weeks with no trouble, and at least while we're here..." He sighs. "At least while we're here, she knows where to find us. Soon we'll start seeing signs of life, we'll see planes in the sky again and the cellphone service'll come back, and that'll be our signal that everything's getting back to normal. Then we can go get some gas and.... And things *will* get back to normal, I promise." He ruffles the fur on the back of my neck again. "Everything's going to be okay. And I bet Julie'll show up tomorrow."

We sit in silence as the late afternoon sky starts to darken. By the time the sun has begun to disappear, the shadows of the forest are much longer, reaching almost all the way to the cabin's steps.

***

I don't sleep during the night. Neither does Jon. He sits at the table, near the gun, while I stay out on the porch, watching the dark forest. After a while he sets a lamp burning, which makes the interior of the cabin brighter but also makes everything outside seem much darker. The whole world is so silent, it's as if Jon and I are the only living things left.

CHAPTER EIGHT

"I DON'T SEE ANYTHING. Do you see anything, buddy?"

Having set out from the cabin at first light, we're now at the top of the hill, which means we're on the highest point for miles and miles around. From here, we can see not only the entire valley but also the main road in the distance, snaking through the forest. Even further away, the sprawl of the city spreads to the horizon, and I can't see any sign of cars moving on the roads.

Looking up at Jon, I can tell that he's a little more worried than yesterday.

"You know," he says with a faint, nervous smile, "I was thinking things through during the night, and I realized that there's no way things won't go back to normal. I mean, even if the shit has really hit the fan, it's just going to take a few days before the government and the military get everything back under control. The world just can't collapse. Do you know what I think happened? I think terrorists took out the grid, something like that. Hackers or whatever. I bet there's a whole lot of panic going on right now, but order's gonna get restored. And you and me, buddy, we're just sitting up here on a hill, keeping well clear of the whole mess."

He reaches down and pats my head.

"If you ask me, we're the smart ones. And Julie will be okay, because she's smart too. I guarantee you, whatever's going on down there in the city, she's staying safe. She's probably working around the clock to help other people, and not sleeping at all, but that's just the kind of girl she is."

He pauses for a moment.

"I think maybe when all of this is over," he continues, turning and leading me back down the side of the hill, "I might change my plan a little. Instead of asking her to move in with us, how about I ask her to marry me instead? I've been thinking about it for a while, but I reckon now's the time. You wouldn't mind that, would you? And if a kid or two comes along after a few years, you'll get a whole new buddy. It'll be a big change, though. Instead of just you and me for most of the time, we'll have a full house. But you'll always be my pal, and nothing will ever change that. You understand, right? Wouldn't you like to get old with me in a loud, happy house?"

I don't know what any of those words mean, but I like hearing his voice. He's clearly still worried, but it's better when he talks. Last night he was silent as he sat at the table, and I could tell his pulse was racing. Humans always give off so many little signals that make it obvious how they're feeling, although I'm not certain they're very aware of those signals. Sometimes, I even think that maybe I have an advantage in that area.

"Tire tracks," Jon says suddenly.

He stops, and I stop too. It takes a moment, but finally I see that the dirt road has changed slightly, as if another car has passed through while we were up on the hill.

"Maybe it's her," he stammers, setting off through the grass. "Maybe Julie's here!"

I run after him, although I have to be careful to make sure I don't get too far ahead. It takes a while for us to reach the edge of the forest, and I can tell that Jon is already getting a little weak, but he doesn't slow much.

Eventually we get back to the cabin, and I'm shocked to see a second car parked out front.

"That's not Julie's," Jon says cautiously, slowing a little just as the cabin's door swings open and an older man steps out onto the porch and stops next to the rifle, which is leaning against the wall.

***

"What do you mean?" Jon asks as he and the man sit at the table inside. "What kind of outbreak?"

"It's been going on for a few days now," the man replies wearily. His name, as far as I can tell, seems to be Richard. "There were reports in the news about people getting sick, but there were so many other big stories around, I don't think many of us paid a whole lot of attention. And then the power went out and the phones stopped working, and that's when it really seemed serious." He pauses. "So is it just the two of you up here?"

"Go back a moment," Jon says. "You said people were getting sick. What was wrong with them?"

"I don't know. At first, it was just like a kind of fever. I heard about a few friends catching it, and I started taking precautions, you know? Just to make sure I didn't pick it up myself. I thought it was like some kind of flu, and the TV said not to worry too much. But then..."

He pauses, staring down at his trembling hands. His heart is pounding and I can tell he's scared.

"I keep thinking I'm going to wake up," he continues finally. "The things I saw after it got worse... Sick people in the streets, healthy people trying to defend themselves... When it finally got really bad, it just escalated so goddamn fast. Before you knew it, all the sick people were dying and then they..."

He falls silent for a moment.

"Then they what?" Jon asks.

Richard pauses, before glancing at him.

"They died," he explains. "All of a sudden, it seemed like people were dropping like flies. And that seemed bad, but it got worse 'cause then they started to... come back."

Jon stares at him. "What... What do you mean by that?"

"I didn't believe it at first," Richard continues. "I thought it was a joke, just a kind of prank people were playing. But then I saw it for myself. All these dead people, once they'd been cold for a few hours, they just started to get back up, except this time they weren't really themselves, you know? They were... Like, you could see they were dead, but they were walking around and they went after everyone else." He sighs. "I know this sounds crazy. I saw it with my own eyes, and I still don't quite know whether to believe it. Maybe I just lost my mind, maybe..."

His voice trails off. After a moment, he looks down at me and smiles, and then he reaches over and starts stroking the back of my head. I let him, for now, but his touch feels stiff, as if he's more tense than he wants to let on.

"You're making it sound like there was some kind of zombie outbreak," Jon says eventually. "I mean, that's... It's ridiculous."

Richard nods. "I know."

"Things like that just don't happen."

"I know."

"So you must be..."

"I must be what?" Richard asks, still stroking my fur. "Making it up? I wish that were the case. If you don't believe me, you've got a car, go see for yourself. It's chaos back there."

They sit in silence for a moment. Richard seems to be enjoying stroking me, but Jon looks more worried than ever.

"Finally I just figured I had to get out of there," Richard continues. "People were dying, and more and more were getting sick. I don't have any family, not anymore, so it's not like I had to go searching for anyone. I just grabbed whatever I could fit in my car, and I drove away. I didn't even know *where* I was going, to be honest, but I knew I couldn't stick around. If I'd stayed, I'd be..."

He pauses.

"I'd be dead by now, I reckon. Everyone in the cities was..."

Another pause.

"It seemed to spread so fast," he adds finally. "Faster than anyone could do anything about, anyway."

Getting to his feet, Jon heads over to the counter and grabs a couple of water bottles. He freezes for a moment, just staring at the bottles, and then slowly he turns to look at Richard.

"You want me to believe that the whole world out there has just... collapsed? Seriously?"

"Before the power went out," Richard replies, "they were saying on the TV that people were getting sick all over the country, and abroad too. America, Europe, Asia... It seemed like everywhere was getting hit. Air travel was spreading it, they reckoned. They announced they were shutting all the airports temporarily, but I guess that was too little, too late. No-one seemed to know where the sickness started, or what to do about it." He looks down at me. "This is a nice dog you've got here. He must be very useful."

Jon pauses. "So how do I know *you're* not sick?"

"You'll just have to take my word on that. Trust me, anyone who gets this thing, they deteriorate pretty fast. The TV was saying symptoms set in after just a few hours. It seems like flu at first, but it quickly gets worse.

To be honest, I *was* scared I might be infected, but it's been a few days now since I last saw anyone, and I'm sure I'd be dead by now if I was a carrier."

He stares at Jon for a moment.

"What about you? How long have you and your dog been up here?"

"A week now. My girlfriend was supposed to join us a few days ago."

"So you came just before it hit, huh?"

Jon nods. "Looks that way."

"There aren't many people left," Richard continues. "I'm sorry to break it to you, but when I drove out of the city the other day, the streets were... Well, let's just say that there was no sign of anyone. I think a few people, the smart ones, headed west, hoping they'd run into some help out there. There was talk of some kind of rendezvous or meeting place at the Rarrah Valley, where survivors might be able to get together. Maybe I should've gone that way too, but this doesn't seem like the time to be mingling with large groups of people. I ended up coming out here instead, and then last night I spotted a light up here. I very nearly kept on driving, but I figured a light probably meant someone was alive. So I figured I'd come take a look."

"You went past the gas station?" Jon asks cautiously. "Did you see..."

"Two of them," he replies, nodding. "Yeah, they're down there. I damn near hit one of them with my car, but I had to keep driving. These things, once they come back from the dead... They're vicious. Slow, but vicious. I saw..."

He sighs again.

"I don't even want to think about what I saw. I'll tell you one thing, though. I don't know if it's ever going to go back to normal. I kept waiting for the cavalry to show up, but I think the cavalry's probably sick too."

"It'll get better," Jon tells him. "It has to."

"You reckon?"

"Of course." He carries the water over and passes a bottle to Richard. "The world is *not* going to collapse into chaos just because a few people got sick."

"It's not just a few, my friend, it's -"

"It's still not going to happen!" Jon sounds agitated now. "There are doctors, people who can figure it out."

"The doctors all seemed completely overwhelmed. I reckon they were the worst hit, too. They were on the front-line when people started going to hospital, so most of them..."

His voice trails off.

"It can't be that bad," Jon says firmly. "Someone'll take charge."

"I wish I agreed with you," Richard replies, "but I saw it with my own eyes. I saw bodies in the streets, and I saw those *things* too." He takes a swig of water. "I hope I'm wrong, but it sure *looked* like the end of the world." Glancing down at me, he forces a smile and ruffles the fur on the back of my neck, but I immediately get to my feet and hurry over to Jon, settling next to him.

"It's okay," Jon says, reaching down and stroking my back. "Everything'll be okay, I promise."

He sounds worried, and I'm worried too. Richard

might smell okay, but there's something about him that I really don't like, even though he's smiling at me and trying to be friendly. My instincts are telling me to be careful around this new arrival. He's lying about something.

CHAPTER NINE

"WHAT DO YOU THINK?" Jon whispers a short while later, as he takes a few more logs from the pile around the back of the cabin. "Should I let him stay? You've had a good sniff of him. Do you think he's crazy?"

I brush the side of my face against his leg, just to get a little more of his scent on me, and more of mine on him. If I reinforce our shared pack identity, maybe he'll realize that Richard doesn't belong with us.

"Everything he told me sounded insane," he continues, still keeping his voice down. "He was describing some kind of zombie apocalypse, and he kept a completely straight face the whole way through. I know we saw some pretty strange stuff at the gas station, but that doesn't mean the whole world is falling apart. Maybe this Richard guy is just some lunatic who thinks he can play a prank on us. Things can't be as bad as he made out."

He pauses for a moment, clearly lost in thought.

"Maybe he can stay for one night," he adds finally, stepping past me and carrying the wood back around to the cabin's front door. "At least until we get this all figured out. If he's lying, he'll trip up eventually. And if somehow he's telling the truth... I guess we need all the information we can get."

I follow, and when we get to the other side of the cabin I see that Richard has opened the trunk of his car and is taking out some boxes. Even from here, I'm picking up on the smell of food wafting from the trunk, but there are other scents too. Lots of different people have touched the boxes, some of them only a few hours ago. Stepping closer, I tilt my head slightly in an attempt to get a better sniff.

"I know it's not much," Richard says, turning to Jon and holding one of the boxes out, "but I'm afraid it's all I can offer right now. I don't mean to intrude on you, and to be honest I think I might head off tomorrow, but if you don't mind me resting here for the night... I guess I'm offering to share with you. Seems like the right thing to do, in the circumstances."

"I'll see what I can find for us to eat this evening," Jon replies, as a few spots of rain start to fall. "I guess if what you said earlier is true, we should start thinking about conserving supplies."

I step closer to the open trunk. There's not just food in there, there's also something else, maybe a trace of blood.

Suddenly the trunk slams shut, and Richard ruffles the top of my head. I pull away, not liking the way he touches me.

"I bet you'd love to get in there, huh?" he says with a smile, before turning and carrying the box over toward the cabin. "It's going to rain, maybe even a storm. If you want my advice, I think you should gather every spare container you can find, and use them to collect water. You never know when a good stock might come in handy, although..."

He sets the box down, and then rifles through the contents before pulling out a bottle of dark brown liquid.

"I happen to have a bottle of whiskey here, and... Well, I don't much fancy drinking it alone. I reckon opportunities for a little companionship are only going to get less common soon, so if you like, I'd happily open this and share it with you. One for the road, so to speak."

"I never thought I'd be so glad to see a bottle of whiskey," Jon replies, before heading into the cabin. "I figure we might as well cook outside. I'm not even very hungry, but we need to keep our strength up."

"We sure do," Richard mutters, watching as Jon goes inside. Turning to me, he stares for a moment, as if he's studying me. "Well, you sure look like a nice hound," he says finally, coming closer with the bottle still in his right hand. "I bet a good dog would be useful out here. Are you a decent barker, boy? Can you bark if you see or hear someone approaching who maybe shouldn't be around?"

He reaches out to pat me, but I step back.

"That's okay," he continues. "You'll get used to me. Maybe you can even hop in the car with me when I leave. I could use a dog."

I don't know what he's saying, but everything about this man makes me nervous. He has the eyes of a liar, and I've noticed that he seems to be studying Jon's every move, almost as if he's trying to figure out his weaknesses. Jon appears to be oblivious, apparently thinking that Richard can be trusted, but I'm not going to let my guard down tonight. I haven't slept for days, but pure fear is keeping me awake.

He puts a hand on the side of my face.

Pulling back, I let out a faint growl.

"What's wrong," he continues, "don't you like me?"

I keep my eyes fixed on him. I can't afford to let him think that I'm weak.

"Looks like you've got some meat on your bones too," he mutters, peering around to look at my flank. "Never know when that might come in handy, either."

He tries to pat me again. This time I slip past him and hurry to the steps, making my way up and then through the door until I find Jon in the kitchen. Sitting next to his feet, I turn and see that Richard is already following. I want to bark, to warn him away, but Jon seems to have invited him inside so I guess I have to give him a chance. If he tries anything, however, I'll be ready.

***

"No, I'm sorry," Richard says later, as the three of us sit on the porch and watch the sunset. Rain is pouring down, crashing against the roof and hissing as it hits the grass. "I don't remember hearing anything about the hospital, at least not near the end. I know they were pretty much on the front-line when the sickness broke out. I guess they must've been overwhelmed."

He grabs the bottle and holds it out toward Jon.

"Refill?"

"Just one more, thanks," Jon replies, watching while Richard pours more of the liquid into his glass. "I think I need to keep a clear head."

"You and me both," Richard replies, setting the bottle back down and leaning back in the chair. He has a glass of the brown liquid too, but he's only drunk a few sips so far. Less than Jon. "I was thinking, if I pass a well-stocked liquor store, I should get some more. Might not get another chance. Not ever." He sniffs. "Of course, wine's more my fancy. I didn't have any family before this all started, but I must admit, I'm rather heartbroken by the thought that I might never again taste a decent bottle of red."

"Things'll get better," Jon mutters, taking another look at his black rectangle.

"None of the phones are working," Richard tells him.

"I know, but they have to come on again some time."

"Do they?"

Jon nods.

"Why?" Richard asks.

"They just have to. The world can't disappear."

"Who said anything about the world disappearing? The world is still all around us. Humanity, on the other hand, is in a rather sorry state."

"That'll change."

Richard smiles. "Maybe this is our inevitable fate as a species. Maybe this is Mother Nature's way of cutting us back down and changing the order. We became too arrogant."

Jon mutters something under his breath as he continues to tap the rectangle.

"What's her name?" Richard asks finally.

Jon turns to him. "What do -"

"I can see it in your eyes," Richard continues with a smile. "You're not like me. You've got someone out there, someone you're worried about. Come on, there's no point pretending."

Jon pauses for a moment. "Her name's Julie," he says finally. "She's a doctor, she works in the ER. That's why I asked you about the hospital."

"Right." Richard nods. "I'm sorry I couldn't give you better news. She's dead, you know."

"You don't -"

"Yes I do," Richard adds, interrupting him. "I do know. They're all dead, barring a few straggling survivors here and there. Unfounded hope won't do you any good, my friend. God knows why you and I are among the survivors, but we must face the truth."

He raises his glass.

"A toast. To the hoards of mankind who died over the past week. All those millions, probably billions. To their memory, and to the future."

He holds his glass close to Jon.

"Not going to join me in a toast?"

"Julie's still alive," he says firmly. "I know what she's like. If anyone -"

Richard starts laughing.

"She's smart," Jon continues, before taking another big sip from his glass. "If anyone can muddle through, it's her. I know she'll be fine."

"Here's hoping," Richard replies, holding his glass up. "A toast to your girl Julie, then, and to her chances. Who am I to crush your rampant optimism?"

They clink their glasses together. Jon takes a big gulp, but Richard merely sips a little while keeping his eyes fixed firmly on Jon. I never like it when Jon drinks this kind of strange liquid, and I can see from the look on his face that he's already getting sleepy.

"It's a real nice place you've got here," Richard continues, looking toward the forest as the rain continues. "High ground, good visibility, far from the main road. Hell, I'd never have stumbled upon the place if I hadn't spotted a light up here last night. Plus, you've got that lake, so there's always going to be water. Good soil, too. Nice and remote." He pauses, clearly lost in thought. "A man could keep himself alive in a place like this. Or he'd have a good chance, anyway. No-one to blame but himself if he messed it up."

In the distance, there's a faint rumbling sound from the sky, and I immediately edge a little closer to Jon. He doesn't seem scared about the weather, though, so I try to stay calm. I've heard the sky rumbling before and it always passes eventually.

"Plus the dog," Richard adds, looking down at me and smiling that same smile that always sets me on edge. "Looks like a tough chap. And I see you have a rifle. Myself, I don't think I'm cut out for the rugged, survivalist lifestyle, but maybe you can make it work. Roaming the apocalyptic landscape and -"

He pauses, before grabbing the bottle.

"Oh, but where are my manners?" he asks, leaning closer to Jon and pouring some more liquid into his glass, this time all the way to the top. "Have some more!"

"I really don't think I -"

"Nonsense, just enjoy it! You're worried about your girl, and there's nothing you can do right now to see if she's alive or dead. That's got to be weighing on your mind. Have a drink to steady your nerves."

Jon sighs. "I have to go to the city," he says as he takes another sip from the glass. "I have to look for her."

"You don't want to do that."

"I have to!" He takes another, longer sip. "If there's even a chance that she's alive, I have to see if I can help her."

"A noble sentiment, my friend, but one that's going to get you killed. There are still plenty of those creatures in the city. They might be slow and they might not last long, but there are so many of them, it's hard to run away from one without running straight into another. And they do rather seem to bite."

"I have to try to find her," Jon says firmly.

"You might not like what you see if you're successful."

Jon turns to him. "What do you mean?"

"Just that a lot of people in the city are..." He pauses.

"A lot of people are what?"

"You might find your girl and wish you hadn't," Richard continues. "I don't think many people avoided the sickness. Now, I imagine that after a few days, maybe a week or two, those walking corpses are just gonna drop. They can't last forever. But until then, there's an awful lot of dead people wandering the streets. They might look like bloated, rotting versions of their old selves, they might even be wearing the same clothes, but there's nothing left of their minds. If I had a girl and I saw her like that..."

His voice trails off.

"I don't know that I'd want to see," he adds finally. "But if I *had* to see her, there'd only be one thing I could do to help her now. And that would be to put a bullet in her head, and maybe a few in the rest of her, too. However many it takes to drop those bastards. Could you do that? Could you put her out of her misery?"

Jon hesitates. "If you mean -"

"Could you aim a gun at her rotten face and blow her away?"

Jon flinches.

"Because that's the kind of decision you might have to make if you *do* find her. Not very romantic, is it?"

Jon stares at him for a moment, his eyes filled with horror, before taking a long sip from the glass. He shudders once he's finished the liquid, and this time he doesn't protest when Richard leans over and gives him a refill.

Worrying that Jon might be getting too sleepy, I paw his leg, but he simply reaches down and pats the side of my face.

"It's okay, Harry," he tells me. "We're going to get Julie back. I'm not giving up on her. Not ever."

He continues to drink, as Richard keeps talking. With each sip, Jon seems a little more tired, but at least he's starting to become less tense. Finally, with the rain still pounding down and darkness having fallen, and with occasional rumbles still filling the sky, I realize that Jon has fallen asleep. I paw at his leg again, but he doesn't respond.

"Poor guy," Richard says, leaning closer and taking a look at Jon's face. "Didn't take much to knock him out, did it?"

He tries to pat my head, but I pull away.

"What's up? Don't you like me?" He looks at the half-empty bottle. "Good job I don't really drink, or I'd regret giving away so much good whiskey. Never had a taste for the stuff, myself. It's wine for me, all the way."

Getting to his feet, he lets out a faint gasp as his bones creak. He smiles at me as he steps past, and then he heads into the kitchen. I let out a low growl, annoyed that he thinks he has the run of the place, and I watch as he heads to one of the drawers and pulls it open. He reaches in, and after a moment he takes out a roll of dirty paper. It's the same kind of paper I've seen Jon sometimes giving to people at stores. Flicking through the notes, Richard seems to be counting how many there are.

"I'll take these," he mutters, before moving over to the cupboards and taking a look inside. "Not that money is going to be much use nowadays, but one never knows. Sorry, my little friend, but it's a dog eat dog world out there now. A man has to do whatever it takes in order to survive. Even if that means slipping sleeping medication into a bottle of whiskey."

He grabs a box from the counter and starts filling it with the food Jon brought.

"On the plus side," he continues, "your owner is going to learn a very valuable lesson when he wakes up. There are a lot of people out there who wouldn't simply leave him snoozing. They'd cut his throat and take his cabin, and to be fair that's not a bad idea, but..."

He holds up a pot and examines the contents for a moment.

"Decent coffee," he says with a faint smile, before adding it to the box. "I'll have to save that for a special occasion. By the way, dog, do you happen to know if your owner has any other weapons? I'm sure the rifle is all well and good, but I could really use a handgun or some decent knives."

Snarling as he heads over to the other side of the kitchen, I watch as he opens the other drawers and takes out some knives. I'm sure he doesn't have permission to be doing this, so I bark a couple of times, partly to warn him that he has to stop and partly so that Jon will wake up.

"Keep it down," Richard says with a grin, before grabbing my lead from the hook on the wall. "I feel bad for this, but I think maybe I could use you on my travels. A good guard-dog could be a real life-saver." He steps toward me, with the lead in one hand and a knife in the other. "Come on, boy. Time to come with me. I'll be your new Daddy!"

I bark again, while backing toward the door.

Sighing, he stops and stares at me for a moment.

"You're going to wake your owner if you're not careful," he mutters, but then he seems briefly lost in thought. "Jesus Christ, what's wrong with me? I have to do it, don't I? What am I, some kind of wimp?"

He pauses, before setting the lead aside. After looking down at the knife for a few seconds, he glances at me with a hint of fear in his eyes.

"I'm not going to last long in this world if I can't even stand the sight of blood. I need to push myself over that line, I need to toughen up and the best way to do that is..."

His voice trails off for a moment, and I can tell his pulse is racing. Suddenly he glances toward the open door, looking out toward the porch where Jon is still fast asleep.

"I can do this," he says finally, as if he's trying to work up the courage to do something that horrifies him. "I can kill a man. I have to. If I do it now, then next time I have to defend myself, I won't hesitate. I'll be less of a pussy." He pauses again, before stepping toward the door. "Sorry, pooch, but I have to do this. I've been a coward all my life, but now I'm going to step up. I might as well pop my murder-cherry while I have the chance."

CHAPTER TEN

BARKING AT RICHARD AS he steps toward me, I hold my ground, ready to strike if he gets too close to Jon.

"Oh, you're a loud one, huh?" he says, adjusting his grip on the knife. "Well, I think I'd better get this done fast."

He tries to step past me, but I back away until I'm at the door. Jon looks to still be asleep, so I turn back to Richard and see that he's still coming closer with the knife.

"Don't worry," he mutters, "I won't make him suffer. Believe me, I want this over and done with. I'm a good person, I've always stuck to the rules, but the world has changed now. And I need to change with it, if I want to survive. So I'll just do this, and then you and I can head off. You'll start to like me soon, and respect me, so just -"

Suddenly filled with a sense of blinding panic, I

rush at him. He swings the knife toward my face but misses, and I bite down hard on his arm, sinking my teeth deep into his flesh. Letting out a cry of pain, he drops the knife and stumbles out through the door, but I keep my jaw clamped shut, even as my teeth start grinding against the bone of his arm.

"Fucking animal!" he hisses, grabbing my throat and then slamming me into the wall.

His blood is running into my mouth, but I refuse to let go. After a moment, however, he raises me high above the ground and then punches me, sending me crashing down. Before I can get up, he kicks me hard in the belly, and the flash of pain is enough to make me loosen my grip. Letting out a brief yelp, I fall onto my side but immediately get stagger to my feet, just as Jon stirs.

"Your fucking dog bit me!" Richard yells, clutching his arm as blood run down to the elbow. "That fucking thing is insane!"

"No way," Jon stammers, still sounding a little groggy. "Harry would never -"

"Look at my fucking arm!" Richard shouts, briefly moving his hand away to reveal the torn flesh. "He bit me through to the fucking bone!"

Jon stares down at me with pure shock in his eyes, but I quickly step past him and snarl at Richard, forcing him to back away down the steps until he's out in the pouring rain. For the first time, he actually seems scared of me.

"Harry's not a violent dog," Jon says firmly. "I don't know what happened, but you must have provoked him and -"

"He's a fucking monster!" Richard yells.

He steps closer, but I immediately start barking. Clearly terrified, he backs away again.

"What were you doing?" Jon asks him. "Why did he attack you?"

"I wasn't doing anything!" he hisses. "That fucking maniac just launched himself at me."

"No," Jon replies, "that's not like Harry. I know this dog better than I know most people, and he wouldn't turn against you unless he felt threatened. You did something that upset him."

"He's probably got rabies!" Richard splutters, as the pouring rain washes more blood down his injured arm. "You need to get rid of that goddamn little shit!"

He steps closer.

I snarl again, and then I bark.

He flinches and steps back.

With rain still crashing down and just a single light shining on the porch, Richard's face is marked by patches of blazing light and deep, black shadow.

"It's okay, buddy," Jon says, patting the back of my head. "I trust you. I know there's no way you'd ever attack someone unless you had a good reason."

"Seriously?" Richard shouts. "You're going to trust that thing?"

"Were you in the kitchen?" Jon asks suddenly, stepping over to the doorway. "Why are the cupboards all open? Why's there a knife on the floor?"

Richard hesitates for a moment, before hurrying back up the steps. I bark at him again, but this time he tries to kick me. I'm too quick for him, however, and I push against his legs, causing him to slip on the wet wood. He tumbles back and lets out a cry as he falls down onto the grass, and I quickly hurry back to my spot at the top of the steps and turn to him again. Whatever else happens, I have to defend Jon and the cabin.

"Fucking animal!" he hisses.

"Were you trying to rob me?" Jon asks incredulously. "Where's the money from the drawer?"

"It's every man for himself now!" Richard replies, his voice trembling with anger. "Do you really think you can trust anyone? We're all just fighting to survive." He lets out a gasp as he examines the bite wound on his arm. "Do you have any medical supplies? You owe me that much, at least. This thing could get fucking infected!"

"I don't owe you a goddamn thing," Jon replies, before turning and heading inside. "I'll give you back the food you brought, though. And then you need to get the hell out of here."

I can tell from the look in his eyes that Richard is considering another attack, so I keep snarling, determined to make him stay back. A moment later, however, I spot a hint of movement behind him, as if someone else is coming this way through the darkness. I lower my front a little, ready to spring forward if necessary, but the wind and rain are making it difficult to pick up any strong scents. For the first time in my life, there are so many impressions all around, I feel as if the world is filled with chaos.

"What the fuck are you looking at?" Richard

asks, clearly unaware that someone is approaching him from behind. "You'd have been better off with me anyway. At least I know how to survive. At least I'm not some naive, dumb-ass hick who can be plied with a bottle of whiskey and -"

Suddenly he screams and clutches his throat, and when he stumbles forward I see that the man from the gas station's parking lot has bitten deep into his neck.

"Get it off me!" Richard yells, with blood spraying from the wound. He tries to turn away, only for the man to drag him down onto the grass and bite his neck again.

"What the hell's going on out there?" Jon shouts, rushing back onto the porch but stopping as soon as he sees the rotten man tearing a thick knot of flesh and meat from Richard's bloodied throat. "What the..."

"Help me!" Richard screams, reaching toward us with a trembling, blood-stained hand. "For the love of God, kill it!"

Still barking, I take a step forward, hoping to scare them both away. Only Jon and I should be here, and I want everyone else to leave the cabin and the field right now. Richard is trying to crawl to the bottom of the steps, but he's already lost a lot of blood and the rotten man is still biting huge chunks away from his neck and shoulder. Already, enough meat is missing for Richard's bones to start glistening in the rain.

"Stay back," Jon stammers, grabbing my collar. "Harry, this is -"

"Help me!" Richard shouts again, rolling onto his back and trying to put the attacker away. Suddenly, however, the rotten man bites down hard on his belly, digging his teeth through the shirt and clawing at his flesh. Sobbing, Richard lets out a gurgled moan as more blood sprays from his ravaged neck, but he can no longer even try to drag himself toward us. Instead, his shaking hands are simply clutching the wet grass as more rain comes down, and I can just about hear a juicy sucking sound as his belly is torn apart.

"That thing's insane," Jon says, before turning and grabbing the rifle.

Still barking, I take a step back and watch as the rotten man continues to feed on Richard.

"I'm sorry," Jon says firmly, stepping past me and aiming at the rotten creature, "but I have to do this."

Suddenly the gun fires, blasting the creature's face apart and sending it slumping down against Richard's trembling body.

"It must have walked all the way up here from the gas station," Jon says, taking a cautious step forward while still aiming the gun at the spot where the creature's body fell. A moment later, the headless torso starts twitching, and Jon shoots it again, this time blowing the upper part of its chest clean away, and finally the meat remains slump down onto the rain-soaked grass.

"Help me," Richard gasps, his voice shuddering as he reaches a hand up through the rain. "Please..."

Although I just want to go back into the cabin and ignore everything that's happening, I follow Jon down the steps, while still snarling at the headless creature in case it moves again. There's very little light out here, but I can just about make out the sight of rainwater crashing down against Richard's bloodied chest, washing blood and other liquids out onto the grass. His guts have been partially pulled out, glistening in the rain.

"I don't want to die," he groans, trying to grab the end of the gun. "Help me. I don't... I don't want to..."

"There might be another one," Jon says, looking out at the darkness. "There was a woman at the gas station too, she might be closer."

"Help..."

Jon hesitates, before propping the gun at the top of the steps and then making his way down cautiously to Richard's bloodied form.

I bark, to warn him that it's too dangerous.

"I don't think I can move you," Jon stammers. "He almost..."

"Get me inside," Richard gasps. "Hurry!"

"I don't -"

"Get me inside!" Reaching out, Richard grabs Jon's arm for a moment, although Jon quickly pulls away and takes a step back. "You can't leave me out here! What are you, a monster? Get me into that fucking cabin right now!"

"I have a First Aid kit," Jon says, turning and hurrying back up the steps. "Wait!"

"I don't want to die!" Richard yells, reaching forward and digging his fingers into the grass.

I step back, keen to keep away from him.

"Do you hear me?" he snarls through gritted teeth, staring at me as he starts dragging himself to the bottom of the steps. He lets out a cry of pain, but he keeps coming, pulling himself forward inch by inch until finally he slumps down again. "What the fuck are you looking at?" he asks. "There's no way I'm going to die. I'll find a way, I'll..."

He tries again to drag himself toward me. Turning, I hurry back up the steps and over to the door, and when I look inside I see that Jon is in the bathroom, sorting through the contents of a small metal tin.

"Help me!" Richard screams, his throat filled with blood now. "What the fuck are you doing? You have to help me!"

I watch Jon for a moment longer, before turning and looking back down at Richard. His eyes are wide open, but something seems different about the expression on his face. Heading over to the top of the steps, I watch him for a moment, and finally I realize that even though rain is falling against his eyes, he's no longer blinking. I sniff the air, but the bad weather make it hard to pick up a decent scent. He's not moving at all, though, and I think he might be dead.

"Okay," Jon says, hurrying out with the metal tin and then making his way down the steps, "I found -"

He stops suddenly, staring at Richard's corpse.

"Richard?"

No reply. He pauses for a moment, before turning to me.

"That thing," he says finally, "the creature that attacked him..."

His voice trails off for a moment, and then he looks back down at the dead bodies.

"It looked like some kind of zombie," he

stammers. "I know that sounds crazy, and it *is* crazy, but I swear..."

He pauses, before coming back up the steps and setting the metal box down. Keeping his eyes fixed on Richard, he grabs the rifle again.

"Should I..."

Whimpering a little, I take a step back as he aims the gun at Richard's head.

"Should I do this?" he asks, his voice trembling with shock. "What if he... What if he comes back somehow, like those other people? What if they all come back?"

He hesitates, before lowering the gun again.

"I'll bury him in the morning," he says finally. "We'll keep all the doors locked, we won't sleep, and then at first light once the rain has gone..."

He pauses, before turning and heading inside.

"Harry! Get in, right now! In!"

I don't need to hear that command twice. Hurrying into the cabin, I'm relieved as Jon swings the door shut and turns the key. He takes a step back, and I can tell he's not sure what to do next.

"This isn't what it looks like," he says finally. "It can't be. We'll wait until morning, then we'll be able to see better and we'll know what really happened. Everything's going to be fine, buddy, I swear. We just..."

His voice trails off, and he stands in silence, staring at the door. Above, rain is still pounding against the roof.

"Julie'll come," he adds finally. "She has to. Then we can get the hell out of here."

CHAPTER ELEVEN

BY THE TIME THE MORNING SUN starts rising in the distance, Jon and I are in the bedroom. He's still holding the rifle in his arms, and he's sitting on the floor next to me, with his back against the bed. Neither of us slept during the night. We both stayed right here, watching the door and listening in case there was any hint of movement outside.

Now that the storm has passed, however, light is streaming through the rain-spattered window and the only sound comes from dribbles of water running down off the roof.

"I should go take a look," Jon says finally, turning to me. He seems exhausted, with rings under his eyes. "I should, right? I should go and..."

He pauses, before gasping as he gets to his feet.

Letting out a faint whimper, I paw his leg.

"It's okay, buddy," he continues, his voice filled with fear. "I'm going to be real careful. And don't worry, we've got plenty of ammo for the rifle. That's one of the advantages of not really liking the goddamn thing. I never even opened the box of ammunition until yesterday."

He heads through to the cabin's main room, and after a moment I follow. The night's storm has changed the scents coming from the other side of the front door, and it takes a few seconds before I realize I can smell death. I wait as Jon opens the door, and then finally he swings it open to reveal the two dead bodies down at the bottom of the steps. I hesitate, worried that they might stir, but the only movement comes from beads of rain that dribble down their sides.

Richard's dead eyes are still open, covered in spots of water.

"Fuck," Jon says, stepping out onto the porch with the gun still in his hands. "I was kinda hoping..."

His voice trails off.

"Well, you know. That none of it actually happened. That it was all just some kind of nightmare."

His hands are trembling, and I can tell he's shocked by the horrific scene.

"What do I do?" he asks finally, turning to me. "What the hell am I supposed to do with them? Even if everything Richard said yesterday is true..."

He stares at me for a moment, before looking down at the bodies again.

"I guess I have to move them," he continues. "I don't want to touch them, though. I'll find some other way. And then when this is all over, I'll have to explain to the cops..."

He pauses.

"And it *will* be all over," he adds finally. "Soon. I can feel it. Everything's going to go back to normal."

***

It takes most of the morning, but Jon finally manages to move the two bodies. He uses a couple of branches, which allow him to push the bodies around without actually touching them. I keep back, watching from the porch, because something about the scent from Richard's body is making me nervous. Somehow the smell isn't changing properly, and I let out a few cautious growls every time Jon uses the branches to push Richard further from the cabin.

Finally, once he's done, Jon comes and sits next to me on the steps.

"Should I burn them?" he asks, a little out of breath. "I can't just leave them like that, can I? It's not like I can call the cops right now and get them taken away, so..."

He pauses, before getting to his feet.

"I'll burn them," he continues, reaching down and patting my head. "I can explain everything to the cops later, I can try to make them understand, but right now I figure I have to deal with the fact there are two dead bodies out here. I'll just use a little gas, not a lot, and then..."

He seems momentarily lost for words.

"Richard's car probably has something in the tank. Maybe enough for us to get out of here, Harry. I guess that's something we need to consider, but let's just do one job at a time, huh?"

I watch as he heads over to Richard's car. After fiddling with some kind of hose, he manages to get some dark, foul-smelling liquid to come dribbling out into a bucket. To be honest, I'm more focused on sniffing the scent that's coming from the bodies on the wet grass, because one of them – Richard's, I'm almost certain – seems to be somehow getting stronger, with a more pronounced and active smell than I'd expect from a corpse. I want to go closer and get a better sense of what's happening, but I don't think it's safe.

As Jon carries the bucket over to the bodies, I let out a bark to warn him.

"It's okay, buddy," he replies, pouring the bucket's contents over the two corpses. "It's not nice, but I've got this."

The liquid obliterates the other scents that were coming from the bodies, which makes me feel a little calmer. Still, I know that something isn't quite right, and I watch with concern as Jon heads to the other car and then returns with a little rattling box.

"I've never burned a corpse before," he mutters, glancing at me. "And now I've got two! New life experiences for everyone, huh?"

He stops next to the bodies, staring down at them, and I can tell he's worried.

I bark again, hoping he'll heed my warning and step back.

Instead, he continues to look at the corpses, as if he's lost in thought. Finally he opens the little box in his hands and takes out what looks like a tiny piece of wood.

"I don't know what to say, really," he continues finally. "I've never been a religious guy, Harry, but at a time like this, I'm thinking maybe..."

He pauses, and then he glances up at the clear blue sky above. He hesitates for a moment, before mumbling something under his breath and then striking the piece of wood against the side of the box. A small flame bursts to life, which he then drops onto the bodies.

At the very last second, Richard's body twitches.

Suddenly flames burst across the two corpses.

I bark several times, but there's no further sign of movement other than the blazing, roaring flames that are already sending thick black smoke high into the clear blue sky.

Letting out a faint, worried whimper, I step back from the edge of the steps, and then I turn around a couple of times before settling again, watching the flames. I need to make sure that Richard doesn't suddenly start moving again.

Jon simply stands on the grass and watches the fire, before coming over and taking a seat next to me. For the next few minutes, we both stare in silence as the flames burn. Jon doesn't say a word, which is unusual for him. Instead, he strokes the fur on the back of my neck for a little while, and then his hands falls still, resting on my flank. It feels good to have him so close, and I'm glad he's keeping well away from the burning bodies. Eventually the flames start to die down, and all that's left is a charred and blacked pile of bones smoking in the wet, bright green grass. Even the bones are mostly destroyed, although I can see part of Richard's blackened skull still, and his mouth is wide open. I'm sure it was closed when the fire started.

"Well that was that," Jon mutters. "When they've cooled, I'll take the tarp from round back, and I'll... I guess I'll find some way to wrap them up and then move them further away. Maybe down to the lake."

He turns to me, and I can see the fear in his eyes.

"Hell of a way to spend our day, huh?"

His voice is trembling, and I can't shake the feeling that deep down something has changed in his heart.

"I shot that guy," he continues finally. "Did you see? Maybe he was a zombie, maybe not, but I shot him right in the face. I shot a..."

He pauses, and now I can hear that his teeth are chattering.

"Fuck!" he hisses, getting to his feet and making his way along the porch, before stopping and turning back to me. "I shot a guy, Harry!" he shouts. "Maybe I was right to do it, maybe I'll have to do it again, but I actually aimed a gun at him and pulled the trigger. And then he died, and that asshole Richard died, and..."

He pauses, before sitting and leaning against the edge of the porch. There are tears in his eyes, and after a moment I get to my feet and head over to join him. Settling next to him again, I rest my chin on his lap, and he starts stroking my neck with a trembling hand. I wish I could make him feel better, but for now all I can do is stay close to him as the smell of burned meat fills the air all around us.

"I shot someone," he stammers finally, under his breath. "Fuck. I actually shot him."

After a moment, he reaches down and feels the flesh around his ankle, where there's a small graze in the skin.

"Damn it," he mutters, "I didn't notice that happening. Must have been while I was moving them."

I don't know how long we sit like this. Several hours, with my chin resting on his leg and his voice trembling as he continues to talk out loud. Eventually I go to the top of the steps and settle there, keen to keep my eyes on the burned bones, just to make sure that Richard doesn't move again. I glance back at Jon every few minutes, though, and I can't help noticing that he's still scratching that patch of damaged flesh on his ankle.

CHAPTER TWELVE

JON'S NOT WELL.

I start worrying later that evening, when I notice that he's scratching his ankle a lot while he makes dinner. Then, while he eats on the porch and occasionally passes scraps to me, I realize he seems a little warm, and I can see sweat glistening on his forehead. I tell myself that he's fine, that there's no reason to worry, but after sunset I start noticing that he's touching his wrist a lot, as if he's trying to listen to his heartbeat.

His ankle smells odd.

And there's fear in Jon's eyes.

More than before.

"It's nothing," he mutters several times, forcing a nervous smile as he glances at me. "After everything that happened today," he adds later as we head out onto the porch and look out at the darkness, "it'd be a miracle if I wasn't feeling under the weather. It's probably just shock."

Still, he keeps scratching that wound on his ankle, and he's made it bigger now. There's a patch of blood on his fingertips, and he only gets worse during the night. I desperately need to sleep, but I only doze a few times, since Jon keeps tossing and turning, bumping me as I rest at the bottom of the bed. He's mumbling, too, and I think his temperature is getting higher.

Figuring there's nothing I can do right now, I close my eyes and try to sleep. And I tell myself that tomorrow he'll be fine again.

CHAPTER THIRTEEN

"IT'S JUST A STOMACH BUG," he mutters the next morning, as he comes out from the bathroom. He pulls the door shut, but I heard him on the toilet and I can smell an overwhelming stench of feces. He smiles at me, but he looks hot and drained. "Great timing, huh? Don't worry, I'll be back on top form in no time."

He spends the next few hours on the porch, drinking tea and watching the forest in the distance. It's clear that he doesn't have much energy, and eventually he grabs a blanket from the bedroom and wraps it around his shoulders, which seems odd since he already seems so warm. The skin around the edge of his nose looks red and sore, with the rash extending down onto his upper lip. He's shivering a little, too, and he keeps mumbling under his breath.

"Just flu," he says several times.

He reaches over and pats my neck a lot, too, and I let him. He's sick, that much is clear, but I know that

Jon has been sick sometimes in the past, and his kind of sickness never seems to cross over and make me unwell. All I want is to make him feel better, and to keep him company while he recovers, but at the same time I can't shake the feeling that he's a lot warmer than ever before.

I'm also watching the burned bones, which are still resting in the grass. They haven't moved since the fire died down, but I still don't like the sight of Richard's skull.

"Do you know what I think?" Jon asks later, after he's said almost nothing for several hours. "I think that Richard guy was full of shit. Seriously, look at the whole thing logically, there's no way some sudden sickness could have carved through the population so fast. Maybe there was some vague thing going on, something small, but he blatantly exaggerated the whole deal."

He seems a little happier now, and a little calmer.

"He probably shot through at the first opportunity. The guy seemed like a coward. I mean, hell, he was trying to steal from us, right? I bet he was one of those conspiracy nuts and as soon as people started getting sick, he assumed the fucking apocalypse had arrived, so he loaded his car up and took off. Then he happened to find us and he took the opportunity to spew out his mangled version of events. And that other guy, from the gas station? That was just a coincidence. Coincidences happen, right? He was just badly hurt, out of his mind with pain, and that's why he..."

His voice trails off. He mumbles a little more,

while still stroking my flank.

"That explains it, really," he adds finally. "Yeah, I'm sure of it. Just a series of really messed-up coincidences. And do you know what else I think? I think Julie's gonna -"

Suddenly he starts coughing.

Startled, I watch as he turns away from me, coughing into his hands. His whole body is shuddering, and the cough sounds harsh but dry. It takes several minutes for him to recover, and when he moves his hands from his mouth, his wrists, palms and fingers are covered in a fine spray of blood.

"That's nothing," he stammers, his voice sounding much weaker now. "It's just flu. Even if Richard was telling the truth, which he wasn't, but even if he was... There's no way I could have gotten sick. Not up here, not at the cabin, away from everyone. I didn't even touch the guy from the gas station, so how could it have gotten into me?" He pauses, before turning and forcing a smile. There's blood on his lips, but the rest of his face looks very pale. "It couldn't. So that's final. At the gas station, and then when I was moving the bodies last night, I was careful the whole time. I was really -"

Before he can finish, he starts coughing again. This time some of the blood sprays out between his fingers and hits the wooden floor, and I step back a little.

"It's okay," he gasps, struggling to get his breath back. "Fuck, this is just..."

He pauses, staring at his blood-spattered hand, as if he's in shock and can't quite work out what's happening.

I let out a faint whimper.

Turning, he reaches out to pat my head, but at the last moment he hesitates and pulls his hand back. I think he's worried about touching me. He looks out toward the forest, and for a few minutes he seems lost in thought, as if he's thinking about something far away. Sweat is running down the side of his face now, and I can feel the extra heat from his body. His scent has changed, too, as if something is different deep down in his body.

Stepping closer, I nudge my nose against the top of his arm, to show him that I'm still here.

"It's okay," he gasps, his voice sounding very dry now, almost scratched. He's shivering, too, even though it's a warm day and he's got a blanket over his shoulders. "We'll both be fine. And Julie's gonna get here soon."

***

Later, while Jon is sleeping on the porch, I make my way around to the other side of the cabin, and I look out at the fields. The whole world seems strangely quiet now, and all the distant din of the human world is not only gone, but almost hard to remember.

It feels as if we've been up here at the cabin forever, and I have to struggle to remember what life was like in the city.

Sniffing the air, I realize that most of the smells seems like natural things. The grass, the forest, even scents drifting from the lake, carried all the way here on the breeze... Before, even up here at the cabin, I could always smell cars on the roads and other, occasional signs of human activity for miles around, but now the world seems to have calmed. Despite my concerns about Jon, I can't help looking out across the field and watching the lake's glittering water in the distance, and just taking a moment to let the scents of the natural world linger in my nose.

I wouldn't mind if things stayed like this. I just need Jon to get better first.

When I eventually head back to Jon, I find that he's still sleeping. His head has tilted to one side, and a faint dribble of clear mucus has begun to run from one corner of his mouth. There's sweat all over his face, too, and still a little dried blood on his lips and chin. He looks sick, with pale skin, and I stop before I reach him, worried about getting too close. Still, I've never gotten sick from being around him before, and I remind myself that he needs me. Sometimes, he seems to feel better just when he gets to touch my flank, so I step closer and settle on the ground next to him, listening to the sound of his rapid but shallow breathing.

He'll get better.

He has to.

And until then, I just have to wait.

Suddenly I hear a faint rattling sound from nearby. I hurry to the top of the steps and look toward the trees, but there's no sign of movement. A moment later, I realize that the sound is coming from the burned bones, and I see that the wind has picked up slightly. I start snarling, just in case there's any danger, and I watch for a few seconds as Richard's burned skull twitches slightly.

Finally the wind dies down.

The bones stop moving.

I don't dare stop looking at them, though.

Just in case.

A few minutes later, I hear a faint creaking sound over my shoulder, and I turn just in time to see that Jon's head is moving slightly. His eyes are still closed, but after a moment they start to open. There's some kind of thick, yellowish mucus stuck in his lashes, almost gumming his eyes shut, and it takes a few seconds before he turns and looks down at me. I wait for him to smile, for him to say something that'll make me feel better, but he's simply staring at me with no hint of recognition at all. I'm scared now, but I can't run from him. Jon is my master and nothing can ever make me leave him, even if his expression seems somehow wrong right now. It's almost as if someone else is staring at me from behind his eyes.

"Hey," he whispers finally, his throat sounding drier than ever. His expression changes, relaxing slightly. "Sorry, buddy, I think I..."

He pauses, almost as if he's forgotten what he was saying.

"I think I nodded off there."

He tries to sit up, but the effort is clearly painful and it takes him several attempts. He wipes his mouth with the back of his hand, letting out a faint gasp as he looks around.

"What time is it?" he asks. "How long have we

been sitting here like this?"

I watch him carefully, looking for some sign that he might be getting better, but if anything he actually seems worse. Warmer, too, and with even more sweat running down his face.

Finally, after a few minutes, he tries to get to his feet. He lets out several more pained gasps, but he keeps pushing until eventually he manages to stand, although he's having to steady himself against the wall.

"I need to sleep," he mumbles, turning and starting to shuffle toward the door. "I'll be better after that. I just need... I need water, and I need to sleep."

I follow as he heads inside, and then I watch him stumbling toward the kitchen. He grabs a bottle of water and starts drinking, and he doesn't stop until every last drop is gone, at which point he grabs another bottle and does the same again. Taking a third bottle, he hesitates for a moment, before leaning down and pouring some into my bowl, and then he starts drinking again, tilting his head back as he pours more and more water down his throat. Finally, as if his body can take no more, he lets out a spluttering cough and lets the plastic bottle slip from his trembling hand. Leaning forward, he gasps several times, and I see bloody water dribbling from his lips.

"I just need to sleep," he says again, turning to me and forcing a smile. "Whatever this is, it's just some kind of flu. I'm going to be fine."

He starts shuffling toward the bedroom.

"I'll be -"

Suddenly he starts swaying, and he takes a

couple of quick steps toward the wall before falling and slamming into the bookshelf. He lets out a gasp of pain, and then he pauses for a moment as if he's trying to get his balance back.

"I'll be fine," he whispers, heading once again toward the bedroom door. "I'll get better, Julie will come, we'll go home and everything will start getting back to normal. I promise."

CHAPTER FOURTEEN

HE SLEEPS FOR SUCH A LONG TIME, I start worrying that he might never wake up.

Afternoon becomes evening, and finally the sun sets, bringing darkness. This time Jon isn't around to light candles in the window, so the cabin is plunged into darkness. I jump down off the bed, where Jon is gasping as he sleeps, and I make my way through to the main room, where I see that he left the front door open. Heading over, I look out onto the porch, but all I see is darkness, although a hint of moonlight is catching the edges of the charred bones.

And all I hear is silence.

Not just the kind of silence where there are a few background noises, but absolute silence. Maybe for the first time in my life, I can hear absolutely nothing. Not a single noise, in any direction.

Sitting in the doorway, I realize that with Jon asleep, I have to guard the cabin. There's still a chance that someone could show up, and I need to make sure I know who they are before I let them inside. Julie is okay, and I'd let her come through the door, but anyone else would have to wait outside. I'm exhausted, having barely slept over the past few nights, but somehow I'm able to stay awake and alert, watching the darkness and listening for any sign of life.

And then later, after several more hours have passed, I hear a bumping, stumbling sound from the bedroom.

Turning, I look across the dark room just in time to see a silhouette appear in the doorway. It's Jon, I can tell that, but the way he's standing seems different somehow, as if he's leaning heavily on the side of the door. He's not moving now, and instead he seems to be simply standing and listening to the silence.

"Harry?" he says finally.

Getting to my feet, I head over to him.

"Hey Harry," he whispers. "I need... I need more water..."

He takes a few stumbling steps through the darkened room, before bumping into one of the chairs and almost falling.

"I think you should stay outside for the rest of the night," he continues. "I don't want... I don't want you getting sick. I think there's blood in the bed, and I don't want you to..."

He pauses, and I can hear his labored breath in the darkness.

"You have to stay well, buddy," he says finally. "You can't come on the bed, okay? Not right now. Not until I'm better. It's for you... It's for..."

His voice trails off, and a moment later he starts stumbling toward the kitchen. I wait and watch as he grabs another bottle of water, which he drinks quickly, and then he drinks two more. Finally letting out a gasp, he starts coughing, and it takes several minutes for him to get his breath back. Turning, he starts heading to the bedroom again, and I follow.

"No," he says, stopping and looking down at me, "you stay out here. Please, Harry, I don't want you to... Please, I can't make you sick. Whatever this is..."

I let out a faint whimper, to let him know that I'm still here, but suddenly he reaches down and takes hold of my collar with a trembling hand, before turning and leading me toward the open front door. I try to pull back, but I don't want to struggle too much so I decide to follow, figuring that maybe we're going to sit together on the porch.

"There," he says once we're outside, letting go of my collar and stepping back through the door. "Just for one night, buddy. Just until I'm better, to keep you from getting sick."

With that, he shuts the door.

I immediately hurry over and scratch at the wood, but I can hear Jon stumbling away now, heading into the bedroom. Panicking, I let out a series of barks, to remind him that he's made a mistake, but a moment later I hear a gasp and a squeaking sound, which I know means that he's slumped back down onto the bed. I run around to the glass door that leads into the kitchen, but it's shut.

I bark again and scratch at the door for a few more minutes, before hurrying along the porch and making my way around to the window that leads into Jon's room.

I stare up at the glass for a moment, before barking yet again, and then a few more times until finally I start whimpering instead. He must have fallen asleep and forgotten that I'm out here, but I have to find a way to get inside so I can sit with him and make sure he's okay. I bark a few more times, hoping to wake him, and then I head back around to the front of the cabin and start scratching once again at the door.

The wind is picking up now. Black bones are rattling in the grass.

CHAPTER FIFTEEN

BY THE TIME THE SUN COMES UP, the cabin has been completely still and quiet for several hours.

I'm still on the porch, watching the front door and waiting for Jon to come and let me back inside. He's probably still asleep, but I'm certain that he made a mistake when he left me out here during the night, and soon he'll wake up and realize that I'm supposed to be with him on the bed. For as long as I can remember, I've always slept at the bottom of Jon's bed. That's just how things are supposed to be, and it's wrong for me to be out here when he needs me. I don't care if he's sick, I just want to be with him.

So I wait.

And I wait.

Later, once the sun is high in the blue sky, I get to my feet and wander around to the cabin's other side. I'm hungry and I need water, but there's no way I can leave the cabin. Jon will feed me as soon as he wakes up and opens the door, but as I sit and look up at the bedroom window, I realize that there's still no sign of him.

Finally, hoping that he'll be able to hear me, I start whimpering, while my wagging tail brushes against the boards.

Several minutes later, I let my whimper become a little louder, accompanied by a few half-woofs, while still staring at the window and waiting for the first sign that Jon is awake.

CHAPTER SIXTEEN

NIGHT FALLS AGAIN. I'm still out on the porch, and I'm starving, but all I can do is wait at the door for Jon to finally come and let me in. Occasionally I start barking for a few minutes, although I'm too weak to make a lot of noise. I need to conserve energy.

My nose is twitching, though. There's a dark scent drifting out from the cabin, curling under the door. I start whimpering again.

I can smell death again.

CHAPTER SEVENTEEN

SUDDENLY THERE'S A LOUD crashing sound from inside the cabin. Having waited out here for hours and hours now, I immediately get to my feet and stare at the door, and sure enough the sound is still there. Jon's moving about again.

It's still dark out here, but I step toward the door and claw at the wood, while barking to remind him that I'm out here.

And my tail is wagging furiously.

He's back!

Everything's going to be okay again!

From inside, there's the sound of glass breaking. It's almost as if Jon has suddenly woken and started stumbling about, crashing into the furniture, but at least he's alive. There's still a stench of death drifting out from under the door, but that must be coming from something else inside the cabin. For now, I take a couple of steps back and start barking again, while wagging my tail as I wait for Jon to come and get me.

For the next few minutes, however, all I hear is the sound of him bumping into things. He's obviously still not well, but at least he can come and sit with me for a while, and give me something to eat and drink. All I can think about is the moment when the door is going to open again, but finally I realize that it doesn't sound as if Jon is coming any closer. All the bumping and crashing sounds still seem far away, as if he hasn't made it out of the bedroom yet.

Hurrying along the porch, I head around to the spot beneath the bedroom window and immediately start clawing at the wood and barking to get Jon's attention. A moment later, however, I hear a loud thudding sound and the wooden wall shudders slightly, as if something slammed into it on the other side. I step back, whimpering slightly, and I pause for a moment before barking again. Jon has to be able to hear me, so it's only a matter of time before he comes out and everything is back to normal.

But as the sun starts to rise in the distance, there's still no sign of him.

If anything, the crashing sounds from inside are getting louder and more persistent. I'm still barking, but I'm also starting to think that maybe Jon isn't able to get to the door. Whereas earlier I was relieved to hear him moving about, now I can't help noticing that he sounds as if he's struggling, and moments later I hear him thudding against the wall several more times. I pause, and now there's a very faint grunting sound coming from the other side of the window, almost as if Jon's snarling.

Jon doesn't snarl, though.

He never snarls.

I don't know why I'm hearing a snarl, but I tell myself that it must be some kind of mistake.

Heading back around to the front of the cabin, I start pawing at the door again, dragging my claws through the wood in the hope that Jon will hear and realize that he has to let me inside. I can still hear a series of loud, heavy bumps, and he seems to be stuck in the bedroom, but I know that once he understands that I'm out here, he'll definitely come and look after me. He must know that I haven't eaten in over a day, and that I need water. I trust Jon more than I trust anyone else, even if it's taking time for him to come to the door.

But no matter how loud I bark and how furiously I scratch at the wood, several hours pass and he still doesn't come to fetch me.

***

I don't know how long I've been clawing at the front door now, but I've started to wear several deep grooves into the wood and my throat is sore from all the barking. The sun has risen high and my legs are starting to ache, but I know I have to keep trying. For some reason, Jon still doesn't seem to realize that I'm out here, so I have to get his attention.

I can still hear him banging around in the cabin.

He hasn't stopped once. He's been awake for hours now, but he still doesn't seem to have left the bedroom. If anything, the banging and crashing sounds have been getting louder, almost as if he's becoming more and more furious. I can hear him grunting, too, although he hasn't spoken once, at least not using any words that I understand. Instead, he seems almost to be on the floor, as if -

Suddenly I hear another, closer bump, and I realize he seems to have finally made it through to the front room.

I bark several times, to make sure he realizes I'm here, and then I sit whimpering for a moment. He'll come and turn the handle soon, and then the door will swing open and I can go inside. I'll be able to eat and drink, and then I can sit with Jon while he gets better. Everything will be okay, so long as I can just get into the cabin.

As I wait, I realize I can hear him coming closer. It sounds like he's crawling across the floor, which seems strange, and a moment later I hear him bumping against the other side of the door.

I reach out and paw at the wood.

Suddenly something heavy slams against the door, startling me so much that I instantly step back a few paces. He hits the door again, as if he's trying to force it open, and I can hear a low, persistent snarling sound now. Looking down at the bottom of the door, I can just about make out his shadow. I'm picking up Jon's scent, too, but it seems to have changed somehow, as if some part of him is starting to turn rotten. As he continues to push against the wood, however, I realize that maybe I can see him now if I go to the glass door, round at the far end of the kitchen.

Hurrying along the decking, I stop at the glass door and look into the cabin.

Sure enough, Jon is on the floor, still throwing his weight repeatedly against the front door. He looks frail and weak, as if he's lost weight, and there's dried blood all around his injured ankle. After a moment, however, he looks this way and I see that his eyes have blackened slightly around the edges, while the whites have become a dull yellowish color. He stares at me for a moment, before hauling himself around and trying to get to his feet. When that doesn't work, he half-crawls, half-stumbles toward me, although he quickly falls and lands against one of the chairs, knocking it over and crashing hard against the bottom of the kitchen counter.

I watch with a growing sense of concern as he reaches out and digs his fingernails into the floorboards, and slowly he starts crawling this way.

Wagging my tail in an attempt to make him happier, I realize that although this is definitely Jon, something seems very different about him now. The glass door makes it harder for me to pick up his scent, but as he edges closer it's clear that the flesh on his face seems to have somehow shrunk slightly, as if it's clinging more tightly to his bones, while his mouth is hanging open with dried blood all around the edges. I've seen him when he's sick before, but he's never looked this bad, and as he reaches the mat on the other side of the door I have to fight the urge to turn and run.

Suddenly he lets out a dry, pained cry as he slams his fists against the window, causing the glass to shudder.

I instinctively step back, while keeping my eyes fixed on him.

He lets out another snarl as he slams his fist against the glass. Staring into his eyes, I can't shake the feeling that somehow it's not really Jon looking back at me. He's never been the kind of person who gets angry easily, and he's definitely never been angry with me before, so I don't know what I should do as he hits the glass over and over again. I can't think of anything I've done wrong, but it's almost as if he really wants to hurt me. I turn and start walking away, before turning again and watching as he tries to sit up. For some reason, he seems to be having trouble with his legs, but finally he starts throwing his body against the glass, and he doesn't even seem to care that he's damaging his face. In fact, he hits the glass so hard, he quickly crushes his nose and causes a trickle of blood to run down to his lips.

Not wanting to see him like this, I turn and head back around to the front of the cabin, although then I stop again. I can still hear Jon shouting, but it occurs to me that if I go back and take another look, he might suddenly be better.

I walk all the way around the cabin until I come back to the glass door, but Jon is still the same. He's slamming himself harder than ever against the glass, as if he thinks he can break through.

Turning, I make my way back to the front porch, and then I pause for a moment. I want to help, but he seems so angry and I'm worried that I might be doing something wrong. Still, there's a chance that he might already be better now, so I walk around the cabin again and take another look at the kitchen door.

He's gurgling now as he continues to hammer his body against the glass, which is now covered in red and yellow smears. There's so much anger in his eyes, it's almost as if he wants to hurt me.

But Jon would never hurt me.

I know that.

Since I can't work out what else to do, and all I want is for Jon to go back to normal, I start walking around the cabin over and over again. Each time I come back to the glass door, I hope that he'll be his old self, and each time I find that he's still crying out and trying to break through the glass. I can't leave him, so I just keep doing the same thing over and over, walking around the cabin and coming back to the door, in the hope that eventually he'll calm down. And each time, when I see his snarling, angry face again, I set off on another walk around the cabin, just in case – next time I come to the door – he's back to normal.

If I keep doing this, eventually it has to work.

CHAPTER EIGHTEEN

SOMETIMES, WHEN I GO to sleep, my head is filled with very clear memories of the past, and images of things that happened a long time ago. It's not just images, either. I hear things, and I smell things. In fact, during these dreams, it's always the smells that are most vivid.

I dream scents and odors.

Tonight, for example, I see the old apartment I lived in with Jon. I don't remember much from those days, at least not in terms of what I saw or heard. But the scents are still so clear. The scent of the park, when Jon used to take me for long walks. Or the scent of my bed next to the dining room table, where I'd wait while he worked. Or the scent of the food he was preparing in the kitchen, and of the scraps he'd let me eat. I don't remember what any of those moments looked or sounded like, but the scents are so vivid, even now.

And we used to run together, especially after we

started coming to the cabin. We'd run through the fields, and through the forest, and around the edge of the lake. I want to run with him again and feel the scents of the world rushing against my face. I want to -

Suddenly opening my eyes, I find that the sun has begun to rise. I didn't so much fall asleep as pass out thanks to a combination of exhaustion and hunger, but for a moment I remembered the scents from the days when Jon and I used to run. Now that I'm awake, however, I can hear him still slamming his fists against the glass door on the other side of the cabin, and he still sounds angry. I was hoping that I'd wake up and find that he'd gone back to normal, but as I get to my feet and start traipsing along the porch, I'm scared that he'll still be angry when I go and look at him.

As soon as I get back to the glass door, I'm shocked to see how much blood is now smeared all over the inside. Jon is still slamming his fists against the glass, and it looks as if he's managed to damage his hands, tearing some of the flesh away until the bone is visible beneath. A couple of his fingers are dangling now by threads, almost entirely mashed away. It's hard to see properly through so much blood, but I can just about make out the shape of him on the other side, and after a moment I lower my head a little and peer through a clearer patch of glass.

I feel a shudder pass through my chest as I see that some of the flesh looks to be peeling away from his face. After a moment, his eyes twitch and look toward me, and he immediately lets out another cry of anger as he throws himself against the glass with more force than ever.

I step back, filled with a growing sense of panic. Jon has always been so stable in the past, and I've often been able to understand what he's doing and why. Even when I *didn't* understand, I trusted him implicitly and I knew that if I just followed him, everything would be okay. My whole life, that rule has stood firm and kept me safe, but for the first time I'm starting to wonder whether Jon is still someone I can trust. He's my master and I've never doubted him before, but if he's lost his mind, maybe there's nothing I can do to help him.

Still, I can't just leave, so I decide to walk around the cabin again, hoping that when I get back to the glass door, he'll be back to normal. My legs are aching and I just want to settle down and sleep, but my belly is empty and the gnawing pains of hunger are starting to fill my mind. I'm thirsty, too, but I don't dare leave the cabin and go down to the lake, not until I'm certain that Jon is okay. He's always pulled through for me before, he even made the pain go away when I got my paw caught in a door and I had to go see the vet. He always looks after me.

I circle the cabin for a few more hours, but nothing changes and Jon still sounds angry.

Finally, too tired to walk, I drop down at the top of the steps and take slow, deep breaths. I need to eat soon, and my belly is starting to hurt. It's hard to know what to do, though, and after a moment I close my eyes, hoping that if I can go to sleep again, everything will be okay when I wake up.

I drift for a moment, before suddenly hearing the

sound of a car's tires screeching along the dirt road.

Opening my eyes, I look across toward the dirt road just as a red car comes racing into view. I get to my feet and watch as the car screeches to a halt, and for a moment I'm filled with fear as I realize that someone else has arrived. A moment later, however, the car door opens and a woman steps out, and I feel an immediate rush of relief as I see that it's someone I recognize.

Julie!

Julie is finally here!

"Harry!" she shouts, clearly scared as she rushes toward the cabin. "Thank God you're here! Where's Jon?"

I run down the steps, overjoyed to see her, and she crouches down next to me and runs her hands along my flank.

"Hey, boy," she stammers, "you're so thin. Are you guys okay? Where's Jon?"

I lean closer and lick the side of her neck, but my tongue feels dry.

"Jon?" she shouts, getting to her feet and stepping past me. She hurries up the steps and onto the porch, and then she stops as if she's suddenly heard the grunts and crashing sounds from inside the cabin.

I watch the back of her head, waiting to see what she'll do. I like Julie, she's smart like Jon and I trust her. She'll make everything better again.

After a moment, she takes a step back as Jon continues to hit the door. Finally, she turns to me with tears in her eyes.

"That's not..." She pauses. "Harry, tell me that's

not Jon. Please, I thought you guys would..."

She turns back to look at the cabin's front door, and a few seconds later there's a loud bump on the other side, as if Jon has made his way back over and is now trying to get out to her.

"Please no," she says, her voice trembling as she makes her way along the porch and round to the other side.

I make my way up the steps, not wanting to follow and look through the glass door this time.

I wait, scared in case -

Suddenly Julie lets out a brief, shocked cry, and I hear her running back this way. She stops as soon as she sees me, and tears are streaming down her face.

"Tell me that's not him!" she sobs. "Please, Harry, that can't be Jon in there..."

As if to answer her, there's another loud roar from inside the cabin, and a series of bumps as if he's still trying to break out through the glass door.

"It's not Jon," Julie whimpers, stepping away from the cabin until she's standing next to me at the top of the steps. "It can't be. I got here as fast as I could, but I was so sure that Jon would be okay. He's *always* okay, he always knows how to look after himself. This can't happen to Jon. It's happened to so many other people, but not Jon."

I look up at her, hoping that she'll know how to put everything right. Maybe if she goes inside, she can make Jon go back to normal. She's always made him happy before.

Inside the cabin, Jon is once more throwing

himself against the door, desperately trying to break out. At the same time, he's letting out a low, guttural snarl that never seems to end. And just as it seems that he has to give up, he starts hitting the wood even harder, and I let out a whimper as I take a few more steps back.

"Oh God," Julie sobs, sitting on the edge of the porch and staring at the wooden door as it continues to shudder. Tears are streaming down her face. "Please, not Jon..."

***

"I can't leave him like this," Julie says eventually, after we've listened to Jon's fury for a little longer. Her voice is trembling more than ever. "I can't... I can't just drive away. I can't."

She pauses again, before getting to her feet. Her heart is pounding as she steps over to the table by the door and picks up the rifle, which has been resting there ever since Jon used it on the creature that attacked Richard. She opens it and takes a look at one of the inner parts, and then she snaps it shut again.

"One shot," she whispers. "I can't let him suffer like this. I saw so many people at the hospital, I saw what happens to these things."

She turns to me, and more tears are streaming down her face.

"They just get worse, Harry," she continues. "I've seen them, they just rot and fall apart. It's not really Jon in there, not anymore. You understand that, right?"

She takes a deep breath.

"This is the only merciful thing I can do for him now."

She hesitates for a moment, before a shudder seems to pass through her body.

"I can't do it," she stammers, turning and heading back down the steps. "I'm getting out of here. Come on, Harry, you can come too. I've got food. Not a lot, but enough, and then we'll get to the rendezvous point and everything'll be okay."

I watch as she opens the trunk of her car. I can't believe that she's actually going to leave without helping Jon, and when I look back at the cabin, I realize he's screaming louder than ever.

"Harry?" Julie calls out to me. "Do you want this?"

I turn to her again, and I see that she's holding out a handful of canned meat. My stomach is so empty, it hurts, but no matter how much I want that meat, I can't bring myself to walk away from the cabin. Even though I'm drooling at the prospect of food, I turn back to the cabin and watch the door, still hoping that Jon will suddenly come out and that everything will be okay again.

"He's gone, Harry," Julie continues, with a hint of desperation in her voice. "That's not him anymore, it's just something in his body. We started to analyze the sickness at the hospital, but then everything went to hell. There's one thing I'm sure of, though, and that's... When they come back, it's not really them. It's just their bodies."

She keeps talking, but I focus on the door. I still

believe that Jon will come out eventually.

"I have to get going," Julie says, and I hear her getting back into her car. "I'm sorry, Harry, but there's nothing else we can do for him. Harry, come get in the car."

I stare at her for a moment, before turning back to the cabin.

"Get in the car!" she shouts, her voice filled with desperation. "You dumb dog, get in the bloody car!"

I don't look at her. I keep my eyes fixed on the door, and a moment later I hear Julie starting her car's engine. The vehicle's rumbling sound continues for a few minutes, before stopping again, and then I hear her climbing back out.

I wait, but finally I turn to her.

"I can't leave him like this," she whispers, wiping tears from her eyes. She still has the rifle in her hands as she steps toward me. "You know I love him, don't you?" she continues, reaching down and ruffling the fur on the back of my neck. Her hand is shaking. "You know I do. I've loved him for so long, and I love him so much, and that's why I can't just leave. I have to put him out of his misery. Either there's a glimmer of his soul left in there and he wants the agony to end, or there's nothing left and this is just the final indignity. Whatever... I saw enough at the hospital for me to know that this is what I have to do now. I have to do it because I love him."

She pauses, before stepping past me and making her way along the porch.

I let out a faint whimper, and she turns to me.

"It'll be quick," she says. "I promise, Harry. He won't suffer."

I don't know what she's talking about, but I turn back to the front door as I hear Jon still desperately trying to break through. A moment later, I realize that Julie is out of sight now, having made her way around the side of the cabin. I take a few cautious steps forward and look at the front door for a moment longer, before heading along the porch and looking along to see that Julie is at the glass door.

She pauses for a moment, before reaching out and sliding the door open.

And then she raises the rifle.

"I'm sorry," she sobs, as I hear the sound of Jon scrambling toward her inside the front room. He's snarling louder than ever. "I love you so much. I'm sorry. I love you. I -"

Before she can finish, she fires the gun. A blast rings out and she takes a step back, and there's a heavy thud from inside the cabin.

Finally everything falls still and quiet.

I stare along the porch, watching Julie, waiting for Jon to step out through the door. After a moment, however, I realize that I can't hear him at all.

"Oh God," Julie whimpers, dropping to her knees and letting the rifle fall from her hands, as she continues to stare through the door. "Please forgive me. I didn't know what else to do. I couldn't leave him like that, I just couldn't..."

She puts her hands over her face and starts weeping uncontrollably. I've never seen her like this before, but usually when she's upset Jon makes her feel better. This time, however, there's no sign of him.

I make my way cautiously along the porch until I reach the open glass door. Looking inside, I see that Jon is slumped just a few feet away, with most of his head having been blasted clean away. There's not much blood, since his body seems to have become very dry over the past few days, but I can see some bones poking out through the stump at the top of his neck, and there are more pieces of bone and meat sprayed across the floor.

"I'm so sorry," Julie sobs, and her whole body is shuddering now as she continues to weep.

I watch Jon's body for a moment, as I slowly start to realize that he's not coming back. I can't smell him at all now. With the glass door having finally been opened, it's clear that the interior of the cabin reeks of death, and the scent is coming almost exclusively from Jon. The part of him that gave him his unique scent is gone, which means that *he's* gone.

I pause for a moment longer. I want to go through the door and sit with Jon, to maybe check if there's anything I can do to bring him back, but the stench of death is too strong and I can't bring myself to take a step forward. Instead, I walk over to Julie and sit next to her. I curl into a tight ball, hoping that maybe if I close my eyes for a while I might wake up and find that Jon is back.

Deep down, however, I know that he's gone forever.

Finally Julie gets to her feet. Her legs are

shaking and she grabs hold of the railing as she stumbles back along the porch. When she reaches the far end, she hesitates for a moment before leaning over the side and vomiting. Then, she makes her way around to the front of the cabin, disappearing from view. A moment later, I hear her sobbing again, wailing this time as if she's in actual, physical pain.

And then she falls silent.

For the next few minutes, I simply rest on the porch and stare through the door, watching Jon's lifeless body in case there's any chance he might stand up.

Eventually, however, I hear Julie coming back this way, and I turn to see her carrying a metal can along the porch.

"I have to do this," she tells me, sniffing back more tears. "One of the things we learned at the hospital, before everything fell apart, was that fire..."

Her voice trails off, and then she turns and shakes the can, spraying the inside of the cabin with the same foul-smelling liquid that Jon used on the dead bodies earlier. Some of the liquid lands on Jon, and I get to my feet as I realize that Julie suddenly seems more determined, as if she has a plan.

A moment later, I hear a scratching sound, and I look up to see that Julie is holding a small piece of wood that's burning at one end. She hesitates, watching as the flame burns, and then she tosses it through the doorway, causing the interior of the cabin to immediately start burning.

"Come on," she says, picking me up and carrying me along the porch, away from the flames.

"He's gone, buddy."

I pull back, trying to slip free.

"He's gone!" she says firmly, keeping hold and trying to drag me along. "Harry -"

Turning suddenly, I look over her shoulder, only to see flames roaring out from the door and already sending thick plumes of smoke into the sky.

"Please don't hate me, Harry," Julie says, sounding a little breathless. "If you'd seen what people become when they get this sickness, you'd know that I did the only thing I could. That wasn't Jon, not anymore. I couldn't leave his body stumbling about like that. It would've been obscene."

She carries me all the way to her car and then sets me down, keeping hold of my collar while holding some more meat toward my mouth.

"You need to eat," she continues. "Harry, food! Dinner! I'm sorry I shouted at you just now, but seriously, you need food."

I turn away, looking back toward the cabin as the flames spread all the way through to the front door.

"Harry -"

Pulling away, I slip free and run away from her car, but I stop when I get to the bottom of the steps. Staring up at the door, I can see smoke escaping from the interior of the cabin, and I realize that there's no way Jon is going to get out of there. I step forward, but a wall of heat pushes me back and finally I settle on the grass, placing my chin between my front legs and watching as the cabin continues to burn. Even if there's no chance of Jon ever coming back, I've spent my entire life with him and I don't know what to do next.

So I'll wait right here.

Maybe something will happen, something I don't understand right now, and he'll suddenly appear.

"Harry!" Julie calls out. "I have to get out of here! Come on, I'll take you with me!"

I barely even hear her voice. Instead, I focus on the sound of the flames, and I listen in case there's any hint of Jon's voice. Julie is still calling for me, but I can't go with her. I belong here, in the spot where I last saw Jon, because I know that he'll come back if he can.

Suddenly I feel Julie's hands on my sides, and she picks me up again. I try to jump free, but she's holding me too firmly as she turns and carries me toward the car.

"I can't leave you here," she says, putting me onto the back seat before slamming the door shut. "Jon wouldn't want that."

Everything about her car smells unfamiliar. I've never been in here before, although after a moment I realize that maybe there's *one* scent that I recognize. Jon has been in here, not recently but maybe a week ago or even longer, but it's the first time in several days that I've picked up on his pure scent.

As Julie gets into the front of the car, I lean my head through the gap between the seats and try to get closer to Jon's scent. My heart leaps at the thought that he might be here, even though I know that the scent isn't fresh. Still, just the fact that I can smell him again without there being a hint of death mixed in with the scent is enough to make me feel happy again, even though there's no sign of him.

"I did what I had to," Julie says, watching as the cabin continues to burn. "I'm a doctor, Harry. I did the sensible, logical thing. It was right for Jon, and it was right for everyone else too. If I'd left him trapped in there, someone else might have stumbled up here and..."

Her voice trails off.

"We have to get to the rendezvous point," she continues after a moment. "That's the last thing I heard, anyway, before everything went dead. It's only only chance. They said survivors should head to a rendezvous point in the Rarrah Valley, and that we could start turning things around. Maybe I can help, they must need medical staff. I know it might not be a good idea for so many people to gather together when there's still a chance of this sickness spreading, but they'll have precautions in place. They have to. This can't be the end of the world."

She pauses, before turning to me. There are still tears running down her face.

"You're lucky the disease only seems to affect humans. Dogs aren't even a carrier."

Reaching out, she strokes the side of my face. She tries to smile, but the effort seems to be too much and she bursts into tears, leaning closer and pressing her face against mine.

"I didn't want to do it," she sobs finally, sitting back. "I swear, if there'd been any other way, if there'd been even a chance to save him..."

She stares at me for a moment, before starting the engine and backing the car away from the cabin. As she turns the wheel and drives back to the dirt-road, I look through the rear window and watch the burning cabin as it gets further and further away. Even once we're a fair way along the road, I can still see smoke rising into the blue sky, and I let out a faint whimper as I remember the last time I drove this way with Jon.

A few minutes later, Julie stops the car at the side of the road and starts sobbing again. This time she's really weeping, and she seems barely able to catch her breath as she leans forward and rests her head on the steering wheel.

PART TWO

CHAPTER NINETEEN

"OKAY, CALM DOWN," Julie says firmly, as the girl continues to scream. "Just try to stay calm and we'll fix this."

Still sitting on the car's back seat, I watch out the window as she kneels next to an injured man, whose lower body is covered in blood. His legs are crooked somehow, as if they both go the wrong way at the knee, and there are several dark patches on the tarmac. There's a girl next to him, still shrieking and crying as she continues to panic.

"What's his name?" Julie asks the girl. "I'm a doctor. Tell me his name, and tell me what happened."

The girl yells something back at her.

"Tell me what happened!" Julie says firmly. "I need to -"

Suddenly the girl reaches out and grabs her by the throat.

"Stop that!" Julie hisses, shoving her back

before slapping the side of her face, which at least gets her to stop screaming. "I'm a doctor. I need to know what happened before I can help him!"

As she continues to talk to this new girl, I turn and look out at the deserted town. Ever since leaving the cabin, we've just been driving and driving for hours on end, and I'd begun to sleep on the car's back seat. I kept hoping I'd wake up and find that Jon had returned, but each time I opened my eyes I simply found that I was still in the car, with Julie still driving. And then, just a couple of minutes ago, I was woken by the sound of the car coming to a screeching halt, and by the sound of screams outside. I don't know where we are, but I don't like it and I want us to get going again.

"He was hit by a car," the girl sobs. "We were trying to flag down a ride, we just wanted to get out of here but some asshole kept on speeding and hit him and..."

Her voice breaks down and she starts letting out a series of whimpered cries.

Meanwhile, Julie is kneeling next to the injured man, and she's started touching his bloodied face and gently tapping him, as if she's trying to make him wake up.

"What's his name?" she asks finally.

"Scott," the girl stammers. "Please, you have to save him." She leans closer to the injured man. "Scott, it's me! Say something!"

"Can you hear me, Scott?" Julie continues. She uses her fingers to open the man's eyelids, although they quickly slip shut again. "What's *your* name?" she asks, turning to the girl.

"Melissa," she replies, "but please, that doesn't matter right now. You have to save Scott!"

"Was he showing any signs of sickness before he was hit?"

"What?"

"Sickness!" Julie continues, her voice filled with frustration. "Any fever or aches, any -"

"No!"

"Absolutely nothing at all? No flu-like symptoms?"

"No!" the girl hisses. "Why aren't you listening to me? He was hit by a car, you dumb bitch! He needs help!"

Hearing a scratching sound, I turn and look the other way, just in time to see some garbage getting blown along the dusty street. There are buildings lining the road, but they all look empty and abandoned, with broken windows and doors that have been left hanging open, while tire marks criss-cross the sidewalks as if cars left here in a hurry. I pause for a moment, filtering out the girl's continued screams, and I realize that the rest of the town seems completely still and quiet, as if there's no-one else around. A moment later I hear footsteps coming toward the car, and I turn again just as Julie leans into the back and reaches for a bag on the floor.

"He's not going to make it," she whispers to me. "We'll be out of here soon, just... Stay in the car, Harry. Be a good dog."

She checks the contents of the bag. Her hands are trembling.

"I need an ER room, not a First Aid kit," she mutters, glancing at me again. "There's not much I can do for him, but I've got to try. The girl's the only one I can help here."

With that, she's off again, taking the bag around the side of the car and over to the bleeding man on the ground. I watch for a moment, and although I want to jump down and go to see what's happening, I'm put off by the fact that the girl is constantly letting out these horrified, pained cries. She seems completely consumed by panic, and her whole body is shuddering as she yells at Julie. Meanwhile, Julie has already opened the bag and is taking out some items. I don't know what she's doing, exactly, but she seems calmer than before, as if finding these people has somehow re-focused her attention after everything that happened at the cabin.

For the first time, Julie is actually making me feel a littler better.

Still, all I can think about is Jon. After watching Julie work for a moment longer, I turn around on the car's back seat and settle down again, curling up tight and resting my head next to my paws. I still think that if I can just sleep for a while, I might wake up and find that Jon is back. In fact, I'm sure that's exactly what will happen, so I close my eyes and try to ignore the girl's continued shouts and shrieks. All I have to do is sleep, and everything will be okay again. I'll be with Jon, back at the cabin.

CHAPTER TWENTY

OPENING MY EYES, I realize that although I've managed to sleep for a while, nothing seems to have changed. I'm still in the car, and there's still no sign of Jon. All I want is to get him back, so maybe I just need to sleep again. Eventually he *has* to return. He can't be gone forever.

Still, at least the girl has stopped screaming.

Lifting my head, I realize I can smell Julie's scent, which means she's still nearby. I could go back to sleep, but I want to know what's happening, so instead I get to my feet and make my way cautiously to the car's open door. I sniff the air again, to make sure that there's no sign of danger, and then I jump down onto the cool tarmac and carefully walk around the car, stopping when I see that Julie and the girl are still sitting with the bloodied man, and that Julie still seems to be doing something with the items she took from her bag.

I sniff the air again, and then I head over to

them, while making sure not to get too close to either the man or the girl. The only person I trust here is Julie.

I smell blood.

Fresh blood.

And fear.

"He's a little more stable now," Julie's saying to the girl as I reach them, "but there's not much more I can do for him out here. He needs to get to a hospital."

"He's going to be okay, isn't he?" the girl sobs, as she runs a hand across the side of the man's face. "Scott, can you hear me? This lady's a doctor and she says you're going to be just fine."

"He needs surgery," Julie tells her.

"Then we have to get him to a hospital, like you said."

"It's not that easy."

"We have to!"

"Moving him would be a huge risk," Julie continues, as she pours some kind of clear, strong-smelling liquid onto her hands. "I don't think he'd survive even being moved to a car right now."

"But you said he -"

"If we had an ambulance, that'd be different. If we had proper equipment..." She pauses, and for a moment she seems lost for words. "All I've got is a couple of bags with me. That's not nearly enough to..."

Her voice trails off.

"But he's going to be okay," the girl continues after a moment. "You said that, you said he'll be fine. You're a doctor, so you save people, that's what you do."

"That's not quite what I -"

"You'll be up and about in no time," the girl adds, forcing a smile as she continues to stroke the man's face. "This lady's a doctor and she's going to make you all better again."

Julie turns to her.

"If you need to operate on him," the girl sneers, "then fucking operate on him!"

"We're on the side of a road," Julie points out.

"So? I've seen movies! Doctors can, like, improvise!"

"His legs are shattered," Julie continues, with a hint of desperation in her voice. "His pelvis, hips..."

As I reach Julie, she continues to work on the man's injuries. Her hands are covered in blood, but it's fresh, bright blood, and it doesn't smell rotten at all. I can tell she's sad, but it's a different kind of sad to how she seemed in the car before we stopped. Now her sadness seems focused on the blood-covered man, and when she glances at me I can immediately tell that she's worried. Even worse, her heart is pounding and her scent has changed a little; she's scared, as if she's expecting something bad to happen at any moment.

"Is it safe to have that *thing* here?" the girl asks.

Turning, I see that she's eyeing me with a hint of suspicion.

"Dogs aren't carriers of the sickness," Julie tells her.

"You don't know that for sure."

"Actually, I do. It's one of the first things that was determined when this thing struck. Dogs and other animals don't seem affected at all, and they don't even carry it. The virus seems to die very quickly outside the human body, so it more or less requires person-to-person contact."

"Dogs are still dirty," the girl continues. "You should chase him off."

Julie runs her hand along my back. "It's okay, Harry, you just -"

"Shoo!" the girl shouts suddenly, clapping her hands at me. "Get out of here!"

Startled, I take a step back.

"Run, you little fucker!"

Suddenly the girl kicks me hard, hitting my flank, and I let out a faint whimper as I run around to the other side of Julie.

"Don't do that to him!" Julie says firmly. "He's not dangerous! Leave him alone!"

"What kind of dog is he, anyway?" the girl asks as tears run down her face. "He's just this stupid little runt."

"He's a Jack Russell, and he's staying!"

"But you can't take the risk," the girl continues. "Even if there's a chance -"

"Do you want to talk about taking risks?" Julie asks, interrupting her and sounding a little annoyed now. "I just stopped my car and came to help your bleeding, dying boyfriend, even though as far as I knew he could have been infected with the sickness. I only had your word to go on that he was fine before he got hurt, but I took the risk because I couldn't just drive on and leave the two of you like this. So if anyone here is taking a risk, it's me. Or do you want me to take the dog, get back in the car and leave you two here?"

The girl stares at her, clearly shocked, before looking at the man again.

"I just want Scott to be okay," she whimpers finally. "We were camping when all of this shit came down, so we weren't in town for the start. By the time we got home..."

Her voice trails off.

"So we packed up and started driving," she continues, choking back tears as Julie gets back to work, "but we ran out of gas. Then we started walking, and we got to this place, wherever the hell it is." She looks around at the abandoned buildings, and once again her eyes are filled with a sense of hatred. "Some backwater little hick town, I don't even know its name. Probably full of inbred fucking assholes before everything went to shit. And then we saw a car headed this way, coming real fast, and Scott wanted to try flagging it down so we could get a ride."

She runs her hands through the man's hair.

"And the driver hit him?" Julie asks.

"He didn't even slow down. I think he actually sped up and..." She pauses, with fresh tears filling her eyes. "Scott wasn't even in the middle of the road. He was being careful, but at the last moment the driver swerved and... I think he hit him on purpose. He slammed into him so hard, he spun him through the air and sent him crashing into the wall of that store, and then..."

She bursts into tears, sobbing hysterically as she places the side of her face against the man's chest.

"And then the asshole just kept on driving," she whimpers finally. "He knocked Scott down like a goddamn bowling pin and then he sped off into the distance. That was about two hours before you showed up. Ever since then, I've been trying to keep him alive but I don't know how. I'm not a fucking doctor."

"He lost a lot of blood," Julie replies.

"But he's going to be okay," the girl continues, sniffing back more tears. "You said it yourself, he's going to be fine."

"He lost at least -"

"That doesn't matter now you're here."

"There's also a head injury. It looks like his skull -"

"But he'll be fine!" the girl hisses.

Julie hesitates. "I didn't quite say that he -"

"I know he will," the girl adds, her voice trembling with fear. "I just know it. Scott isn't going anywhere. He's strong, he's healthy, he's young, and he's gonna get better real fast. Give it a few more hours and he'll start waking up, and then he'll be able to stand again, and then it'll be like none of this ever happened." She turns to Julie. "You have to stay. You have to make sure he's okay."

Julie hesitates for a moment. "I'm on my way to -"

"You have to stay!" the girl hisses, as if she's starting to panic again. "You're a doctor! You, like, legally have to stay until you know he's fine!"

Again Julie pauses, while still working on the man's injuries. She seems torn for a moment, as if she's not quite sure what to do next. After a moment, she turns and looks around, as if she half expects to see someone in one of the streets.

"There are none of those fucking monsters here," the girl tells her. "If that's what you're scared of. We've been here for a few hours, we'd have seen them by now. All we've seen are rotten corpses."

"Do you know if there's a pharmacy anywhere in this town?" Julie asks, turning to her. "Somewhere I might be able to get some better medical supplies?"

CHAPTER TWENTY-ONE

"IT'S OKAY," JULIE SAYS a few minutes later, as she and I make our way along the dusty, abandoned street. "The sickness, whatever it is, doesn't last long outside the human body, so I don't think there's any chance of us breathing it in or getting exposed by dirty surfaces. Even rotten bodies probably aren't a danger, but don't go licking anything, just in case. Understood?"

She stops as we reach the edge of a small town square. She's been talking to me a lot since we left the cabin, and at first I was worried in case she expected me to understand her. Now, however, I'm starting to think that she's a lot like Jon. She talks to me because it's a way of talking to herself.

"Now where?" she mutters. "Any ideas, Harry?"

Turning, I look back the way we just came. I'm glad we left the girl and the man behind, although I think we're probably going back to them soon. I wanted to just get back into the car and leave the town, but Julie started walking this way and I was worried about letting her go off alone, so I followed in case she needs my help. Jon would want me to stay close to her until he comes back. Keeping Julie safe is my new job.

My flank still hurts a little, though, from where Melissa kicked me.

"What I *am* worried about," Julie continues, as we set off across the square, toward a set of buildings on the far side, "is bumping into more infected individuals who are still on their feet. Melissa said she hasn't seen or heard any sign of movement around here since she and Scott arrived, but that doesn't mean there can't be something trapped somewhere. Or headed this way." She glances down at me. "I'm relying on your amazing sense of smell, Harry. Okay? If you pick up anything that seems wrong, anything at all, let me know with a growl or a bark."

I still don't know what she's saying, but I know that she seems calmer than before, and much calmer than the two people we met just now. At least until Jon returns, I feel as if I should follow Julie and let her lead the way.

"We've got to keep moving," she mutters, stopping in front of a building that has a green cross above the door. She pauses, before reaching down and picking up a rock. "If we stop for too long, that's when we're in trouble. If we keep moving, eventually things'll get better and we won't have to think so much about..."

Her voice trails off, and she stares at the store's window for a moment before suddenly throwing the rock and shattering the glass.

I take a step back, shocked.

"It's okay, Harry," she says, reaching down and patting the top of my head. "We'll make a note of everything we take, and when all of this is over we'll come back and pay properly. We'll pay for the window, too. We're not thieves, we're just doing whatever's necessary to survive, that's all." She looks down at me, and I can see the sadness and fear in her eyes. "It's going to get better, you know. All this madness is going to end, and everything's going to go back to normal. Well... Almost everything."

She pauses again, before stepping forward and peering into the store's dark interior.

"Hello?" she calls out. "Is anyone here?"

She waits.

"I think the place is empty," she mutters finally. "It's okay, Harry. You just stay out here. I wouldn't want you cutting your paws on the glass. I'll be right back, so just stand guard out here, okay?"

She climbs through the gap and into the store. I try to hurry after her, although I stop when I realize that I can't reach up to the bottom of the window. Instead, I sit and wait as I listen to the sound of her walking about inside. After a few minutes, I turn and look back across the town square, but there's no sign of anyone and I feel as if this whole place has been completely abandoned. Still, I'm starting to pick up on certain scents that are making me worried, and finally I get to my feet and walk over to the top of the steps, where I stop to sniff the ground.

People were scared here.

I can usually tell when humans have been scared. I can't explain how, but something changes, something in their whole body, and in extreme cases they leave traces after they're gone. Their sweat changes.

Stopping next to a bench, I realize I can smell human urine on the ground, but the urine seems different to normal. It's as if someone was right here just a few days ago, and whatever happened to them, they released urine at a time when they were terrified. Now that I'm on the trail, I'm picking up other smells, too, and I make my way cautiously along the front of the building until I reach the far end, at which point I look along the next street and immediately pick up a scent of rotten flesh. I freeze, and a moment later I spot what looks like dead human on the ground, several meters away with lots of blood all over the ground and the wall. There's a small black bird perched on the body's shoulder, pecking at its meat.

Taking a step back, I start barking.

The bird turns and looks toward me, with a chunk of pink meat dangling from its beak.

I bark again, but still the bird just stares. It seems completely unafraid, as if its only business is death.

"Harry? Where are you?"

Still barking, I hear Julie clambering out through the broken window and hurrying this way. When she reaches me, she lets out a faint gasp just as the bird flies up to the top of a nearby wall with its piece of flesh.

"Did the body move?" Julie asks, her voice filled with tension. "Did it..."

She pauses, before stepping past me.

"It looks like it was hacked to pieces," she continues. "I saw that before a couple of times. When people were worried about a body coming back, they took an ax to it and made sure it was immobile. At least that way, if it tried to get up it wouldn't have any arm or legs. A crude method, but definitely effective. Looks like this guy was set on fire too."

She turns to me, and I see that she's cradling lots of little boxes and packets in her arms.

"It seems like the survivors from this town took off," she adds. "Either that, or they died in their homes and..."

She looks around, as if she's worried about seeing or hearing something in one of the nearby buildings, and then finally she turns to me again.

"I'm going to do what I can for the guy at the side of the road," she continues finally, "and then you and I are going to get going, okay? We can't stay here too long. Like I said, we need to keep moving. We'll patch that Scott guy up, giving him the best possible chance, but then we have to try to reach the rendezvous point at the Rarrah Valley. That's where people will be, or at least... It's our best shot."

She steps back past me and starts heading across the town square again.

"Harry! Stay close!" she calls back to me. "Harry, come!"

I stare at the burned corpse for a moment longer, sniffing the air, and after a moment the black bird lands on the shoulder again. I watch for a moment as it pecks at a fresh patch of meat, and then it turns and stares at me with two dark, beady eyes. It looks so hungry.

Startled, I turn and hurry after Julie.

***

"Put your hand right there," Julie tells the girl a short while later, once we're back at the side of the main road. "Press hard. You need to learn how to change his dressings."

"Why can't *you* do it?" the girl asks, as she places her hands on the injured man's leg. "You're the doctor."

Julie hesitates for a moment. "I don't know how long I can be -"

"You're not leaving us, are you?" the girl continues, her voice once again filled with panic. "Please, you can't leave us! You're a doctor, you have to stay! You're not allowed to leave patients behind!"

"I just -"

"Please!"

Julie pauses again, glancing at me for a few seconds, before turning back to the girl.

"Of course we'll stay," she says finally, with a hint of reluctance. "But I still want you to learn how to do this, so press down on the bandage. Make sure it's nice and tight."

The girl stares at the bandage for a moment, before shaking her head and pulling back.

"It's gross."

"You have to learn!"

"You're the doctor. You do it."

Julie opens her mouth to argue, before sighing as she grabs another roll of tape. She glances at me, and I can see that she's annoyed, but after a moment she starts working on the man's injuries again. After a moment, she turns to the girl. "We were in luck at the pharmacy. I can apply some dissolving stitches, but I'll need to close all the wounds properly before nightfall. I'm going to need some kind of wire, and a flame. And right now, you have to press here."

"But -"

"Do it!" she says firmly. "If you don't, he'll die!"

The girl hesitates for a moment, before pressing a finger on the bandage.

"That's good," Julie continues. "Now whatever you do, don't let go."

CHAPTER TWENTY-TWO

BY THE TIME NIGHT FALLS, Julie has been working for hours and I can tell she's exhausted. She gets the girl to start a small fire close to the spot where the man is still unconscious, although the girl struggles and eventually Julie has to do that as well. At least the flames provide some heat as the temperature continues to drop.

While the light from the fire is welcome, it makes the rest of the town seem much darker, and I know I can't afford to rest. I want to sleep, so that maybe I can wake up later and find that Jon is back, but I figure I have to stand guard while Julie is still busy. Jon would want me to keep her safe.

Finally, after what feels like an eternity, she gets to her feet and heads over to the car. I hesitate for a moment, before hurrying to join her.

"Hey," she mutters, sounding exhausted as she takes some items from one of the boxes on the back seat.

"Are you doing okay there, Harry?"

She glances back toward the girl.

"She's not a lot of help," she adds. "I guess she's just in shock."

She takes a slice of ham from a packet and crouches down, holding it out for me.

"You need to eat," she continues. "You're no use to anyone if you're weak. Please, Jon would want you to have something, and I'm sure we'll be able to find some fresh supplies eventually. Jon always..."

She pauses, and it's as if the mention of his name has brought fresh tears to her eyes. She wipes the tears away, but more come soon enough.

"Please eat," she adds, holding the ham closer to my mouth. "I know what it's like, I'm not hungry either, but we have to keep our strength up. Come on, ham was always your favorite. Remember how you used to do all those tricks just for a taste? This is a whole slice on offer."

I sniff the ham for a moment, but I feel too nauseous to eat.

"Roll over," she says suddenly.

I stare at her.

"You know this trick," she continues. "Harry, roll over."

I hesitate, before rolling over.

"Good boy," she says, holding the ham out, and this time I eat it automatically. After all, I always get ham after I've performed a trick. By the time I remember that I wasn't feeling well, I've already swallowed.

"Roll over," she says again, holding another

piece of ham.

I do as I'm told, momentarily feeling pleased that I can follow a command. Again, I eat the proffered ham before I even have a chance to realize that anything is wrong.

"Now let's try like this," she continues, holding up yet another piece. "Eat, Harry. Please."

This time I take the ham and swallow it almost whole. Now that I've started to eat, I feel a little better.

"I'll try to find something healthier for you soon," she explains, "so don't get used to the ham lifestyle."

She takes another slice and seems like she's about to eat it, but then she hesitates. After a moment, she holds it out for me.

"I'll eat later," she mutters. "Right now, I..."

Her voice trails off for a moment, and then she looks past me and watches the silhouette of the girl and the man against the fire. Once again, I can tell that she's sad.

"He's not going to make it," she whispers. "Even if I could get him to a hospital, it'd be touch-and-go, but out here there's no chance at all. All I can do is try to ease his pain, and to be honest that means making sure he doesn't wake up. His hips and legs and shattered, he's lost a lot of blood, and that head injury means he probably hasn't had a hope ever since he was hit. The brain damage would be too severe." She pauses. "I should just let him go now, but I can't do that. I have to try. Still, I doubt he'll last the night."

She hesitates for a moment.

"I saw worse at the hospital," she adds finally. "In the first few days, when people were starting to come in but we still didn't know what was actually wrong with them, and we were learning about it by seeing what was happening right in front of our eyes... I remember the first time I saw one of those *things* start to move again after it was supposed to be dead. I don't think this Scott guy is infected, but I can't be sure. If I ever seen another of those creatures again..."

She pauses, and then she smiles.

"Listen to me, talking to a goddamn dog," she mutters, patting my flank. "You're a good listener, Harry."

She seems upset, and I can see more tears glistening in her eyes. Stepping closer, I nudge her arm with my nose, and she reaches over to stroke the fur on the back of my neck. Maybe it's because she was taught by Jon, but she has a very similar touch, and she reminds me of the way he'd absent-mindedly pat me while he was thinking about other things. And now, as Julie continues to stroke my fur, I can tell that she's starting to fall asleep, and I turn just in time to see her head dipping forward before she jerks back.

"I just need to get a few hours," she mutters. "I'll be able to work better once I've slept. It's been days since I managed. We'll sleep in the car, with the doors locked. Just for a little while, okay?"

She heads back over to talk to the girl, and finally she comes back to the car. There's not much room, even after she's cleared the boxes off the seats, and she tries to get me to sleep in the front. I want to stick close to her, however, and eventually she relents, shifting to make room for me. I curl tight next to her belly and then I close my eyes, ready to sleep again. I tell myself that this time, maybe I really *will* wake up back at the cabin with Jon. Even though I know that something bad happened, I figure that it might un-happen.

It's not long, however, before I wake on the car's back seat, and I realize that something seems to be wrong with Julie.

Although she's definitely still asleep, she's moving about a lot, and she's mumbling under her breath. I can barely see a thing, since there's not even any moonlight tonight, but I can hear Julie's voice and she sounds upset by something, as if she's trying to warn people. A couple of times, I hear her mention Jon's name, and finally it seems as if her voice has changed a little. Now she's begging, and she sounds desperate, and she's saying Jon's name more and more. She twists and turns, and with each passing second she seems to be getting increasingly upset.

"Jon!" she shouts suddenly, sitting up and hitting her head on the car's roof.

I pull back, startled as I slither down off the seat. Looking up, I see Julie's silhouette and I realize I can hear her gasping for breath.

"Damn it," she says after a moment. "Another nightmare. I need some air."

She turns and opens the door, before stepping out into the cold night air. I want to sleep, but instead I get to my feet and jump out after her. I can tell her heart is pounding, and she takes a moment to steady herself before heading back toward the still-burning fire.

I hang back a little, and I can see the silhouette of the girl as she continues to sit with the injured man.

A moment later, I watch as Julie's silhouette kneels next to them, and I can hear muffled voices.

"No!" the girl screams suddenly, pushing Julie away. "He can't be! You said he'd be okay!"

The girl starts sobbing, clutching the man close to her, while Julie's silhouette watches from a little way back. I can tell that something's wrong, and as I cautiously make my way closer to them, I realize that I can already pick up a faint scent of death.

"You said you'd save him!" the girl whimpers. "You promised! What kind of fucking doctor are you, if you can't even keep someone alive?"

Julie's silhouette seems frozen for a moment against the flames, before finally she puts her head in her hands. I step closer and wait for her to rub my fur, but after a moment I simply settle next to her and place my chin on the side of her leg. She's crying again.

CHAPTER TWENTY-THREE

MORNING SUNLIGHT STREAMS DOWN as Julie uses the shovel to add more dirt to the pile, and finally she steps back. She already looks not only exhausted but also thinner than before, and her eyes are sore from crying during the night.

Nearby, Melissa is staring at the hole they've finished filling in. I watched earlier as they dug the hole at the side of the road, and then they put the man's body at the bottom before shoveling all the dirt back in, and now they're both just standing back as if they're not quite sure what to do.

The black bird is watching from a nearby wall. He already looks plumper than yesterday.

After a few minutes of silence, Julie grabs an old tree branch and drives it into the ground at the edge of the grave.

"What's that for?" Melissa asks, her voice trembling with anger.

"It's so you can find the grave again."

"Why would I need help finding it?"

"When this is all over," Julie replies, "and things start going back to normal, you might want to come back and -"

"Back to normal?" Melissa stammers, interrupting her. "Are you fucking insane? How the hell is anything ever going to go back to normal? The whole fucking world has turned to shit!"

"But soon -"

"But soon nothing!" Melissa hisses. "Do you think someone is gonna come along and save us all?"

"There was talk of rendezvous points all over the country," Julie continues, although she doesn't sound like she really believes what she's saying. "Places for survivors to go, places where -"

"Everyone's dead! It's the end of the world, you dumb bitch!"

"I'm sure -"

"You were sure you could save Scott," Melissa adds, turning and storming around the side of the grave, heading toward us. "And how did that go? Obviously you're a fucking awful doctor! Maybe you're not even a doctor at all, maybe you're just some fantasist who likes fucking with people!"

"Melissa -"

As she gets closer, Melissa suddenly turns and kicks me hard in the belly. I let out a pained yelp and pull back, scared she'll try again, but she hurries past and makes her way back across the road, heading toward the buildings.

"Melissa!" Julie calls out. "Where are you going?"

She waits for an answer, but after a moment Melissa disappears down the side of one of the buildings, apparently making her way toward the town square.

I hope she doesn't come back.

"Are you okay?" Julie asks, reaching down and running a hand across my belly. "Sorry, Harry, I had no idea she was going to do that."

She pauses for a moment, but now the whole town seems to have fallen silent again and there's no sign of Melissa. It's as if the girl has simply vanished into the dust, and that's fine by me. All I want is to get away from her and leave this place, and then maybe go back to the cabin. I know things looked bad last time we were there, but I keep thinking that maybe it's all better now and we'll find Jon waiting for us. He's probably worried, and he'll feel much better and much safer as soon as Julie and I get to him.

Nearby, the black bird is still watching us.

"We can't leave her here," Julie mutters finally.

She sighs as she sets out across the road, and I follow closely. We're heading away from the car already, and I have no idea why we're going back into the main part of town. We're just wasting time here and the whole place is starting to smell bad to me. As we pass the blood-stained patch of dirt where the man died, I take care to keep well away, just in case I get too close to his blood, and then I follow Julie down the next street until I spot Melissa up ahead, sitting on the ground with her back against a building, sobbing with her hands over her face.

I slow my pace, not wanting to get too close, but Julie keeps going until she reaches the girl. And then she waits for a moment, as if she's not quite sure what to say.

"What do you want?" Melissa asks finally, looking up at her with sore, reddened eyes. Tears are streaming down her face.

"Before everything went to hell," Julie replies, "there was a message that survivors should go to a rendezvous point. The nearest one to us is in the Rarrah Valley, and that's only about sixty miles from here. I know there's a chance we'll get there and find nothing, but it's the only real plan I have right now."

"Great," Melissa mutters, wiping her cheeks. "Have fun."

"You have to come with us."

Melissa laughs, before bursting into tears again.

"There'll be people there," Julie continues. "The government will have -"

"Are you retarded?" Melissa hisses, suddenly getting to her feet. "You sound like a fucking child, expecting to get there and find that everything's going to magically work out! This is the end of the fucking world, you dumb, incompetent whore!"

Julie shakes her head. "I refuse to believe that there won't be -"

"It's just gonna be everyone fighting among themselves for whatever scraps are left!" Melissa continues, interrupting her. "Why the hell would you want to go to a place where there might be other people, anyway? I don't know if you've been paying attention to the world, but people are shitty to each other at the best of times!"

"No, that's -"

"It's gonna be a thousand times worse now," Melissa adds. "People are going to be killing each other for drops of fucking water! It's gonna be chaos! The whole of society is breaking down, and you wanna go driving straight into a trap?"

"There's no trap," Julie replies. "People are going to start working together, to rebuild whatever -"

Melissa lets out a brief scream of anger as she turns to walk away. After a moment, however, she turns back to Julie.

"You really don't get it," she continues. "Then again, maybe since you're a doctor, you might actually be useful. They might decide to keep you around, instead of murdering you for sport. Or using you as some kind of rape-bag."

"What are you talking about?" Julie asks, clearly shocked. "There's no -"

"That's what people do to other people when there's no-one around to stop them!"

"No," Julie stammers, "you're -"

"Some ass-hole ran my boyfriend down!" Melissa screams. "He literally swerved to hit him! So now do you wanna explain to me how everyone's gonna band together and help each other? 'Cause from what I've seen so far, people are just cruel monsters who're gonna show their real nature now that they don't have society pressuring them to act good!" She takes a deep breath. "And that's the truth, whether you like it or not. If I seem cynical, then maybe that's because you didn't see your boyfriend die today. And maybe you're just fucking naive."

Julie pauses for a moment, as if she's not quite sure how to respond.

"I'm going to get a few supplies," she says finally, taking a step back, "and then Harry and I are going to hit the road. I know you might be right, there might be nothing waiting for us at the Rarrah Valley, or there might be something bad, but at least it's worth a shot. And the alternative is just sitting around, assuming the worst and waiting to die. Maybe that's the easiest approach, but I have to at least try to find other people. So long as there's a chance, I'm going to keep going."

She hesitates, before turning and heading back the way we just came.

"Harry, stay close."

I watch Melissa for a moment, and I swear I can see pure anger and hatred in her eyes. Suddenly she grabs a small rock and throws it at me, missing by just a few inches as I turn and hurry after Julie. I glance over my shoulder a couple of times, to make sure that Melissa isn't following us, and fortunately she's still at the other end of the street. I don't like her, and I want to get as far away from her as possible.

A short while later, however, she comes and joins us in the car, just as we're about to drive away.

"You changed your mind?" Julie asks.

"What am I supposed to do in this shit-hole?" Melissa asks, slumping into the passenger seat. "Starve to death?"

"There's a chance everything'll be okay," Julie tells her.

"And there's a chance we'll get raped and murdered."

Julie takes a deep breath. "I don't -"

"We'll die," Melissa continues, interrupting her. "I don't know how, but it'll happen. We'll probably get shot once some asshole decides we're not useful anymore. Or we'll get hurt and end up dying somewhere in the dust."

Julie shakes her head. "We'll find a way. We'll be okay."

"Whatever. That's what you said about Scott, and you let him die. You can't be a very good doctor."

Julie doesn't reply. Instead, she starts the engine and turns the car around. Looking out the window, I see the black bird over by the patch of blood on the tarmac, pecking at small chunks of blood flesh. After a moment it glance at me and lets out a loud cawing sound. Its beak is glistening in the morning sunlight.

A few minutes later, as we speed away, I watch as the town disappears into the distance behind us, and then I turn and see that Melissa is already curled on her side, facing away from Julie and looking out at the barren land. I still don't like this girl, and I wish she hadn't come with us, but Julie seems not to mind and I suppose I have to assume that Julie knows better.

Settling on the back seat, I close my eyes and wait to sleep again. Maybe this time Jon will come back.

"There'll be someone waiting for us at the

Rarrah Valley," Julie says finally, although there's a hint of fear in her voice. "There has to be."

After that I manage to doze, letting the car's motion rock me to sleep. I doze for miles and miles, and I start picking up faint scents that seem to be coming from my dreams. It seems to take forever before I'm able to actually sleep, however, and then suddenly I'm woken again by Julie's voice.

"There!" she says excitedly. "I told you there'd be someone here!"

Sitting up, I look straight ahead and see cars parked in the distance. Hundreds of cars, glittering under the midday sun.

CHAPTER TWENTY-FOUR

"YOU HAVE NO IDEA how badly we needed another doctor to show up," the short, balding man says with a smile as he leads Julie past another row of cars. "I was praying for someone like you, just the other night."

"I don't have many supplies," Julie tells him.

"Supplies are one thing, but knowledge is another," he continues. "There are close to five hundred people here, and a few more arriving every day. We haven't even begun to figure out how to deal with them all."

As they continue to talk, I make sure not to get too far from Julie. This place is loud and noisy, with people seemingly living out of their cars, and I can't help noticing lots of strange looks from everyone. They're watching us with a hint of caution, as if they're worried about our arrival, and everyone seems a little dirty and angry. There's an overwhelming stench of bodily fluids, too, and it's clear that this huge camp isn't particularly clean. At least I can smell food, though, and for the first time since leaving the cabin I'm actually starting to feel as if I want to eat.

"I'm not sure about the dog," the short man mutters, glancing down at me. "There might be some concerns about -"

"Dogs don't carry the sickness," Julie tells him.

"Still, people might -"

"He's fine," she adds, as they reach a patch of land where several men and woman have been left on pieces of cloth. "He's my dog now and he's useful. He stays with me."

"But -"

"If he goes," she says firmly, "then I go with him."

The man hesitates for a moment, before shrugging.

"I'm not gonna argue with a doctor," he mutters, as another man comes over to greet us. "Speaking of which, Doctor Julie Carpenter, allow me to introduce you to Doctor Hugh Evans. Doctor Evans, I'm pleased to inform you that we've just doubled our medical staff."

"Pleased to meet you," Evans says, reaching out and shaking Julie's hand. He's wearing white gloves. "And relieved, too. As you can see, we're a little short-handed around here."

He glances down at me.

"Is the dog yours?"

"He stays," Julie tells him. "He's clean and he's well-behaved."

"I'm sure he is," Evans continues, stepping

closer and giving my head a quick scratch. I let him, and I'm already getting a good feeling from this man.

"What kind of facilities do you have for checking new arrivals?" Julie asks, as I follow them past several groaning, injured people. "I'm assuming the first thing you do is make sure that no-one brings the sickness into the camp."

"Absolutely," Evans replies. "So far we've been lucky. I might be wrong, but at this stage I'm starting to think that the sickness was mainly confined to built-up urban areas. It was able to spread quickly, but it kills its hosts too quickly for them to travel much beyond the center of the infection zone. The primary vectors for transmission appear to be physical contact, which gives me hope that we'll eventually be able to get this thing under control. Speaking of which, obviously I'll need to run a few tests on you and the girl."

They both turn and look past me. Following their gaze, I see that Melissa is still with us. She has her arms folded across her chest, and she looks annoyed.

"Melissa," Julie says, "we need to -"

"I heard," she mutters darkly. "I'm not deaf. What exactly are you gonna do to me?"

"It's a brief physical exam," Evans explains. "People with the sickness always develop small lesions around the naso-labial fold, and we've found that they initially present as small bumps that can be felt. Do you mind?"

"Go ahead," Julie replies, and she waits while Evans touches her face.

He pushes his fingertips against the area around

her nose and upper lip, before stepping back.

"All clear," he says, turning to Melissa.

"I can touch my own face," she says sourly, reaching up and rubbing her nose. She sighs. "See? I'm fine."

"I'm afraid I need to check for myself," he explains, stepping closer to her.

"So there have been no cases at the camp at all?" Julie asks.

"None," he replies as he touches the flesh around Melissa's nose, "but we have to remain vigilant. I've been recommending certain measures that I think should be put in place."

"And who's in charge? Some kind of government agency?"

He turns to her, and it's clear that he's a little uncomfortable.

"There's been no sign of any government intervention at all," he tells her. "We've been waiting, assuming that someone would organize help, but so far we seem to be absolutely on our own. At first I was hoping to some day see a convoy show up, but now..."

His voice trails off.

"See?" Melissa says, raising an eyebrow as she turns to Julie. "I told you, it's the end of the world and we're all on our own. I mean, what is this place, anyway? A bunch of losers living out of their cars? It doesn't exactly look like the start of a recovery."

"We're working on some improvements," Evans replies. "Right now, our priority is checking everyone's health and determining what our next move should be.

We're certainly not planning on staying here forever."
He turns to Julie. "A man named Simmons is running
the place right now. Before the disaster struck, he was an
emergency planner for a federal agency, so we figured
he has some expertise. At some point, we need to make
things a little more democratic, but right now we're in
survival mode."

"So where do you need me?" Julie continues.
"I'm ready. Put me to work."

"What about you?" Evans asks, turning to
Melissa. "Where do you think you can help?"

With her arms still folded, Melissa simply
shrugs.

"What did you do before all of this?" Julie asks.

"Do?" She pauses. "I didn't *do* anything. I went
to school and I worked Saturdays in a diner, but that's
about it. Why, is there a diner around here? Do you need
someone to take milkshakes and sodas to morons?"

"We'll find something for you," Evans
continues, before glancing at me again. "Sorry, pal, but
we can't have you in the medical area. I'm sure you're
clean and well-behaved, but we still have to be careful.
In fact..." He heads over to a nearby tent, and a moment
later he returns with a length of rope. "I think you should
be on a leash," he adds, reaching down and attaching the
rope to my collar. "For your own safety, as much as
anything else."

"It's okay," Julie says, coming over and patting
my head. "It's not forever, Harry. I'm going to get to
work, but I'll see you later." She takes the other end of
the rope and holds it out toward Melissa. "Can you keep

an eye on him? Just until I'm done here?"

"You want me to look after your fucking stupid dog?" Melissa asks, clearly unimpressed.

"Just until this evening," Julie continues. "I'll figure something else out tomorrow. Please?"

Melissa stares at me for a moment, before muttering a few words under her breath as she takes the rope.

I turn to Julie and let out a faint whimper, before reaching up and placing my paw on her knee. I want to stay with her, but a moment later I feel my collar being yanked as Melissa starts dragging me away.

"It's going to be fine!" Julie calls after me. "I'll fix something else for tomorrow, Harry, I promise! Just behave yourself and I'll see you later! Melissa's going to look after you!"

I try to pull back to her, but Melissa yanks me again, hard enough to hurt. As Julie turns and follows Evans into the tent, I realize I have no choice other than to go with Melissa for now. Even though I don't like this girl, I figure Julie wouldn't send me off with her if it wasn't safe.

"Fucking dog," Melissa mutters, glancing down at me with anger in her eyes. "Is this what I'm supposed to be? A fucking dog-walker at the end of the world?"

CHAPTER TWENTY-FIVE

"THERE," SHE SAYS WITH a sigh, once she's finished tying my rope to a wooden stake in the ground, "that should hold you."

She takes a step back, eyeing me with a hint of contempt.

"Stop looking at me like that, you dumb mutt," she continues. "Seriously, I don't know what you want, but you're not getting it from me. Your fucking owner basically killed my fucking boyfriend, remember? And now look where she's brought us. It's like the parking lot from hell."

She turns as a man wanders over, and I immediately smell some kind of cooked meat. I take a few steps toward him, salivating at the thought that I might be able to eat something, but suddenly the rope around my neck pulls tight and all I can do is sit on the hard, rocky ground. I don't like being restrained like this.

"You want some?" the guy asks, holding his

plate out toward Melissa. "It's actually canned beef, believe it or not. I don't have much left, but I'm willing to share."

"Are you sure?" she asks cautiously.

"When was the last time you had something good to eat?" he continues. "You need to keep your morale up, and good food is half the battle. Go on, eat it all."

She hesitates for a moment, before taking the plate and slipping a slice of meat into her mouth. Letting out a groan of pleasure, she quickly finishes the rest while the guy watches with a growing sense of amusement.

"Thomas," he says finally, once she's done. "Nice to meet you."

"Melissa." She wipes a finger against the plate, gathering some sauce.

"Just lick the damn thing," he tells her.

She smiles.

"I'm serious," he continues. "Lick the plate, Melissa. You want to get every last scrap, don't you? It'd be a waste otherwise. Seriously, I promise I won't laugh." He looks around for a moment. "And no-one else is watching."

She hesitates, before turning her back to him and quickly licking the plate. She's blushing once she's done, and she quickly hands the plate back to him.

"That's better," he says with a smile, and then he glances at me. "Nice dog you've got here, Melissa."

"He's not mine," she replies, "I'm just looking after him for a friend. So..." She hesitates. "Do you have anything else to eat? It's just, I'm starving and I haven't eaten for days."

"Supplies are a little light," he mutters, "but... I could probably rustle something up."

"I'd be so grateful," she continues. "If you have any more of that meat..."

His smiles grows. "Well, I do but..." He hesitates again, watching her with a hint of amusement.

Something about the look in his eyes is worrying me, and I instinctively turn and try to walk away. Once again, I forget about the rope attached to my collar, and I only manage a few steps before I'm held in place. Staring out into the crowd, I look for some hint that Julie is coming back to get me, but all I see are unfamiliar faces. Some of them are watching me intently, and I can't help noticing the hunger in their eyes.

"We have to look after each other round here," Thomas is telling Melissa as I turn back toward them and let out a low, worried whimper. "I'd love to help you, but you'd kinda need to give me something in return. Relationships around this place kinda have to be transactional right now."

"I don't have much..."

"I'm sure you've got *something*, Melissa," he continues, with a faint smile. "Everything's got some way they can contribute. An item, or a service maybe. Hey, why don't you come and meet my friends?"

He's saying her name a lot.

She pauses, and I can tell that she's a little worried.

"It's alright," he tells her, "they don't bite.

Listen, I know how it is. People are shit, aren't they? Even in normal times, they're only out for themselves, and with things going the way they are right now..." He sighs. "It's more important than ever to pick your friends carefully, and to recognize your enemies. I'm not gonna lie to you, Melissa, there are plenty of people in this camp who'd gladly put a knife in your back for just one extra mouthful of food. Seriously, that's how bad things are right now."

"You don't need to tell me how much people suck," she replies. "I've seen it first-hand."

"Which is why I'm just suggesting that you come and sit with me and my friends for a while," he continues. "No harm done if you don't like us, but we're a bunch of like-minded people and we think we can work together. A girl like you strikes me as being pretty smart, so maybe you've got something to offer. And I'm *certain* we've got something to offer you in return. Besides, do you really wanna be wandering around all by yourself?"

She hesitates for a moment.

"Okay," she tells him finally, heading over to follow him. "Show me the way."

"Aren't you forgetting something?"

"What?"

He nods toward me.

She sighs. "Oh, he's just -"

"Bring him anyway," he continues, grinning at me. "You never know when he might come in handy."

She opens her mouth to argue with him, before coming over and pulling the wooden stake from the ground. I instinctively turn to hurry away, but she quickly pulls me with her as she follows Thomas through the camp. They're still talking, but I can't help looking over my shoulder and hoping that Julie will come and get me. I try again to pull away, but this time Melissa yanks the rope hard enough to hurt my neck, and I have no choice but to follow.

***

"You want some?" the grinning guy asks, holding another strip of cooked beef in front of me. "Hungry? You want some of this?"

I reach out to take a bite, but he laughs as he pulls it out of the way. I try again, but this time he puts it into his mouth and starts chewing, while smiling at me and then finally bursting out laughing.

"Look at him!" he says, turning to the girl next to him. "He's literally drooling!"

"Poor thing," she mutters. "You shouldn't tease him."

"Watch!" He holds up another piece of meat. "Do you want this, dog?" he asks, letting the meat dangle in front of my nose. "Do you feel -"

He pulls it back as soon as I try to eat, and he quickly drops the slice into his mouth while laughing wildly.

"Oh, that tastes so good!" he continues, grinning wildly. "Oh, so meaty!"

Letting out a faint whimper, I look down at his plate and see that he has several more strips. I'm so hungry, I can barely think about anything other than food, and my belly is starting to hurt. I stare at the guy, hoping against hope that he might decide to give me some of his meat, but he simply moves the plate away and starts talking to his friends.

"Sounds like a deal, then," Thomas says suddenly, coming closer.

Turning, I see that he's brought Melissa back with him. They tied me up next to one of their cars earlier, and then they promptly disappeared for a while. Now Melissa looks different somehow, almost as if she's slightly embarrassed, and I can't help noticing that she's holding Thomas's hand as he leads her between two of the other cars. She smells different, too.

She has Thomas's sweat on her body.

"Everyone," he says with a smile, "I'd like to officially welcome Melissa into our little group. From what I've seen so far, she's a very smart and capable girl, and I think she'll do us proud. She also says she knows the new doctor who arrived today, so she might be able to get us some fresh supplies." He turns to me. "In addition, we now have a dog!" he continues. "Apparently his name used to be Harry, but since that's a bit of a rubbish name, I was thinking we'd come up with something better. I've decided to officially rename him Hannibal!"

Suddenly someone grabs me from behind, pulling me closer and embracing me in a tight hug. I try to wriggle free, but he just squeezes me even tighter, and a moment later two other guys start rubbing their hands across my face, spreading their scent all over my fur.

"Hannibal!" one of them says with a laugh. "He'd better not be a cannibal!"

"Then he'd only eat other dogs, idiot," someone else replies.

"No, cannibals eat humans!"

"You're such a dick, Alex."

"I don't think he'll need much food," Thomas continues, reaching down and patting the back of my head, even though I try to duck away. "Shame he's so small, but we'll keep him lean and mean, so he doesn't get too comfortable. And if he doesn't turn out to be useful after a day or two, there's still some nice meat on his bones, so I'm sure he won't go to waste." He stares at me for a moment, before laughing again. "Don't fret it, Hannibal. I reckon you'll learn the ropes and fit in just fine. Just remember to bite any assholes who try to bother us."

I try again to pull away from all the people who are holding me tight. I don't like feeling their hands all over my body, but they refuse to let go, even when I let out a warning growl.

"Sounds like he's pissed off about something," Thomas mutters. "That's good. We want a dog who shows a bit of personality."

Grabbing my face, he holds my mouth shut while pulling my lips apart.

"Nice teeth, Hannibal!" he continues, before letting go and stepping back. "I've got a good feeling about you, little dude."

As they continue to talk, I finally manage to get free. I turn and try to hurry away, only for the rope to once again pull me back. I try to twist loose, and then I paw at the rope for a moment, before realizing that there's no way I'm going to be able to get free. Still, I make my way around to the other side of the stake and try again, and when this doesn't work I go back to the side where I started.

"Look at the dumb idiot!" one of Thomas's friends says with a laugh, before reaching over to me and poking my flank with a metal fork.

Feeling a brief burst of pain, I let out a whimper and scurry to safety, settling on the ground as far away from him as possible.

"That's your first lesson," the guy continues, holding the fork up as if he's threatening to hurt me again. "Don't trust people. People are bastards. And if you don't believe me, Hannibal, just look around at everyone else in this camp. Human nature's a bitch, and it's a dog-eat-dog world."

With that, he flashes the fork toward me again. I pull away, and he starts laughing as he turns to the others.

"Alex," one of his friends says with a laugh, "you're such an asshole!"

Melissa is sitting with Thomas, still holding his hand, as everyone laughs and talks. After a moment she glances at me, and her eyes narrow slightly before she turns and whispers something into his ear. He chuckles and looks toward me, and then he kisses her on the lips.

Resting my head on the ground, I figure all I can do is wait for Julie to come and get me.

CHAPTER TWENTY-SIX

"FIRST ORDER OF BUSINESS!" the man's voice announces, squealing slightly as it comes through the megaphone at the front of the crowd. "We now have four hundred and ninety seven people here at the camp, following five new arrivals today. One of those new arrivals is Doctor Julie Carpenter, who will be providing some much-needed assistance at the medical tent."

Hearing Julie's name, I sit up and look through the crowd that has gathered at the far end of the camp. There's no sign of her, but it's been several hours since I last saw her and I'm convinced she'll come and find me again soon. She wouldn't just leave me with Melissa.

"What about the five hundred rule?" a woman shouts suddenly. "You're not going to ignore that, are you?"

"We have to prepare for more arrivals," the man tells her. "I'm confident we can deal with a population of six hundred if necessary, and we can't turn people away."

"Of course we fucking can," Thomas mutters, sitting nearby. "People who don't have anything to offer, anyway. It's survival of the fittest now."

He takes a drag on his cigarette, before passing it to Melissa.

"Careful with that," he tells her. "Those things are like fucking gold-dust these days."

People are still talking at the front of the crowd, but I have no idea what they're saying. The sky is starting to dim now, as late afternoon rolls into evening, and I'm still tied to the same wooden stake as before. No-one has really paid me very much attention over the past few hours, which is a relief, but I tried chewing through the rope without any luck at all. Despite my best efforts, I'm going to have to wait for Julie to show up. Either that, or maybe eventually I'll go to sleep and wake up back at the cabin with Jon.

"What about people who are getting sick?" a voice shouts suddenly. "I've noticed people coughing a lot today!"

"There's nothing to indicate that there's anything other than a mild cold going around," the man at the front replies. "I'm sure you all remember how the sickness developed very rapidly. The one good thing about that is the fact that if it hits the camp at any point, we should know very quickly, and Doctor Evans has an emergency containment procedure in place, ready to roll out if the worst happens. In the meantime, I want to remind you all to be very conscious of hygiene rules. Remember to wash and -"

"That'd be easier if we had more water to go around!" a woman tells him. "Seems to me, that's another good reason why we shouldn't let the population go above five hundred."

There's a murmur of agreement from elsewhere in the crowd.

"Every new arrival is a risk!" a man adds. "I know this might sound bad, but we also need to think about the elderly. If they can't contribute to the camp -"

"We've already discussed this," the man at the front tells him. "We decided that -"

"*You* decided, Simmons!" another voice yells. "Maybe it's time we started putting things to a vote, instead of letting you and your doctor friend run the place like a pair of dictators!"

Again, several people nearby seem to agree with that point.

"Doctor Evans and I are best-placed to deal with the current situation," the man continues, "but obviously there'll come a time when we need to establish a new system. For now, we have to focus on hygiene, because otherwise we might have a real problem with disease. I know some people aren't sticking to the sanitation rules, and that kind of sloppiness is far more dangerous than any perceived risk from outside the camp."

"Sounds like bullshit to me," Thomas mutters.

Glancing over at him, I'm surprised to see that he has a handgun in his lap. He's turning it around and around, as if he's studying it, but after a moment he notices that I'm watching him. He stares at me for a moment before raising the gun, aiming it at me, and then slowly lowering it again. After that, he places a finger against his smiling lips, as if to tell me I should be quiet.

"We'll hold another meeting tomorrow morning," the man at the front of the crowd continues, "and then we'll see how much progress we've made regarding the sanitation issue. I should warn you, though, that if we spot any members of the camp recklessly endangering everyone else's health, we *will* consider enforcing some form of punishment. I'm sorry, but we have to be strict here."

As the meeting breaks up, everyone starts talking loudly, as if lots of little arguments have begun at various spots in the crowd. A moment later, I feel someone tugging the rope attached to my collar. I try to dig my feet into the ground, but I'm quickly pulled away by Thomas and his friends, and I have no choice but to follow them. Still, I glance over my shoulder and look for some sign of Julie. She has to be close, but I'm starting to think that maybe she's abandoned me and now I won't ever get away from Melissa and her friends.

***

"Fucking idiots!" Thomas shouts into the wind, as he stands on a rocky outcrop. "Fucking morons! All of you!"

We're several miles from the car-filled camp now. Melissa and the others still have me attached to a piece of rope, and they forced me to follow them as they left the camp and scrambled up a rocky incline that led up to this higher patch of land. Now the camp seems so small in the distance, but I can make out hundreds of little figures milling about and I assume one of them must be Julie.

Sitting, I watch the camp for a moment before lowering my chest and resting my chin on my paws.

"I've got ideas," Thomas continues. "Fuck, I've got so many ideas, and I think I know how we're gonna survive this fucking mess. You guys need to stick with me, and I'll keep you all safe. I'm just figuring out the last details, but soon I'm gonna lead us somewhere better. We're gonna start our own town, one where everything's run right. Better that this fucking camp, and better than anything that went before. We've been gifted a new age, and we're gonna seize it, 'cause it's a fucking opportunity!"

He holds his hands up high in the air, while still looking at the distant camp. He's still holding the gun, waving it at the sky.

"Did you hear that, you bunch of fucking assholes?" he yells, shouting into the wind. "We're the fucking future!"

"Up!"

Suddenly the rope is yanked and I'm pulled back. I turn and see one of the other guys grinning at me. I think his name is Alex, and for some reason the others seem to have let him hold my rope.

"No-one told you to sit down, Hannibal," he sneers.

"Did you hear all that crap Simmons was coming out with?" Thomas hisses, turning to the others. "And they just sat there, like obedient little idiots, taking his orders. I mean, who the fuck put him in charge? He's literally spending his fucking days telling other people where they're supposed to piss and shit! And that's what counts for a leader around here?"

Turning, I try to walk away, heading back to the camp, but I quickly reach the end of the rope and find myself held back.

"Hey!" Thomas yells at me. "I'm still talking here!"

Suddenly a stone hits my flank, just above one of my rear legs. I spin around and let out a pained yelp, but Thomas already has another rock in his hand and I freeze in case he throws it at me.

"We'll find a way to make you useful," he mutters, before turning and looking toward another set of large rocks. "Where did those other idiots go, anyway? I want everyone to hear my ideas."

As he and Alex continue to talk, I look over at Melissa. She's sitting on the ground with her legs crossed, but she doesn't seem to be paying attention to anything that's going on around her. Instead, she's staring at the ground and something about her eyes seems to have changed, as if they've somehow become a little darker and smaller. After a moment she glances at me, and I realize that whereas earlier she looked angry, now she just seems blank and impassive, as if she doesn't really care about anything that's happening around her.

"Over here!" an excited voice shouts suddenly. "Guys, quick! Get your asses over here!"

I turn, just as Alex yanks my rope and forces me

to follow. He, Melissa and Thomas scramble up a small hill until they find their two friends.

"Look!" one of the others yells. "Is that what I think it is?"

He points, and when I look down the other side of the incline I see a figure stumbling toward us. He's still a little way off, and he's moving slowly, but a moment later I realize that I can smell rotten flesh drifting this way. It's the same scent I picked up back at the gas station with Jon, and the same scent I noticed at the cabin after Jon got sick, and I instinctively take a step back while baring my teeth and letting out a low warning growl.

"It's one of the fuck-ups," Alex says, with a hint of awe in his voice. "It is, isn't it?"

"They're called zombies, idiot," Thomas mutters, taking a step forward, "and yeah, it's one of them. So much for the idea that they'd all have dropped dead after a few days. I guess there are still a few lingerers."

"It looks like it's in a bad way," Alex points out. "Is that as fast as it can move? It's fucking pathetic."

"Huh," Thomas continues. "You're right, it doesn't look *so* dangerous. Why the fuck were people ever scared of these things?"

"Shoot it," Alex tells him.

"Why? Are *you* scared?"

"I don't want it coming any closer."

Thomas smiles. "Bullets are precious, my friend," he says after a moment. "Besides, we might be able to have a little fun with this thing."

I let out another snarl, hoping to warn the creature away.

"The dog doesn't like it, either," Thomas continues. "Look at him. He sees and hears and smell things that are beyond our comprehension."

"Classic," Alex replies, nudging my side. "Alright there, Hannibal? What's up, are you scared? I didn't have you down as a pussy."

For the next few minutes, they watch as the rotting creature edges closer. Finally, once it's no more than twenty feet away, Thomas reaches down and picks up a stone, and then he hesitates for a moment before throwing it at the creature. He misses by a couple of feet, but he grabs another and tries again, and this time the stone hits the creature's chest before dropping harmlessly to the ground.

"Five points for a chest shot!" Thomas says with a smile, before turning to Alex. "Reckon you can do better?"

Alex picks up another stone and takes a moment to aim. Then he throws the stone at the creature, although he barely hits its knee.

"One point," Thomas tells him, picking up another stone. "Ten for the head, right?"

Growling a little louder now, I take a couple of steps back as the creature edges closer. Suddenly Thomas throws the stone, and this time he hits the creature's forehead, causing it to stumble slightly.

"Ten points!" Alex laughs. "Not bad. I bet I can do better!"

"Get back a bit, though," Thomas mutters. "We

don't want the idiot getting too close. He might try to eat our brains."

They continue to throw stones at the slow-moving creature, while carefully edging back every few minutes so that it can't come much closer. The creature definitely seems to have noticed their attention, and it's letting out a series of grunts as it stumbles toward us. Alex is still holding my rope, and no-one seems to have noticed that I'm warning them about this thing. I've begun to really show my teeth now, and the hair on the back of my neck is standing up as I let out a couple of warning barks, hoping that I might scare the danger away. Every muscle in my body is tense, ready to fight.

"This is getting boring," Thomas says eventually, before glancing down at me. "You know what I'd like to see?" He pauses for a moment. "I'd like to put our new recruit to the test. I have the utmost faith in him, but I think he needs to demonstrate his abilities. I want proof that he can protect us against a zombie attack."

"Are you kidding?" Alex asks, his eyes alive with glee as he starts giggling. "That'd be insane!"

"Dogs don't catch the sickness or spread it," Thomas continues, crouching next to me and patting my flank, "so what's the danger? Do you want to prove your worth, Hannibal? If you're gonna be our guard dog, we need good, solid evidence that you can take one of these fuckers down." He turns to Alex. "Give me the rope. And you brought the stake, didn't you?"

He takes the piece of wood from Alex and drives it into the ground, and then he attaches the other end of the rope.

"I've got faith in you, Hannibal," he says finally. "All you've gotta do is kill the bastard, okay? Let's see your wild streak come out. Don't hold back."

He places a hand against the side of my face, firmly enough that I know not to fight back.

"Let your true nature out, Hannibal," he continues. "Free yourself from whatever restrictions your previous owners placed upon you. Connect with your true soul. And kill the fucking zombie."

With that, he and the others hurry back, stopping about fifty feet away as if they want to watch what happens next. I turn and hurry after them, but the rope around my neck quickly holds me back and I turn to see that I'm tied to the stake. A moment later, I catch the rotting creature's scent on the breeze, and I see that it's stumbling toward me. Immediately, I'm filled with a sense of pure, unbridled panic.

"Go on, Hannibal!" Thomas yells from a distance. "You can do it! Kill the bastard!"

As the creature approaches, I bare my teeth again and let out a low growl, slowly increasing the volume in the hope that a warning will be enough. By the time the creature reaches the wooden stake, however, it's only about ten feet away and still showing no sign of fear. I bark a couple of times, as loud as I've ever barked before, but the figure stumbles closer and closer until finally I have no choice but to run past and around to the other side of the stake.

I bark again, but the creature stops for a moment and then turns. Its dull, rotten eyes stare at me for a few seconds, and then it starts stumbling toward me once again.

"Get him!" Thomas shouts from the safety of the rocks nearby. "Do it, Hannibal! Don't hold back! You're a dog! Act like one!"

"My money's on the zombie!" Alex yells. "We're gonna see guts spill! I bet you all a meal that the dog gets ripped open!"

Still barking, I hold my ground as the creature once again stumbles toward me. I know deep down that I should attack and bite its leg, but the stench of death is overwhelming and my instincts are telling me to keep as far away from this thing as the rope will allow. Even a warning bite might be dangerous, since the creature seems to be carrying some kind of infection. It looks a little like a human male, with scraps of clothing hanging from its thin body, and it's letting out a constant, low gurgle.

Suddenly it stumbles and reaches for me.

I turn and run, hitting the limit of the rope and then ducking a different way. I feel the rope catching on something, followed by a heavy thud that shakes the ground, but I keep going until the rope pulls tight again. Turning, I see that the creature has fallen, and I realize that it must have tripped over the rope.

I try to run again, but the rope prevents me from managing more than a couple of paces.

"Good tactic!" Thomas shouts. "Now go for the kill, Hannibal!"

"The dog's got brains!" one of his friends adds. "Maybe you're gonna lose this bet, Alex!"

"Go fuck yourself!" Alex yells with a laugh. "Some mangy dog isn't gonna bring down a fucking zombie! No fucking way!"

Still groaning, the creature struggles back up, and for a moment it seems to be struggling for balance. After a few seconds, however, it lurches toward me again, and I back away until the rope pulls tight. All I want is to run and find Julie, to warn her, but the rope won't let me get far and the creature is already coming closer again. My heart is pounding as I bare my teeth, followed by more barks, but nothing seems to be scaring this thing. It just keeps coming, and finally I have no choice but to run in a circle again until I'm on the far side of the stake.

When I turn again, the creature is already coming this way.

"Who's gonna get tired first?" Thomas shouts. "The dog or the zombie? Come on, Hannibal, don't let some rotten sack of shit bring you down! Prove yourself, hound!"

I start barking again, louder and faster than before, but the stench of death and rotten flesh is overwhelming as the creature stumbles toward me. I try holding my ground, still hoping that I can scare the creature away, but finally I have no choice but to run. I duck past the creature's hands, and then I feel the rope tugging against my collar. There's another thud, and this time I struggle to pull free. Once I eventually get to the far side of the stake, I turn back and see that the creature once again tripped over my rope. Short of breath, I watch as it rolls onto its front and stares at me, and I wait for its next move.

For a moment, the creature simply watches me, but then it looks down at the rope. My heart is pounding. I wait, and slowly the creature reaches out and puts its hands on the rope, while still letting out a series of grunts and groans.

"I think you might have a problem, Hannibal!" Thomas yells. "No-one can run forever! You're gonna have to get stuck in!"

I continue to bark as the creature holds the rope in its rotting hands, and then slowly I realize that it has begun to pull on the rope, trying to drag me closer.

I dig my paws into the ground, but the creature is stronger than I expected and after a moment I'm yanked forward. As if it has begun to realize that its approach is working, the creature looks at me for a few seconds before pulling on the rope again, dragging me closer. No matter how hard I try to push my paws into the dirt, I'm powerless to hold myself back as the creature – having finally figured out how this works – starts pulling harder and faster on the rope, dragging me closer and closer.

Nearby, Thomas and the other humans are cheering and shouting.

Turning, I try to run, but a moment later the rope is pulled again and I'm dragged closer to the creature. The stench of death is all around me now, and a sense of pure panic is rushing through my body. I dig my paws into the dirt, but I'm powerless to stop the creature as it drags me even closer, and now the stench is stronger than ever. I can hear the creature grunting and snarling, and finally I turn and see that I'm just a couple of feet away. It reaches its rotten hands further along the rope, until it's almost close enough to touch my flank, and then it pulls again.

This time, pure instinct takes over as I realize that I can't pull away. Instead, I take a step toward the creature and then I jump straight over its body, landing on the other side and pulling as hard as I can manage to get away. I can already feel the rope snagging on some part of the creature, but after a moment I'm able to drag myself a little further. Every muscle in my legs is aching with the effort, and I'm terrified that the creature is about to yank me back, but I pull as hard as possible as I feel the rope straining.

"No!" Alex shouts in the distance. "That's not fair!"

"Do it!" Thomas yells. "Harder! Get the fucker! Go for it, Hannibal!"

Ignoring them, I continue to pull on the rope. I don't know why the creature hasn't grabbed me yet, but all I can think about is that I have to get away. Finally I feel the rope starting to slip slightly and I manage a few more paces, and then I look back over my shoulder. The rope is caught around the creature's neck and has begun to dig deep into its rotten flesh. With its eyes still fixed on me, the creature is on its back, as if now I'm starting to drag it across the ground.

Turning, I keep pulling, still trying to get away, until finally I feel the rope slip free with a sudden jolt and I'm able to run several feet until it tightens again.

I look back, and this time I see that the rope was

caught around the creature's neck and has finally broken all the way through its rotten meat, tearing the entire head away.

The creature's hands twitch for a moment, and the eyes blink on the decapitated head, and I start barking furiously to warn it off. I'm breathless and trembling, but still terrified in case the headless creature is still able to come for me.

"You win!" Thomas shouts, hurrying closer but still keeping well clear of the creature as he comes and pats the back of my neck. "Hannibal, you legendary beast, you killed a zombie!"

"I think technically it's still, like, moving and stuff," one of his friends points out.

"Yeah, but not for long," Thomas adds, grabbing an old tree branch and raising it high above his head. "Looks like you lost the bet, Alex. I'm gonna enjoy eating your meals for a day or two."

With that, he brings the branch crashing down against the creature's head, crushing the skull and splitting the forehead. He keeps hitting the corpse with surprising force, this time aiming at the torso and smashing the rib-cage a little more with each strike. Finally the creature's hands stop twitching, but Thomas starts screaming as he hits it again and again, crushing its chest and spine until pieces of broken rib start flicking up into the air. He only stops once he runs out of breath, at which point he tosses the branch aside and steps back, breathlessly admiring the shattered corpse.

"And that," he mutters, turning and coming over to me, "is how to kill a fucking zombie." He slams a hand into my flank, patting me hard, before walking past and kicking some stones on the ground. "Fuck! Yes! Now who's the fucking boss around here? Huh? Who's the boss? It's me, you fucking assholes!"

"You just lost me a bet, you furry piece of shit," Alex says, untying the rope from the stake and then turning to me. "You realize that, right?"

He hesitates, before stepping closer and kicking me hard, catching my right rear leg.

I let out a yelp and pull away. He kicks at me again, before holding back at the last moment as I flinch, and then he starts laughing.

Still out of breath and exhausted, with my heart pounding, I look over at the crushed zombie and then I see that Melissa is watching me from nearby. Whereas the others all seem either annoyed or exhilarated, Melissa still appears to be very calm. She's simply staring at me, barely even blinking, with no trace of emotion on her face at all.

CHAPTER TWENTY-SEVEN

"HARRY!" JULIE SHOUTS SUDDENLY. "Harry! Wait!"

As we reach the edge of the camp, I turn and see Julie running through the crowd.

"Harry!" she gasps, dropping to her knees next to me and putting her arms around me. "Thank God! I was starting to worry!"

"His name's not Harry," Thomas tells her, still holding the rope that's attached to my collar. "His name's Hannibal, and he's our guard dog."

"He's *my* dog," she replies, before turning to Melissa. "Where have you been? It's starting to get dark!"

"You told me to look after your stupid dog," Melissa mutters, her voice sounding bare and empty, "so I looked after your stupid dog. You should be grateful."

"Give me the rope," Julie says, reaching out toward Thomas.

"He's *our* dog now," Thomas replies. "He's one of my followers. I'm gathering followers."

"He looks injured," Julie continues, leaning around to look at my rear leg, which has been hurting on the walk back down to the camp. "He's bleeding! What happened to him?"

"It's none of your fucking business," Thomas tells her, as he and his friends surround us. "Like I said, whatever might have happened in the past, Hannibal's our dog now. We arranged things fair and square with Melissa, we needed a guard dog and he's turned out to be quite the zombie killer. He's useful, he has a role to play in our little group."

"Are you okay?" Julie asks, wiping some dirt from my face as she looks into my eyes. "Harry, it's me! I'm so sorry I let these people take you. I was busy helping patients." She leans closer and kisses the top of my head, and I feel a flash of relief as I pick up her scent again.

Suddenly I'm yanked back.

"Like I said, lady," Thomas sneers, "he's our dog now! So get your filthy fucking hands off him, okay? And don't even -"

"Go to hell!" she hisses, trying to grab the rope from him, only for him to step back. "Melissa, did you give my dog to these people?"

"Who says he's *your* dog?" Melissa asks. "He's not a piece of property."

"I'm not arguing about this," Julie continues, unfastening the rope from my collar and picking me up. I immediately feel a flash of relief as I feel her heartbeat against my flank. "Come on, Harry, it's getting late, we need to eat and think about sorting out how we'll sleep tonight."

She steps back, carrying me away from the others.

"Hannibal!" Thomas says firmly. "You're with us! Come on, boy!"

I glance back at him, and after a moment he comes closer and reaches out for me.

I immediately bark before letting out a low snarl, and this stops him in his tracks. I bare my teeth, warning him to stay away, and finally he steps back.

"The fucking mutt looks rabid anyway," he continues, staring at me for a moment longer before glancing at Julie. "You're the new doctor, aren't you? Maybe you can *buy* the dog back. You must have some medical supplies sitting around somewhere, right? My friends and I wouldn't mind a few pills and bottles, just something to take the edge of the fucking monotonous misery of this place. That seems fair, right?"

"Go to hell," she says again, turning and carrying me away through the crowd. "Come on, Harry, let's get moving."

"We'll come and collect payment later, then!" Thomas calls after her. "Have a think about what you've got to offer! You're taking our dog, bitch, so we're gonna want something in return! You can't just ignore us! We'll come and collect on the debt!"

***

"I'm so sorry I let Melissa take you away like that," Julie says a short while later, as we sit on the ground next to her car. Behind her, the sun is starting to set, casting an orange glow across the sky. "I had no idea she'd barter you away to a bunch of idiots. Please forgive me, Harry. I'll do better tomorrow, I promise."

She opens a small bottle and pours a strange-smelling liquid onto a piece of cotton wool.

"This might sting a little," she continues, "but I need to disinfect that cut on your leg. I'm sure there's nothing to worry about, but we have to be careful. Just trust me, okay? It's for your own good."

She reaches down and presses the pad against my leg. I feel a flash of pain, but I don't pull away. Whatever Julie's doing, I trust her and I'm sure she's right. All that matters to me right now is staying close to her and not seeing Melissa or her friends ever again, so I sit patiently and wait while Julie continues to work on my wound. Finally she sits back and smiles at me, even though I can tell that she's exhausted.

"I'm not a veterinarian," she mutters, "but I guess a cut is a cut, whoever's leg it happens to be on."

Turning, she leans against the side of the car and place a hand on my flank, stroking me gently as she looks out at the sunset.

"I miss him," she says after a moment. "I bet you do too, huh? You miss Jon?"

I turn to her, feeling a flash of excitement at the mention of that name, and then I look around at the other people sitting next to their cars. Hoping that I might spot Jon coming this way, I sniff the air, but the only scents

I'm picking up right now are coming from the food that people are cooking nearby.

"I didn't mean to get you excited," Julie says, still stroking my fur. "Sorry, Harry, maybe I shouldn't say his name around you anymore." She pauses for a moment, watching the sunset. "Did I do the right thing at the cabin, Harry? He was so far gone, but I keep thinking that maybe I could have found some way to undo the sickness. I've not heard of anyone recovering, it's a death sentence and I thought I was putting him out of his misery, but now I keep wondering whether..."

Her voice trails off for a moment, and she nuzzles her faces against my fur.

"What if someone finds a cure? I could never live with myself if..."

She pauses.

"No, there's not going to be a cure," she continues. "I've seen enough of this thing to know that once it takes control of a human body, it doesn't let go. At least it seems to be contained right now. Our best hope is that it just dies off and then we can begin to regroup. I know this camp isn't perfect, Harry, but there are already plans for us to start moving and find a better place to set up. And you know what else? I still believe that people are fundamentally good. Nothing I've seen here has made me change my mind or lose my faith in humanity."

She kisses the side of my neck.

"We're going to pull through this. Not just you and me, but all of us. I can feel it in my bones. One day this nightmare will be over and there'll be hope again."

Feeling another burst of pain in my injured foot, I settle next to her and rest my head on her lap, while staring at the horizon.

"The sunset's beautiful tonight," she whispers after a few minutes, still running her hands through my fur. "I've got a feeling the sunrise will be beautiful in the morning, too."

Later, once night has fallen and we're in the car, I sleep next to Julie on the back seat. There's not much room for both of us, but we manage, and I'm determined to stay close to her. There are voices in the distance, and it's clear that plenty of other people in the camp aren't sleeping tonight, preferring instead to sit around the fires. But the pain in my foot is getting a little better and although I wake several times, I'm too exhausted to keep from sleeping for long. Once or twice, I realize that Julie seems to be crying, so I lick salty tears from her face and she smiles.

All I need now is for Jon to come back, and everything will be okay again.

CHAPTER TWENTY-EIGHT

"A COUPLE MORE HAVE been spotted about two miles from here," Doctor Evans continues, as he and Julie sit next to the medical tent the following day, eating bread and meat. "I think they're drawn to us. I can't even begin to imagine how that works, but it could become a problem."

It's almost noon, and the sun is bright in the sky above. Julie has spent the morning working with Evans, helping the injured, but this time she's kept me close. I'm not actually allowed into the medical tent itself, so instead I stay at the entrance and keep guard. Most people who come past take a moment to pat me and say a few words, and so far I've seen no sign of Thomas, Melissa or any of the others from yesterday. Hopefully they won't ever come near me again.

"Do you think the worst is over?" Julie asks Evans. "Those things... I don't want to call them zombies, because that just sounds too crazy, but whatever they are... I mean, they must have a finite limit, right? There's only so long they can keep moving before their bodies just rot away and they collapse."

"That's the theory we're working with at the moment," he replies. "There's definitely evidence to suggest that it's the case. The creatures that have been seen coming this way have always dropped before they can get too close." He takes another bite of bread and chews for a moment. "When all of this is over, I really want to get involved with some kind of study, to really understand what this sickness is, and how it works and where it came from. That's the only way we can make sure it never comes back."

"You and me both," she continues. "After I lost..."

Her voice trails off.

"You lost people you loved?" he asks.

She nods.

"I lost my wife and my two sons," he tells her. "I saw them after they'd come back. I keep thinking I should have done something, I should have destroyed them, but I couldn't bring myself to do it. I just drove away. Now I'd give anything to go back to that moment and put them out of their misery. I left them stumbling about in our town." He pauses. "They're probably gone by now. They probably collapsed and rotted away. I hope so, anyway. Better that, than to think of them still on their feet."

Hearing raised voices nearby, I turn and see that a small crowd is gathering not far from the tent. Some kind of argument seems to have arisen, and I instantly tense as I realize that people seem angry.

"Great," Evans says with a sigh, "looks like it's time for the daily dose of panic."

"What do you mean?" Julie asks.

"Every day some new rumor spreads," he continues. "Someone says they heard that zombies are surrounding the camp, or that the sickness has reached us. I swear, people around here actually seem to *enjoy* panicking. I guess if they've got nothing better to do with their time..."

"No-one's coming to help us!" a woman shouts in the distance. "We're sitting here, waiting for some kind of miracle to arrive, but we're all alone! We need to come up with a plan and haul our asses out of this valley, or we're just a bunch of targets!"

"The government might still show up," a man replies. "They can't have just vanished."

"They told us to gather here!" the woman yells back at him. "We did our part, so where are they? In case you hadn't noticed, we only have enough food for about six more days, and that's assuming we don't get a whole load of new survivors showing up!"

"Maybe they told us to gather together so they can finish us off," another woman suggests. "This was a planned extermination!"

"Give it a rest," a man says with a sigh. "If I hear one more conspiracy theory from you..."

The arguments continue, and eventually the man with the megaphone starts talking again. There was a discussion like this yesterday, but this time people seem a lot more agitated and worried, and it sounds as if a physical fight might break out at any moment. Even Julie seems concerned, as she and Doctor Evans join the back of the crowd and listen to the growing clamor from all the arguing voices. The man with the megaphone is still trying to keep order, but he's starting to get drowned out by people shouting at one another.

Eventually Evans pushes through the crowd and starts speaking from the front, using the megaphone. He seems to be trying to calm everyone, although he doesn't seem to be having much impact. Limping over to join Julie, I stand with her and watch her face, hoping to see some sign that she's less worried, but it's very clear that something is causing her a lot of concern. Finally, feeling as if the atmosphere is turning increasingly hostile, I glance back over toward the medical tent just in time to spot a figure sneaking through the entrance.

I look up at Julie again, but she doesn't seem to have noticed. I nudge her leg, but she's too focused on listening to Doctor Evans, so I turn and head over to the medical tent's entrance.

Looking inside, I see that Melissa is taking some small bottles from a shelf. As soon as she sees me, however, she freezes.

"Don't bark," she whispers. "There's nothing wrong, you little shit, so keep your mouth shut."

She takes a few more bottles, before coming back over to the entrance.

"That's right," she continues, keeping her voice low. Reaching down, she starts patting the side of my face, although after a moment she starts holding my mouth shut, as if to ensure that I stay quiet. "Just mind your own business, okay? You're just a dumb little asshole, and none of this concerns you."

"What have you got there?" Julie asks suddenly.

Melissa steps back, startled as Julie comes over to join us.

"Have you been in the supply cupboard?" Julie continues. "Melissa -"

"My friend's in pain," Melissa replies. "Please, he needs these..."

"I'm sorry to hear that," Julie says, "but we don't have enough supplies to go around. Bring him to see me, and I can work out what to do for him. You can't just take medicine."

"But my friend -"

"Please, Melissa," Julie continues, stepping closer, "put the bottles down. Don't make me tell you again. No matter how worried you are about your friend, stealing supplies is not the answer."

"It's not stealing," Melissa snaps, her voice filled with anger. "The whole camp owns the medicine supply. We're entitled to our fair share."

"There are people who -"

"Why are you always such a bitch?" Melissa adds.

Julie flinches, and I can tell she's annoyed.

"You think you can just tell everyone what to do, don't you?" Melissa continues. "You think your smarter than the rest of us."

"I really don't think that. I just want to try to make sure our supplies are reserved for the people who really need them, and that there's no -"

"If you're such a good doctor," Melissa mutters, interrupting her, "then why did you let Scott die?"

"I did everything I could for him," Julie replies. "He was very badly hurt. You must have seen that for yourself."

"Whatever."

Pushing past her, Melissa tries to head into the crowd, but Julie grabs her arm and pulls her back.

"What's your problem?" Melissa asks.

"My problem is that you're taking medical supplies," Julie says firmly. "There are people who need those, and I can't let you walk away like this. Please, Melissa, don't make me force you to put them back."

"And how would you do that?" Melissa spits back at her.

"I'll find a way."

Melissa stares at her for a moment, before suddenly moving her arms to her sides and letting the various items tumble down onto the ground.

"Happy?" she sneers, shoving Julie back before turning and hurrying into the crowd.

Sighing, Julie gets down onto her knees and starts gathering the supplies.

"Who put you in charge, anyway?" a nearby woman sneers, eyeing Julie with obvious disdain. "Just because you and that other doctor know how to bandage up a few scrapes, there's no reason why you should get to decide who's given pain-killers and who's left in agony."

Julie sighs. "We have limited supplies and we have to ration all the -"

"Don't tell us what we have to do!" a man shouts angrily. "You're a doctor, right? So you're here to help people, not to act like some kind of dictator!"

Julie opens her mouth to reply, but the crowd is breaking up angrily now and finally she turns to me.

"I'm just trying to do what's best," she stammers. "You understand that, don't you? If I give pain-killers to everyone who asks for them, we'll be out of stock by the end of the day."

"I guess the guard dog needs a little more training," Doctor Evans mutters as he comes over to join us. "I don't know how much longer people are going to stay calm around here. Some of them are talking about leaving today and going off to find a better place. I can't entirely say that I blame them. The mood's deteriorating fast."

"So let them go," Julie replies. "No-one should be forced to stay."

"They're demanding to take their share of the supplies."

She pauses for a moment. "We need to stick together," she says finally, while reaching down to stroke my flank. "We *do* need to find somewhere better than this, though, and maybe -"

Suddenly there's the sound of an engine roaring to life, and I turn to see that several cars have been started.

"Great," Evans says with a sigh, "now people are getting ready to leave. They think they'll be better off on their own."

Over the next few minutes, five or six cars pull

209

away from the camp and head off across the valley. Then there's a lull for a while, followed by some more arguments in the distance, and finally a couple more vehicles leave. Julie and Doctor Evans get back to work in the medical tent, but I can tell that the atmosphere all across the camp seems to have changed and soured, and eventually another car leaves. At the same time, the man with the megaphone is talking again, and I think he's trying to make people calm down.

I watch the crowd for a moment, before spotting a familiar face. Melissa is staring at me, and once again her face seems strangely blank. I wait for her to look away, but she continues to keep her eyes fixed on me until finally, unnerved, I head over to the medical tent's entrance and settle on the ground. I try to rest, but eventually I glance back and see that Melissa is still out there, still watching. I know I can't be the first to look away, so I hold eye contact with her, but she doesn't look away either.

She wants something.

CHAPTER TWENTY-NINE

"TWENTY-ONE CARS DEPARTED TODAY," Doctor Evans says later, as the sun begins to set on the horizon, "carrying a total of forty people away from the camp. And they took supplies with them. Worse, there are plenty of other people talking about leaving tomorrow. I think Simmons is losing control of the place. The camp is falling apart."

"They have every right to leave," Julie points out.

"They're scared," Evans continues. "That's all it is. They're acting irrationally because they're letting their fears take control. Most of them will be dead within a couple of days." He pauses. "We're running low on almost every key supply. Unless we start rationing the pain-killers and antibiotics more strictly than ever, we'll be all out in about two days' time. Maybe even sooner."

"And then what?" Julie asks.

She waits for Evans to reply. When he simply

looks over toward the horizon, however, she reaches down and strokes the back of my neck.

"Someone'll come to help us," she says finally, with a hint of sadness in her eyes. "I don't know how I know. I just do. Somewhere right now, the surviving members of the old government are getting together and working out what to do next. They know about the rendezvous points, so we just need to stay here until they show up. They'll have supplies, and then we can start getting back to normal. We just have to be patient and keep going until then."

"You don't really believe that, do you?"

"I believe people are fundamentally good," she tells him. "I also believe that some remnants of the old world are still in place. They have to be."

As they continue to talk, I turn and look back toward the medical tent. I heard a faint scrabbling sound a moment ago, but now I don't see anyone. I've worked out over the past couple of days that no-one is supposed to be in that tent unless they're accompanied by Julie or Doctor Evans, but I'm certain someone else is close. Getting to my feet, I walk over to the tent's entrance, but the door is still zipped shut. Still, after a couple of seconds, I hear the scrabbling sound again, and this time I realize it's coming from around the rear of the tent.

I glance at Julie and Doctor Evans.

They don't seem to have noticed.

Heading around the side of the tent, I hear a faint whispering sound. When I get to the next corner, however, there's still no sign of anyone and the whisper has abruptly stopped. Now all I hear is the chatter of people around nearby camp-fires, and all I smell is meat cooking on grills. I'd dearly love to go over and beg for some of that meat, but I know I can't abandon my post at the tent, so I make my way all the way around until I get back to the front, where Julie signals for me to join her.

"Are you okay?" she asks, stroking my flank again as soon as I'm back with her. "You seem like you're on edge, Harry. Are you picking up on all the bad vibes?"

I nudge my nose against her arm, before turning to once again look over at the tent. Sometimes my instincts tell me that something is wrong, even though I can't work out *exactly* what's setting them off. Right now, for example, the tent looks completely safe, yet I can feel deep down that something or someone is hiding from me. I let out a faint growl, before turning to Julie and seeing that she's smiling as she watches me.

I glance back at the tent again, before turning to Julie and placing a paw on her arm.

"What's up?" she asks. "Are you trying to tell me something?"

"Why don't you just call him Lassie and be done with it?" Evans asks.

Julie watches me cautiously for a moment, before getting to her feet.

"Show me," she says, as if she's starting to realize that something might be wrong. "Harry, what is it? Show me?"

"Ignore the dog," Evans mutters. "He probably just wants food."

"I think it's something else," she replies. "I think

he's trying to tell me something."

I turn and head toward the tent, and I'm relieved to hear that Julie is following. Stopping at the door, I look at the zip, and a moment later Julie reaches down and pulls it open I step inside, but I can immediately tell that no-one has been in here since we left a few hours ago. I take a quick look around, before hurrying out and making my way around to the tent's rear. Whereas a moment ago there were no unusual scents here, now I realize that Melissa has been here very recently, most likely in the past few minutes, along with Thomas and the others.

I let out a faint whimper.

"Harry?"

Julie stops as she reaches me.

I look down at the spot where I think Melissa was standing, and after a moment I paw at the ground.

"You're starting to freak me out a little," Julie says as she comes over and pats my head. "Whatever's bugging you, there's clearly no-one here now. What do you say we head back to the car and get an early night? I've had a hell of a day, and -"

Hearing another engine nearby, she turns and looks back the way we just came. Following her gaze, I see another car driving away.

"More people abandoning the camp," she mutters, sounding disappointed. "They're losing faith."

She hesitates for a moment, before turning and heading back around the tent. I follow, but when we get to the front she stops and looks toward the spot where she was sitting with Doctor Evans.

"Where did he go?" she whispers.

Picking up his scent, I make my way to the tent's door, although I stop as soon as I pick up the familiar smell of blood. A moment later I hear a faint bump from inside, too, and I immediately take a step back and start growling.

"What is it?" Julie asks.

There are more scents in the air now. Melissa is in the tent, along with Thomas and at least one other person besides Doctor Evans. The hairs on my shoulders are standing up and I step back, letting out a rumbling growl.

"We just looked in there," Julie mutters, before stepping past me and heading inside. "There's no -"

Suddenly she lets out a gasp, and there's a heavy thump as she's dragged through the entrance. Rushing after her, I see that she's struggling with someone, and she's quickly pushed down onto the ground.

"Don't make a sound," Thomas whispers, placing a finger against his lips. "It's in your best interests to keep quiet, okay? We're only taking what we need."

I snarl at him, and he glances at me with a hint of disdain.

"Don't challenge me, mutt," he sneers. "I'm leading my people away from this hellish place. We just need some supplies for the journey."

"You can't take the medicine," Julie says firmly, getting to her feet. "It's for people who -"

Before she can finish, he punches her, sending her thudding to the ground.

I rush forward, but suddenly Alex grabs my collar and pulls me away.

"I told you she'd interfere," Melissa mutters, as she loads more bottles into a box. "She just can't leave well enough alone."

Gasping with pain, Julie sits up.

"I told you not to trust people," Melissa tells her. "What did you think this was, some kind of magical utopia where people would suddenly *not* be complete assholes to each other?" She smiles. "Human beings are cruel and vicious and monstrous. They always have been, and they always will be." She puts some more bottles in the box. "It's survival of the fittest these days, and that means getting away from places like this. Thomas has a plan."

"The only people I've seen being cruel and monstrous around here," Julie replies, her voice tense with pain, "are the ones who've been saying people are cruel and monstrous all along."

"Is that right?" Melissa asks, before pausing. "Huh. Well, I guess maybe you have a point. Still..."

Her voice trails off.

Suddenly Thomas smashes the handle of a gun against the back of Julie's head, sending her slumping to the ground.

I immediately lunge at him and start barking, but Alex pulls me back and wraps a length of rope around my mouth. I struggle and try to kick him, but he pulls the rope tighter.

"Like your new makeshift muzzle?" he asks, holding me firmly. "From now on, you bark when we want you to bark. Got it?"

I try again to get free, but he kicks me hard in the side and I stumble back. Julie is on the ground, not moving at all, and a moment later I spot Doctor Evans slumped in the far corner of the tent. There's blood on the side of his face.

"Let's just focus on getting everything packed up," Thomas mutters. "I want to get away from this dump before anyone else notices what we're doing. Let's leave this miserable place to die. We're gonna head west, 'cause west is where the ocean is, and I figure it's always best to go toward water. And when we get there, I'm going to establish a new colony of enlightened souls."

Alex turns to him. "But what about -"

"You don't have to come," Thomas adds firmly. "No-one's making you do a fucking thing."

Alex mutters something under his breath, while still holding my collar tight.

"I'm gonna get the cars ready," Thomas continues, reaching down and grabbing my collar before leading me toward the exit. "You guys get your asses moving, okay? Food, water, medical supplies, anything you can lift, bring it all to our two cars. The future is waiting for us, and I know how to get there."

Keeping hold of my collar, he starts pulling me out of the tent. I turn to go back to Julie, but Thomas quickly yanks me outside. When I turn to growl at him, I find that I can't open my mouth, and I remember that my jaws have been tied shut using a rope. No matter how hard I struggle, I'm powerless to stop Thomas as he drags me toward a nearby car.

CHAPTER THIRTY

"FUCK!" ALEX SCREAMS, LEANING out the window as the car races along a dirt-track road. "Let's get the hell away from this shit-hole! To the future! Are you with me?"

The others are all shouting too. I turn and look back out through the car's rear window, and I see the camp rapidly disappearing into the distance. All I want is to go and find Julie, to make sure she's okay, but suddenly Melissa grabs my collar and pulls me back down onto the seat.

"Forget it," she says, with no hint of emotion on her face. "You're coming with us now. We're following Thomas."

"We're just gonna keep driving," Thomas announces from the driver's seat. "Fuck, it'll be dark soon, but I don't care. We're just gonna keep the pedal down and -"

He pauses.

"Fuck! Look!"

The others stare out at the road ahead. Turning, I see a figure in the distance, struggling toward us.

"It's one of those fucking zombie assholes," Alex says with a faint smile as he turns to Thomas. "I think you have a duty to deal with this bastard."

"Way ahead of you," Thomas mutters, not slowing down as the car races toward the figure.

Before I can react, the car slams into the figure at full-speed, causing the torso to break apart and sending arms and legs clattering over the roof. Thomas hits the brakes, bringing the vehicle screeching to a halt, and everyone turns to see the wrecked and mangled figure behind us. Despite the speed of the impact and the fact that its limbs are missing, the rotten torso is still twitching and shuddering, but suddenly Thomas puts the car into reverse and drives back again.

"Get her!" Alex yells excitedly.

Melissa is just staring out the back window as the car grinds closer to the creature.

The car slams into the figure, this time crunching over the torso at lower speed. The entire vehicle shudders and jolts, and finally Thomas brings it to a halt again. Everyone looks out the front, seeing that the creature is more mangled than ever, with its chest having been crushed into a series of knots. Still, however, it refuses to stop moving, and after a moment the head turns to us and snarls once more.

"It just won't fucking stay dead," Thomas mutters, laughing as he drives the car forward. "I think the key thing is to get the fucking head off."

This time he drives even more slowly, and I hear the creature's bones cracking under the wheels as the car rides over the corpse. Thomas and his friends are still laughing and hollering, and Melissa is still sitting with a vacant expression on her face, and after a moment the car stops so that they can all look out the back, where the creature has been smeared against the road but is still, somehow, trying to get to its feet.

For the next few minutes, Thomas keeps driving over the figure, each time crushing its body a little more. His friends shout encouragement, but it takes a while before the creature stops twitching and they're all satisfied that the smeared patch of flesh and bone on the road isn't going to move again. In some strange way, they actually seems disappointed once the job is done, but they're still chattering excitedly.

"We're gonna park up for the night," Thomas says suddenly.

Alex turns to him. "I thought you wanted to -"

"I've changed my mind," he continues, as he starts driving the car along the road once more. "I need time to think, and to figure out our next move. We'll find a safe spot and we'll stop until sunrise."

"But -"

"I'm in charge," Thomas adds breathlessly, keeping his eyes on the road ahead. "You all just have to trust me."

***

With the rope still tied tight around my mouth, holding

my jaws shut, I'm pulled by the collar until I jump down out of the car. It's dark outside now and I immediately turn, wanting to climb back up and return to the camp, but Alex drags me away from the car and then kicks me hard, sending me stumbling forward into the darkness.

"Untie his fucking jaws," Thomas mutters.

Alex turns to him. "But what if he -"

"He won't fucking bite you. Not if he's afraid of you. I'm officially making it your job to discipline that flea-bag. If anyone or anything approaches us while we're here, I want it to give us a warning."

"Did you hear that, Hannibal?" Alex asks, stepping over to me. "You've got a job to do. Doesn't that make you proud? Everyone wants a job."

He pauses, before suddenly kicking me hard in the ribs.

I stagger back, but he immediately does it again, and this time I stumble and drop down onto the cool ground.

Leaning down, he removes the rope from around my jaws. I start snarling, but he kicking me in the ribs and I let out a pained whimper as he attaches another rope to my collar. I've never been in so much pain.

"Do you know who's your boss now?" he sneers, leaning closer until his face is just inches from mine.

I pull back, scared in case he hits me again, but after a moment I realize I need to hold my ground. Baring my teeth, I start snarling again.

"Who's your fucking boss?" he shouts, grabbing my collar and holding me steady. "Do you hear me, dog? Who's your fucking boss, you little cocksucker?"

"He doesn't speak English, dumb-ass," Thomas mutters, coming over to look down at me. "You don't communicate with him using words. You use actions. Body language, that sort of thing."

He pauses for a moment, before taking a step back.

I snarl at him.

"Fine," Alex says, slightly out of breath, "but what kind of -"

Suddenly Thomas kicks me hard in the face, harder than I've ever been hit before, and I let out a yelp of pain as I fall back. I can taste blood in my mouth, but Thomas steps closer again and I instinctively start cowering and whimpering, terrified in case he hits me again. All I can hope is that by submitting, I'll make him see that I'm no threat.

He starts laughing, and then he turns and heads back over to the others.

"We need to start a fire," he tells them. "I'm fucking freezing out here, and I can't think properly when I'm cold. And get out whatever booze we've got left. Fuck saving it, let's have one more big blow-out. We'll find some more later, we'll track down a fucking store or something."

"Who's your fucking boss?" Alex asks again, leaning down to me.

I pull back, scared in case he hits me.

"Yeah," he continues with a grin. "That's better. Now remember, if you catch so much as a whiff of one of those zombie assholes, you start barking, okay? You can still bark, can't you?"

For the next few hours, once they've got a small fire started next to the car, Thomas and the others sit around talking and drinking. They take some items from the car's trunk, too, and drink from little bottles that were originally in the medical tent. I have no idea what they're discussing, but they sound angry and at one point a couple of them even get into a fight, scrabbling with one another while the others watch and cheer. I stay as far back as possible, hoping that they'll forget I'm here. All I want is to go back to the camp and find Julie, and make sure she's okay, but I know that I'm not allowed to leave, and that I'll be beaten again if I try. Besides, I'm tied to the stake again, and there's no way to get free. So instead I just sit here, watching the fire, hoping that somehow everything will be better in the morning.

Eventually, once Thomas and his friends have started to fall asleep, I hear the faintest of noises in the distance. I turn and look out into the darkness, but there's no sign of anyone. Still, I definitely heard a rumbling sound, even if it's stopped now. My ribs and leg hurt too much to let me sleep, so I simply watch the darkness in case there's any sign of movement.

CHAPTER THIRTY-ONE

SEVERAL HOURS LATER, the noise returns.

Thomas, Melissa, Alex and their two friends are fast asleep, and I've spent the night watching as the fire slowly begins to die. Now, however, I can hear a scratching, stumbling sound somewhere in the darkness, although I'm not picking up the smell of death. Instead, as I lift my head and look around, I realize there's a more familiar scent getting closer.

Julie.

I sit up, and after a moment I hear the sound of my own tail brushing against the ground as it wags. Getting to my feet, I step toward the source of the scent, and now I can hear the faintest hint of footsteps. After a few more seconds, I'm able to make out a shape moving in the darkness, and finally I limp around the side of the car just in time to find Julie creeping closer.

I instinctively run to her, but the rope quickly pulls me back.

THE DOG

She smiles as soon as she sees me. She has bruises on one side of her face, and she puts a finger against her lips as I reach her, warning me to stay quiet, and then she comes over and unties me.

Crouching down, she pauses for a moment, listening to the sound of Thomas and the others as they continue to sleep.

She waits, and then she crawls toward the car and reaches into the open trunk, carefully taking out one of the boxes that originally came from the medical tent. Getting to her feet, she heads back the way she just came, and I follow. We walk silently for several minutes until we reach her car, which is parked out of sight around a bend in the road. She takes a moment to set the box in her trunk, and then she turns to me. With the first light of morning starting to show on the horizon, I can see her better now, and it's clear that she has several cuts on her neck from where she was beaten yesterday.

"I'm not letting these assholes steal the camp's medical supplies," she whispers, holding up a gun. "I borrowed this from Doctor Evans. Don't worry, I'm not going to shoot anyone, but I'll wave it around if I have to. There are people at the camp who'll die if they don't get this medicine." She pauses, before leaning down and stroking the side of my face. "And I came for you too, Harry. Jon would never forgive me if I let anything happen to you."

I nuzzle my nose against her wrist, relieved that she's back, but then to my horror she turns and starts making her way back toward the spot where Thomas and the others are sleeping. Hurrying after her, I paw at her leg, but she doesn't stop. Trying to warn her, I bark.

"Quiet!" she hisses, turning to me.

I paw at her leg again.

"You've got to be quiet, okay?" she continues, her voice tense with fear. "Quiet, Harry! Quiet!"

I paw at her leg for a third time. All I want is for her to take me away from this place.

"They've been using some of the drugs they took, right?" she whispers. "Mixing them with some of the alcohol they stole? Don't worry, I think they'll be out for a few more hours." She looks down at the gun, and I can see that her hands are trembling. "No-one else was willing to come with me. Most of them are busy trying to figure out whether or not they should cut and run, the whole camp is falling apart but..."

She pauses, and for a moment I think she might be able to change her mind.

"I keep thinking about Jon," she continues. "I was so sure I was doing the right thing back at the cabin, but now I keep wondering whether... Maybe I should have left him trapped in there. I was so busy trying to do the right thing, but..."

Her voice trails off.

I paw her leg yet again. Why can't we leave?

"I have to do this," she adds finally. "This is the right thing. I can't let fear get the better of me again. I've been a coward too many times before. This time I need *all* the medicine, not just some of it."

With that, she sets off again, and I have no choice but to follow. The rope is still attached to my collar, trailing behind me along the dusty ground.

Sticking close to her, ready to defend her if necessary, I'm relieved when we get back to Thomas's car and there's no sign that anyone is awake yet. They drank so much last night, and the whole place stinks of alcohol. I stand guard while Julie takes another box from the trunk, and then I follow her back down to her car. Her heart is pounding, but once again she immediately turns and heads back up the hill to get another box. I follow reluctantly, still hoping that soon we can drive away and never see Thomas or the others again.

There was a time when everything was okay. I want to go back to the cabin, to the days when Jon and I just used to go for long walks and runs, and when -

Suddenly Julie cries out, and I turn to see that Thomas has grabbed her from behind and pulled her away from the car.

I run to help, but I'm quickly pulled back and I turn to find Alex holding the rope that's trailing from my collar.

"Drop it!" Thomas shouts, slamming Julie's arm against the side of the car, causing her to let go of the gun. "That's better."

He shoves her to the ground and then kicks her hard in the ribs.

Barking, I strain to get away from Alex, but he pulls me back again and then pushes my face down into the mud.

"Some fucking guard dog," he mutters darkly, as I hear Julie crying out again and again nearby. "Whose fucking side are you on, anyway?"

Grabbing my collar, he pulls me around the

other side of the car. I turn and snarl at him, but he quickly smashes a fist into the side of my neck, causing me to cry out. My injured leg gives way, and he starts dragging me across the rocky ground until we reach the spot where the night's fire is now dying out. Morning sunlight has begun to light the scene, and I'm shoved to the ground as Julie screams in the distance.

Despite the pain in my legs and ribs, I try to get up. I have to go and help her.

Luke kicks me again, before leaning close to my right ear and screaming.

"Stay! You fucking little piece of shit! Stay"

His voice is so loud, I flinch and instinctively recoil. He places the sole his right boot against my back and pushes down, forcing me to the ground. I try to scramble free, but he's hurting my back and all I can manage is a series of faint whimpers.

At the same time, Julie's screams are getting louder, although after a moment they change and become more of a jerky series of pained gasps. I try to go to her, but Alex is pushing down harder and harder against my back. After a moment, he leans close to my ear again.

"Are you fucking dense?" he snarls, finally moving his boot away but keeping hold of the rope. "She doesn't need your help. Trust me, Thomas is giving her everything she needs. Then maybe I'll get a turn."

I growl at him, and this time I don't back down when he steps closer. Instead, I press my paws against the ground, ready to hold my ground and fight back. My back hurts and my leg is agony, but I can't let any of that show right now.

Laughing, he turns to the others.

"Have you seen this fucking thing? It's hilarious! He thinks he -"

I bark at him.

He turns and kicks me hard in the face, sending my scurrying back.

A moment later Thomas appears, dragging Julie by the arm and shoving her forward until she stumbles and falls. I try to run to her, but Alex holds me back and I'm powerless as Thomas heads over to the others, wiping his hands together.

"Can you believe the fucking bitch was trying to steal *our* medicine?" he asks. "The fucking nerve, am I right? Here we are, trying to strike out on our own and build something that'll actually last, and some whore from the old camp comes and tries to sabotage us. Isn't that somewhat symbolic, my friends?"

"Yeah," Alex mutters with a nervous laugh, "fucking nerve."

I start barking at Thomas. I can see that Julie is hurt, with blood on her face and arms, and I know we have to get out of here.

"Shut that dog up," Thomas continues, as Melissa gets to her feet and walks over to Julie. She has a gun in her hand. "Seriously, make that fucking dog stop barking, it's driving me up the wall."

Suddenly there's a loud bang as Melissa fires the gun, blasting one side of Julie's face away and sending her body slumping to the ground with blood pouring from the wound.

"Fuck!" Alex hisses.

I bark louder and faster than ever, filled with panic as I try to get free so I can defend Julie and keep her safe. Before I can do anything, however, Thomas steps behind me and grabs my shoulders, hauling me up into the air and carrying me over to the car. Still trying to wriggle free, I bark and snarl in an attempt to make him drop me, but suddenly he shoves me down into the car's trunk.

I immediately turn and try to get out, only for him to slam the trunk shut, hitting my head and knocking me back. As the trunk's door clicks and shudders, I'm trapped in darkness. I bark over and over, trying to get Julie to let me out, and when that doesn't work I start pawing at the metal latch. Filled with panic, all I can do is bark and hope that at any moment Julie will open the trunk and everything will be okay. My whole body is trembling with fear and my throat hurts, but pure terror compels me to keep barking as I hear voices shouting outside.

CHAPTER THIRTY-TWO

I DON'T KNOW HOW long I spend in the trunk, barking and still trying desperately to find a way out, but eventually the car's engine restarts and I feel the wheels turning. Once the car is speeding along the road, I'm bumped and jolted in the trunk, but I keep barking and howling, and my paws are hurting now after scratching for hours and hours against metal.

All I know is that I have to get out of here. I have to get back to Julie and make sure she's okay.

CHAPTER THIRTY-THREE

ONCE THE CAR HAS come to a halt, I hear the doors opening and then footsteps come around to the rear. I wait, snarling and shuddering, and finally the trunk opens.

Blinding light fills my eyes, but I immediately launch myself at Alex, only for him to smash some kind of stick against my face. Pressing the stick's end against my neck, he pushes me down in the trunk. I try desperately to get to my feet, but he presses harder and harder, grinning wildly, until finally he grabs the other end of the rope around my neck and hauls me out, kicking me in the ribs as I stumble down onto the dusty ground.

"Your fucking barking is driving us all nuts," he says firmly. "You're lucky Thomas still thinks you might be useful."

I turn and bark at him, but he kicks me again and I let out a faint whimper.

Turning, I see that we're even further from the camp. The strongest scent is my own blood, but I can also smell the sweat of Thomas and his friends. Looking around, I wait to see Julie, but there's no sign of her, although a moment later I pick up the scent of her blood. Turning, I realize that there's some of her blood on the sleeve of Thomas's coat, and I bark at him as he whispers something in Melissa's ear.

"At least you'll make a good guard dog," Alex mutters, patting my flank, "so -"

Turning, I try to bite him, missing by just a few inches. He pulls back and drops the rope, and for a moment I can tell that he's scared.

"Keep that fucking dog under control!" Thomas yells.

Alex tries to grab the rope, but I pull away, still barking and snarling.

"Did you hear mar?" Thomas continues. "You're the dog wrangler here, or the dog whisperer, whatever it's fucking called. I need time to think, and to plan, so keep that monster on a tight leash."

"He's looking pretty fierce," Alex says cautiously.

Melissa marches over. I snarl at her, but she reaches down and grabs the rope, handing it to Alex. After that, she turns and stares at me with the same impassive expression that she's worn over the past few days. Whereas the others all have pounding hearts, she seems completely calm, and something about her seems deeply unsettling. I snarl for a moment longer, before taking a step back, and now a faint smile crosses her face.

"See?" she mutters, turning to Alex. "It's easy if you're not a pussy."

"Watch who you're calling a pussy," he replies, although he sounds worried.

"Did you ever kill anyone?" she asks him.

"No, but -"

"I did," she continues. "I killed the bitch who let my boyfriend die. So I'm pretty sure I get to call you a pussy."

She turns and heads back over to Thomas. I snarl at her, before turning and barking at Alex.

"Quiet!" he tells me, although his voice is trembling and it's clear that he's not confident at all. "Hannibal, please, be quiet!"

"I need to be able to hear myself think!" Thomas yells. "I'm trying to plan our collective future here!"

"Quiet, boy," Alex continues, stepping closer to me. "Seriously, can you just be quiet? For me?"

He reaches down to pat my head.

"Just be -"

Instinctively I lunge at him, biting his hand. As my teeth sink into his flesh, I taste a burst of blood in my mouth, and I hear him let out a shocked yelp of pain. I let go pretty quickly, now that I've warned him off, but he drops the rope and staggers back, clutching his hand as blood dribbles down onto the dusty ground.

"He bit me!" he gasps. "The fucking bastard bit me!"

"So?" Melissa mutters. "You deserve it."

"Fucking asshole!" Alex yells, stepping toward

me with fury in his eyes.

I bark and lunge at him again, and he immediately pulls back, tripping in the process and landing hard on the rocky ground. I take another step toward him and he scrambles away, and now I can sense his fear.

"Get it away from me!" he shouts, still clutching his injured hand. "Help!"

Still barking at him, I suddenly feel the ground shuddering beneath my paws, and I realize that someone is hurrying toward us. Picking up the scent of Julie's blood, I turn just as Thomas gets to me, but he quickly grabs my collar and pulls me back. Slamming me against the ground, he clutches my throat and squeezes tight, and he refuses to let go even as I desperately snarl and try to kick him away. After a moment, he leans closer until his face is just inches from my mouth, but all I can do is growl and bare my teeth.

"You're starting to piss me off," he says finally. "Granted, that asshole deserved to get bitten, but this is a very serious time for me. I need to make a decision about what to do next. There's a lot of pressure on me, do you understand? Pressure to lead these people. Pressure to keep us alive. Pressure to help humanity grow and evolve to the next stage of existence. This global extinction-level event is an opportunity."

He stares into my eyes, but I continue to struggle, desperately trying to get free.

"Can you smell this?" he asks, grabbing the end of his coat and holding it up so that I can see Julie's blood drying on the fabric. "Do you know what it is?

Does it scare you?"

Filled with fear, I try even harder to get away, but he's holding my throat too firmly.

"This is the blood of a casualty," he continues. "Casualties are inevitable in any uncertain situation. There'll be more, and that's a pity, but the old world is gone now. The world where you got to curl up on a nice blanket is gone. The world where people gave you fucking snacks and treats is gone. Do you understand?"

"He's a dog," Alex whimpers, sobbing slightly. "He doesn't understand anything. I'm sick of him, he's dangerous, let's just put a bullet in his throat and keep moving."

"No," Thomas replies, with his eyes still fixed on mine, "I think we can use this animal. I think it would be a crime not to."

He pauses, before suddenly letting go of my throat, while keeping his face close to mine. I immediately freeze, waiting to see what he does next, but he simply stares at me. His eyes seem strange somehow, as if the darker parts are larger than they should be, while the whites are bloodied.

"Careful!" Alex hisses. "He'll bite you!"

"No," Thomas says calmly, "he won't. Will you, Hannibal?"

He pauses, still looking into my eyes.

"He won't bite me," he continues, "because he's knows I'm the boss. I've dominated him."

He leans a little closer.

"He can feel my breath on his face. He respects strength. He wants to know his place in our hierarchy, and his place is at our side. At *my* side. Once he knows that, he'll settle right down."

I want to bite him, but something about his stare is forcing me to hold back. He seems much more powerful than the others, and I'm scared to make him angry.

"Do it, Hannibal," he whispers. "If you want a chunk of me, take it. Nothing's stopping you. Nothing in the whole world, bite my fucking face if that's what you think you need to do. We're all free animals here. We can all do what we want, so if you *want* to pick a fight with me, be my guest."

There's madness in his eyes, and finally I turn away. Scrambling to my feet, I take a few steps back, but when I turn I find that Thomas is still watching me.

"And that," he adds, turning to the others, "is how to fucking dominate a wild animal. See? He's totally in my shadow now, and he knows who's the boss."

He comes over, and I don't dare try to stop him as he reaches down and pats the side of my face.

"He's my pet now," he continues, running his hand onto my flank and feeling my ribs. "He's lean. That's good, it means he'll stay alert. But he fucking rides with me, do you all understand? Frankly, this animal is more useful than most of you assholes put together."

"I still don't like it," Alex tells him. "I vote that we -"

"Are you challenging me?" Thomas asks, stepping over to him. "If you are, do it now rather than constantly sniping."

"I just -"

"You're not *just* doing anything," Thomas adds, stopping and staring straight into his eyes from just a few inches away. "If you think I'm leading us in the wrong direction, let's hear what you think we should be doing instead."

Alex pauses, before taking a step away from him and looking down at his wounded hand.

"Sorry," he mutters, "I didn't... I wasn't... Sorry."

Thomas stares at him for a moment longer. "Okay," he says finally. "Then I guess that's settled."

"I'm need to change," Melissa mutters, heading over to the car. "Fucking boys are all the same."

"You're gonna to stick by my side," Thomas says firmly, turning to me again. "You're my dog now, Hannibal."

"Wow," Alex says suddenly, his voice filled with a sense of awe.

Realizing that they're all watching something, I turn and see that Melissa is taking her clothes off. She glances at the guys, clearly aware of their gaze, before stripping completely naked and then taking some crumpled clothes from the back seat. She takes her time getting dressed again, and it's clear that she could easily have chosen to go to the other side of the car, but after a moment I realize that I recognize her new clothes. Julie was wearing them earlier.

I start barking, but Thomas places a hand on my nose and I quickly stop. Still, I let out a faint growl as watch Melissa buttoning her new shirt. She's grinning, as if she likes the attention.

"Melissa," Thomas says finally, "you sit with me too. I want you sticking to my side, just like..."

His voice trails off for a moment, and then suddenly he claps his hands together.

"Let's move, people! Let's hit the mother-fucking road and drive to the new future!"

CHAPTER THIRTY-FOUR

BY THE TIME WE reach a small town several hours later, night has begun to fall once again. Thomas forced me down into the car's foot-well, but I knew I couldn't disobey his command so I've stayed curled up, constantly jolted as the car races along dusty roads. Now that we've stopped again, however, I follow the others as they step out of the car, although naturally I keep close to Thomas since he's in charge.

My heart is racing and I'm terrified, but Thomas is my master now.

"Looks like the place fucking burned," he mutters, heading across the street toward a large, blackened building that looks to have been on fire at some point. "Maybe they were trying to smoke out some zombies."

He pauses, before holding his hands out and turning.

"Welcome to the ruins of human civilization.

Look at what the fuckers left behind after they died. Houses as bones of a body that died."

Turning, I spot Melissa at the rear of the car. Her attention seems to have been drawn by something that's stuck to the trunk's lid, as I see a flicker of shock in her eyes.

"I don't like it here," Alex says, his voice filled with fear. "We should be avoiding built-up areas in case there are more of those creatures."

"The creatures are dying out already," Thomas continues. "They couldn't exactly sustain themselves."

"But -"

"Are you questioning my judgment again?" he adds, turning to Alex. "Is that what you're doing?"

Alex shakes his head. "Definitely not. I promise. Sorry."

Thomas stares at him for a moment, as if he's not quite convinced. "Good," he adds finally. "Listen, I don't like this fucking ghost-town any more than the rest of you, but we need supplies. Gas, alcohol, food, alcohol, water, alcohol, medicine, alcohol..." He grins. "Anything we can get our hands on. And maybe even some new cars. A truck would be fucking sweet. So I want everyone to take a look around and grab whatever they can. Don't be pussies now. Break windows if you have to, but get stuff. And meet back here in about an hour, okay? We need to decide whether to stay here or not once it's properly dark."

As the others head off in different directions, I follow Thomas to a nearby building. I don't want to go with him, of course, but I know I have no choice. The rope is still attached to my neck, with the other end trailing on the ground. Thomas is in charge and he's made it clear that I have no right to challenge him.

"That's a good boy, Hannibal," he says with a grin, before using a brick to smash the window of a store. "You know your place. I wish Alex and the other animals were that smart. Don't tell the others, but I honestly think you're the second smartest member of our little gang right now."

Picking me up, he passes me through the broken window and sets me down on the other side. I immediately let out a yelp as I feel a piece of glass cutting my paw, and I pull away with blood dripping from the wound.

"You'll get used to it," Thomas continues. "I just need you to make sure there are no nasty surprises waiting inside. Looks like this was a grocery store. There's gotta be some shit that's still good."

Limping forward, I realize I can smell rotten food. Lots of it. There are a few other scents too, but the most overwhelming is a sense of foul meat, and when I get to the far end of the aisle I spot moldy food behind a glass partition. Hearing footsteps nearby, I turn and watch as Thomas comes over to join me, and he seems faintly disgusted by the smell.

"I think we'll stick to canned stuff," he mutters. "Fuck, that meat stinks. And if *I* can smell it, Hannibal, *your* nose must be fucking buzzing."

As he starts examining items on a shelf, I make my way over to a door in the far corner. Somewhere beyond the stench of rotten food, there's another smell, something human. Stopping suddenly, I realize I can hear a scratching sound from the next room, so I'm much more cautious as I head through the door, and finally I stop as soon as I see a little girl on the floor, with her head leaning against the wall. Her eyes are open, staring straight at me, but she's painfully thin and she smells bad. She's not one of those creatures, I can already tell that from how she looks and how she smells, but she seems very weak and as I take a cautious step toward her, I realize that the scratching sound is coming from her fingers as she drags them against the floorboards.

She lets out a faint gasp and her lips tremble slightly, as if she's trying to say something.

"Found anything through there, Hannibal?" Thomas calls out, kicking some bottles across the floor. "We're in luck, this place has fucking whiskey!"

I wag my tail as I step closer to the girl. Even though she smells bad, I remember being around children sometimes in the park with Jon, and they were always friendly. As I reach her, she keeps her eyes fixed on me, and I nuzzle her hand with my nose.

"Help," she whispers, her voice barely audible at all. "Help me..."

"Fuck!"

Turning, I see that Thomas has come through to join us, and he's staring at the little girl with shock in his eyes.

"Are you okay, kid?" he asks, stepping around her. "You look like skin and bones. Have you just been starving here, with no-one to help you? Did your Mommy and Daddy die?"

AMY CROSS

The girl tries again to speak, but this time only a faint sigh emerges, disturbing the dust that has settled on her lips.

"Oh, you're too fucking far gone," Thomas continues. "Sorry, kid, but I don't think there's anything I can do for you except..."

He looks around, before taking a knife from one of the counters.

"You don't want to be left here in pain, do you?" he asks, crouching next to her. He pauses, watching as she continues to twitch slightly. "I should do this," he continues. "I should know how it feels to end a life, and you're clearly way past the point where you can be helped. How long have you been all alone here like this? Days at least, maybe a week or more? That's fucking awful, dude. No-one should have to endure such absolute fucking pain." Another pause, and then he places the blade against her neck. "How old are you? Seven? Eight? Clearly too fucking young to go through this misery."

She gasps again, and she seems a little more agitated now, as if she's scared.

"My name is Thomas," he tells her. "Before all this shit went down, do you know what I did with my days? I worked a fucking mind-numbing job making fucking sandwiches for fucking loathsome customers in a little town. I was nothing, and I was going to end up living a worthless, meaningless life. But then when everything changed, I felt something stirring in my soul. A kind of..."

He pauses.

"Greatness," he adds finally. "In *this* world, with conventional civilization ruined and tattered, suddenly I have something to offer. Suddenly I can lead other people to enlightenment. I see that now. I can be a prophet of the new dawn. But that's a huge responsibility, and one of the things I have to do is... I have to keep bettering myself, and proving myself, and I think God has put you here in this room specifically for me. In his infinite wisdom, God is signaling me, showing me that he has faith in me and asking me to pass this test. God wants me to help you."

He closes his eyes.

"Give me the strength to do this," he whispers. "I'm not talking to God now. I'm talking to my inner self, to the part of me that makes me who I really am, deep down. Give me the strength to kill this little girl and end her suffering, and to show myself that I have what it takes to lead. Give me the strength to recognize that I'm a leader, and to achieve my full potential. Let me prove myself God as he silently watches."

He sits in silence for a moment.

The girl is still letting out a series of gasps.

Suddenly Thomas slices the knife through her throat. She shudders and gurgles, with blood spraying from the wound, and I step back to keep from getting dirty. Letting out a low whimper, I wait as the girl's body continues to shake, and it takes a few minutes before she finally falls still. Even then, Thomas stays completely still and silent for a little while longer, before sighing and tossing the knife to the ground.

"Fuck, that was intense," he says finally, getting

to his feet and turning to me with a faint, nervous smile. "I had to do it, though. I couldn't let Melissa be the only one who knows what it's like to kill. I needed to break my duck, yeah? I needed to pop my killing cherry and become a man." He steps over the girl's corpse and crouches next to me, and after a moment he looks toward the dead girl. "It's a thing of beauty, isn't it? I feel more alive than ever. This new collapsed world really suits me, Hannibal. I never would've got to experience this feeling in the old world. You're lucky. You just witnessed my rebirth."

I take a step back, wanting to get away from the girl and from Thomas, but he grabs my collar and hauls me closer.

"Not so fast," he says firmly. "I didn't tell you to leave, did I? You need toughening up, my friend. I still see fear and weakness in your eyes. If you're gonna be the faithful hound at the side of a great leader, you need to look the part."

He pauses, watching me intently, and finally I have no choice but to turn away.

Suddenly he yanks me forward and pushes my face down toward the puddle of blood. I try to turn, but he's too strong and I can't fight back as he smears my chin and the side of my face against the ground. By the time he lets go and I pull away, the girl's blood is soaked into my fur and its rich scent is filling my nostrils.

"That'll be good for you," he says with a smile, before reaching down and dipping his fingers into the blood. "It's good both all of us." He wipes some of the blood across his upper lip. "We have to be less scared of death now."

Getting to his feet, he takes a few steps away before stopping with his back to me, framed against the dusty window. Slowly, he raises his arms to the sides, and I can see dust drifting between his fingers.

"I have to lead the people," he continues after a moment, his voice filled with a sense of wonder. "I have to take them to a promised land."

He pauses, before turning and looking down at the girl's corpse.

"I've got a fucking wicked idea!" he says suddenly, grinning wildly. "A fucking *amazing* idea!"

CHAPTER THIRTY-FIVE

I WAS HOPING THAT we'd leave the town, but instead Thomas and the others decide to spend the night in a large building overlooking the main square. One side of the building has been badly burned, but the rest is intact. They've got alcohol and food, scavenged from local stores, and they seem excited. As they continue to drink, they become louder and more animated, and a couple of fights even break out. Thomas remains in charge, though, and the others seem to be recognizing more and more that he's the leader of their pack.

I keep back as much as possible, resting on the floor near a makeshift fire that has been lit near the window. The girl's blood has dried in the fur around my mouth, but the scent is still too strong to ignore and my heart is pounding. I can't even remember what it felt like in the days when I wasn't constantly scared.

"Welcome to the end of the fucking world!" Thomas screams suddenly, raising his arms with a bottle of whiskey in each hand. "Bow down before me, my brothers and sisters, and I shall lead you to the promised land!"

Alex and the others stumble over to him and then get down onto their knees, while shouting Thomas's name over and over. Melissa seems more cautious, preferring to hang back at the edge of the room and simply watch.

"Fuck that stupid rendezvous point at the Rarrah Valley," Thomas continues, before taking a swig of whiskey and then burping. "That was a fucking waste of everyone's time. The old prophets, the ones who pontificated across the airwaves from their Washington homes, were leading us all wrong. The new order isn't gonna be about trying to put the world back together. No fucking way. From this day on, we create our own fucking civilization, and I know the way."

"Amen!" Alex shrieks, before bursting into a giggling fit.

"I haven't led any of you wrong so far," Thomas adds, "and I promise you, everything will be okay if you stick with me. We're in a new world now, a world where the human race survives thanks to quality rather than quantity. Never again will we create cities that swarm with unnecessary populations. Humanity is gonna be more focused, more refined. Better. And do you know what else?"

He pauses.

"What?" Alex asks plaintively.

"We're gonna fucking blow this joint apart," Thomas continues, swaying slightly as he drinks from the whiskey bottle again. Once he's done, he gasps and wipes his lips. "We're the new generation now. We're gonna seize the world and make it better, but first..."

He pauses, before stepping over to the fire and wrapping some cloth around his hand. Reaching down, he picks up a long piece of metal, the tip of which has been resting in the flames for the past few minutes.

"What's that?" Alex asks with a nervous smile.

Thomas stares at the metal tip, which is shaped in a wavy pattern. After a moment he glances at me, and I can see the confidence in his eyes. Finally, he turns to the others.

"I need each and every one of you to prove that you're committed to the cause," he explains, and now his eyes are blinking rapidly. "That's why, when I found this interesting chunk of metal, I realized it'd be the perfect way to brand ourselves. To *mark* ourselves."

"You're wasted," Alex says with a smile, taking another sip of whiskey. "We're not fucking cattle, dude."

"We're animals," Thomas replies. "Absolutely, we *are* animals. The best animals, the strongest animals, but still animals. We need to remember that, so that we don't make the same mistakes as everyone who came before us. I've seen the light, my friends, and I know how the human race must continue. We can rise from the ashes of this disaster and become stronger than ever before, but first we need to recognize the terrible mistakes of our ancestors. And don't worry, I'm going to be the first to mark myself."

"Like..." Alex pauses. "With actual fire?"

"With actual fire," Thomas whispers, staring at

the red-hot metal with a hint of wonder in his eyes. "It was fire that allowed mankind to master the world the first time, and it will be fire that allows us to master everything around us again. And do you know what else? There will be no pain."

With that, he presses the metal tip against his hand. His face remains completely calm, completely devoid of all emotion, as his flesh burns. He keeps the tip in place for a few more seconds before finally he pulls it away.

"There," he whispers, holding his hand up to reveal the red mark. "I did it! I felt the pain, but I told myself to focus on the pleasure instead. Now I want every last one of you fuckers to follow!"

Even above the scent of the girl's blood on my face, I can smell Thomas's burned flesh.

"And just to make you feel better..."

He heads over to the corner and picks up a cotton bag, stained with blood. I let out a faint whimper, already knowing what's coming, and I watch as he carefully takes the little girl's severed head from the bag.

"Fuck!" Alex hisses, and the others seem shocked too.

Except Melissa.

She simply watches.

A few fresh dribbles of blood run from the girl's neck and spatter against the floor.

"Let a child of the old world observe our ritual," Thomas says with a sense of awe in his voice, as he places the head on a chair.

"Dude, that's sick!" Alex stammers. "Fuck,

where did you even get that from? I don't want to see some kid's head, for God's sake!"

"You must be strong," Thomas whispers, adjusting the head a little. "See how the light from the fire dances in her dead eyes. Now let her watch as you mark yourselves."

He turns to them.

"Trust me," he adds with a grin. "I know what I'm doing."

Over the next few minutes, he gradually persuades the others to line up so he can burn their hands. Some of them are more scared than others, but they eventually agree. They all scream as the red-hot metal is pressed against their flesh, and I can only watch with a growing sense of shock as they submit to something so horrific. Humans are difficult to understand at the best of times, but right now they seem completely insane as they willingly do something that leaves them in so much agony.

Perhaps the biggest surprise, however, is Melissa. When it's her turn, she's the only one who doesn't scream, who doesn't even flinch, as the metal is pressed against her hand. She simply stares into Thomas's eyes, without a trace of emotion, and he keeps the metal on her flesh for a little longer, as if he's waiting for her to cry out. It's almost as if they're engaged in some kind of face-off, with her refusing to cry out even as the metal burns deeper and deeper into her hand.

Finally, Thomas takes a step back, and I can see a hint of shock in his eyes. The others seem surprised too, watching the pair of them as if they're not quite sure what's going to happen next.

Melissa looks down at the burn on her hand, before getting to her feet.

"Do you mind?" she asks, reaching her damaged hand toward him.

"What do you want?" he asks cautiously.

"The branding iron."

He hesitates, before passing it to her.

Stepping past him, she places the tip in the flames.

"What are you..." He pauses again. "What are you going to do with it?"

"I had an idea."

I can sense his fear now.

"What kind of idea?" he asks. "I'm not sure I approve of this. The little girl doesn't either."

"You don't know that," Melissa tells him.

"I do," Thomas stammers. "She's saying this is wrong."

A faint flicker of amusement crosses Melissa's face. "You hear her talking to you?"

Thomas turns and looks at the severed head. "Don't the rest of you? She hasn't shut up since I cut it off the rest of her body."

"Just be patient for a moment," Melissa says calmly, staring into the flames. "All good things come to those who wait. Right?"

Thomas smiles nervously.

Still keeping well away from them all, I start trying to brush the dried blood from around my mouth. When I find that I can't quite get my paw into the right places, I switch to rubbing my chin against the floorboards. The smell of blood is getting too strong, and all I want is to clean myself and then get out of here. These people are insane.

"What are you gonna do with that branding iron?" Thomas asks nearby, but I don't even turn and look over at them. "Melissa? I think... I think you should remember that I'm in charge, okay? I'm the leader here."

I want to be alone as much as possible. I used to love being around people, back in the days when Jon used to take me for long walks and I used to get patted and fussed, but now everyone seems to be want to hurt me. Still rubbing my face against the floorboards, I try to ignore Thomas and the others as they shout at one another. Glancing across the room, I see the dead girl's head on the chair, and her eyes are almost looking directly at me.

Instinctively, I get to my feet and move around the edge of the room, hoping to get away from her.

Suddenly Thomas screams.

Startled, I look over and see that he's on his knees. Melissa has pushed the burning metal spike into his mouth, driving it deeper and deeper into his throat as he cries out. He tries to get up, but she pushes down against his shoulder, and there's pure hatred in her eyes as she shoves the tip deeper. Finally, I watch in horror as the tip bursts out through the back of Thomas's neck and blood starts running from his mouth. Twisting the metal around, Melissa slowly pulls it out and then shoves Thomas back until he slumps against the floor. Blood is pouring from the wound now, and he lets out a series of breathless gasps as he tries to crawl away.

"That's for Scott," Melissa stammers, her voice trembling with anger. "I recognized the bumper sticker on your car, asshole. You ran him down like he was a goddamn piece of trash!"

She drops the metal, letting it clatter against the floorboards as Thomas continues to crawl away. Turning to the others, she takes the gun from her belt.

"Dude," Alex says, getting to his feet, "what are -"

Before he can finish, she shoots him in the chest, sending him crashing down, and then she turns and shoots the two other guys as they try to run.

"My Dad used to take me shooting," she mutters, turning to look back down at Thomas as he writhes on the ground with blood pouring from his mouth. "Did I never mention that? So I'm a pretty good fucking shot."

She pauses, before shooting him in the head, sending pieces of his skull and brain across the floor.

"Fucking asshole," she whispers, watching him for a moment longer before suddenly kicking him hard, cracking his face.

I flinch and take a step back.

"Fucking bastard!" she screams, stamping down on Thomas's head over and over again, crushing his skull a little more each time.

Shocked by her sudden outburst, I slink around the edge of the room, hoping to get to the door.

"Where the fuck do you think *you're* going?" she asks suddenly.

Turning, I see her staring at me. After a moment, she aims the gun at my face.

Running out of the room, I hurry along the corridor while trailing the rope from my collar. I can already hear Melissa coming after me, and in my panic I have no idea which way to go. Scrambling in the darkness, I run along another corridor until suddenly I reach the burned part of the building, where some of the walls are missing and late-night wind is blowing through the gaps.

I head over to the far side of the room, but when I look out I see that I'm too high to jump. Instead, I hurry through to another room, hoping that I can find another way down.

Suddenly a shot rings out and I feel a sharp pain slicing across my hip. Whimpering, I start running again, pushing through the agony as I hear Melissa hurrying after me through the dark building.

"Get back here, asshole!" she screams. "You were that bitch's dog! I've got one more bullet left and I'm saving it for you!"

Reaching another room, I find that there's no way out so I turn and head back into the corridor. I spot Melissa's silhouette at the far end, and a moment later there's another shot, this time missing me by inches and blasting charred plaster from the wall.

"That's okay!" she yells, running toward me. "I'll just have to -"

She lets out a sudden cry as the floor collapses beneath her. I hear the sound of wood and plaster raining down, followed a moment later by an agonized scream.

I stand completely still, too shocked to react, but a moment later Melissa cries out again. For the next few minutes, I don't dare move, but she's still shouting and sobbing and finally I realize that there's no-one else left in the building. She killed Thomas and the others, and it's clear that she's in agony.

Despite the pain in my hip and legs, I start limping along the corridor, heading toward the hole that she fell through a moment ago. I still have the little girl's blood dried in the matted fur beneath my nose, and my heart is pounding as I get to the hole and look down.

Melissa is a long way below, flat on her back with rubble all around. Both her legs are broken, snapped at the knees with shards of bone poking out through the bloodied flesh. She's still crying out as she tries to sit up, but it's clear that she won't be able to walk again. For a moment, I stare down at her as she tries over and over again to move, and each time she simply ends up in even more pain. Finally she looks up at me, and for a moment our eyes meet and she falls silent.

And then she screams louder than I've ever heard any human scream before. It's a scream filled with rage and anger and pain, and it seems to be ringing throughout the entire building. She reaches for the gun and aims at me, but all the happens when she pulls the trigger is a series of impotent clicks. Tossing the gun aside, she tries again to get up, which brings even more pain and causes her scream to become even louder. She's sobbing, too, with tears streaming down her face, and the bones protruding from her broken legs are shining in a patch of moonlight that shines down through the building's damaged roof.

"My back," she sobs. "I can't... Help me..."

Finally I turn and walk away, to find another exit. Melissa's screams are still ringing out, and I swear they're loud enough to make the entire building shudder. She's still screaming as I make my way past the bodies of Thomas and the others, and I can hear her even after I'm out of the building. By the time I've limped all the way to the edge of town, she's much further away but her cries can still be heard, filling the entire empty town.

I don't stop.

I don't look back.

I just keep limping out into the barren countryside, desperate to get as far away from humans as possible. My legs hurt and my flank is bleeding, and there's a child's blood smeared across my face and chin. My ribs are stinging too, and I can barely even remember where I came from or how I ended up like this. One thing's certain, though. I never want to see another human again, not for as long as I live.

PART THREE

CHAPTER THIRTY-SIX

I STAY LOW IN the long grass.

Watching.

Waiting.

Listening.

Eventually I hear another faint rustling sound. Closer this time.

Still I wait.

My belly is stinging with hunger and I know I have to time this just right.

Ahead, the grass is swaying slightly. There's a breeze this morning, but one patch of grass in particular is moving more than the rest and the air is alive with the scent of my prey.

Saliva dribbles down my chin.

Finally I spot something small and brown scurrying through the grass, and my instincts kick in. I leap forward, snarling as the rabbit squeals and turns to run. Its attempt to escape is a fraction too late, however, and I bite down hard on its flank, crushing its legs and feeling fresh, warm blood bursting into my mouth.

CHAPTER THIRTY-SEVEN

I SPEND SEVERAL HOURS eating the rabbit. I don't want to swallow too many bones, but at the same time I can't afford to leave even a scrap of meat behind. Still, the process is somehow calming, and my mind empties as I rest in the meadow and gnaw at the top of the rabbit's skull. It might take several days before I catch another meal, so I have to make this last.

This is right.

This is how I want to live now.

This is how I should be.

And then suddenly I hear something in the distance, something that makes me freeze. Something I haven't heard for many, many years.

Human voices.

CHAPTER THIRTY-EIGHT

CREEPING FORWARD, I STAY LOW as I reach the ridge. The voice are much closer now, somewhere down at the foot of the hill. My heart is pounding, but I know I have to see what's happening. Leaning around the ridge, I look down toward the abandoned farmhouse, and that's when I see them.

Five humans.

Two adult males, one adult female, one little boy and one little girl.

The children are playing, but the adults seem to be examining the farmhouse. They clearly have no idea that I'm here, so I remain in place and watch for a few minutes. I honestly can't remember the last time I saw living humans. I've stumbled across corpses occasionally over the years, but many summers have passed since the day I limped away from the town where Melissa lay screaming.

Ten summers at least. Maybe more.

My instinct is to turn and get out of here. This meadow has been a good home for the past few summers, with a fair number of rabbits and mice for me to eat, but I'm sure I can find somewhere else to live and hunt. Still, the humans are a good long way down the valley still, and despite my aching muscles and bones I feel sure I could outrun them even if they suddenly came for me.

I just have to stay alert.

Sniffing the air, I realize I can smell human sweat, but also the scent of food. The humans have brought several wooden carts with them, each loaded down with meat and other items. It has been so long since I ate human food, but suddenly I remember the taste of ham and cheese, and the bacon Jon used to cook in the mornings, and the almost-empty ice cream bowls I was sometimes allowed to lick. For the first time in many years, I allow myself to think back to those days, to a time that had almost slipped from my mind.

I'd love nothing more than to go through those wooden carts, but I don't dare go anywhere near the humans so I get to my feet and turn to walk away. I'll find another meadow. I'll be fine.

"Harry!" a voice calls out suddenly. "Harry! Over here!"

CHAPTER THIRTY-NINE

"HARRY, HELP YOUR SISTER! There'll be time to play later. Right now, you have to help your sister bring more boxes inside. Harry? Harry, get over here and help out! Harry!"

"Does that mean we're staying?" the boy asks, heading to one of the wooden carts.

"There's nothing wrong with the place," the man replies. "The house is sturdy and the land looks good. It's damn near perfect."

"Says who?"

"Says me, now grab a box and help out. Come on, Harry, we all need to pull together."

Still keeping low, I watch as the boy takes a box and starts carrying it into the house. There's food in the box, and it's clearly too heavy for him, but he struggles on nonetheless. Ever since I first heard the name Harry called out a few minutes ago, my interest in these people has become much stronger. I haven't heard that name for a long, long time, and I can't deny that it sparked some deep part of my soul that laid dormant during my time here in the meadow. I think deep down, I thought the humans might be calling me.

But now the truth is clear. When they call for Harry, it's the boy they're after.

I feel a flash of sadness as I realize that he has my name now. I guess I didn't use it for so long, it was taken away and given to someone else.

"You're not done yet, Harry!" the man's voice calls out. "Grab another box!"

"Listen to your father, Harry!" the woman calls out from inside the farmhouse. "Don't leave all the heavy ones for Sophie!"

A moment later, the boy comes out and trudges toward the cart. He's clearly tired and, as he grabs another box, he manages to stumble. Falling down into the mud, he covers his face as the box crashes down on top of him.

"Harry dropped one!" the girl shouts, with a hint of amusement in her voice. "I guess he's a weak-ass after all!"

I let out an involuntary whimper at the sound of that name, and somehow in my head I almost hear Jon's voice calling me, and Julie's too. I've tried not to think about them during my years alone in the meadow, because those memories only make me sad, but hearing the name Harry again has stirred thoughts that I'd hoped might be gone forever.

"Oh Harry," the woman says, coming out from the farmhouse. "You need to remember how to lift properly. Or are they too heavy for you?"

"Of course they're not!" Harry says firmly, although he clearly struggles as he gets to his feet. At the last moment, just before he can reach down to grab the box again, the girl takes it from him and carries it inside. "I had that!" he calls after her. "Sophie! That was mine!"

She laughs.

"Just grab another one," the woman says, following the girl inside, "and try not to make a fuss."

"I had that one," he mutters, turning back to the cart. Suddenly he happens to glance this way, and our eyes meet.

I duck down, out of sight.

"Mom! Dad!" he shouts excitedly. "I saw a dog!"

"Nonsense," the woman replies. "Come on, there's no time for stupid games."

"I saw a dog up there!" he yells. "I swear, I saw a little dog! He looked right at me!"

I wait, hoping that they don't come looking for me. After a few minutes, the voices settle and I dare to take another look. The boy must be inside, because only the two men and the girl are carrying things in from the cart now, and they seem totally engrossed in their work. I've been down to that farmhouse a few times, but the smell of long-gone humans always kept me from staying for too long. Now it seems humans are back, which means I have to be extra careful.

Still, the food scents drifting up from the house are impossible to resist, and I've already come up with a plan.

CHAPTER FORTY

"DO YOU REALLY THINK we can make this work?" the woman asks later as I sneak closer to the house. "We don't know the first thing about farming."

It's dark now, and I've waited hours and hours for this opportunity. I no longer remember many details from my time with Jon at the old cabin, but I *do* remember how he used to put garbage out in a bucket each night. Figuring that these humans might do the same, I've finally come down to take a closer look, and now that I'm right beneath one of the windows I'm able to smell some kind of cooked meat. Still, all the interesting scents so far seem to be coming from inside the house, so it seems that nothing has been thrown out yet. Despite the hunger in my belly, I'll have to be patient.

"We'll manage," one of the men mutters as I slink along the side of the building.

"How?" the woman continues. "It just looks like

grass in all the fields around here."

"There were those wild sheep near the old train line."

"And what are you going to do with those?"

The man sighs. "I admit it's a steep learning curve, but what would you rather do? Keep roaming the countryside, hoping to find something better? This place is already a miracle, Carly. We'll just have to buckle down and make it work. Trust me."

"And what if more of those things show up?"

"No-one's seen one in years. But that's why we decided to stay away from the camps, remember? Out here, away from other people, there's no real risk of us getting sick. And if something *does* show up, that's what the rifle's for."

"And what about other people?"

Silence falls among them for a moment.

"What if other people find us here?" she asks, with fear in her voice. "Those gangs that have been roaming the Mid-West are -"

"This isn't the Mid-West."

"But there are probably others around. We have one rifle, Sam, and how many bullets?"

"We have two boxes of cartridges."

"It won't be enough if someone attacks us. Some of those gangs are very organized."

"Let me deal with that," the man replies. "I have some ideas. Ways we can keep ourselves safe. And no-one's actually seen anything in the area, have they? You're worrying about a threat that's probably hundreds of miles away. That's why we came this far out. There's no-one else here. It's just us."

"I feel like we've become some kind of old-fashioned pioneer family," the woman continues. "I grew up in Manhattan, Sam. With cellphones, computers, cars, every kind of tech... I never imagined I'd end up like this. Even when the sickness started, I thought the government would save us. And now look at us, desperately hoping we can make a go at subsistence farming. And cooking meager scraps in a pot."

As they continue to talk, I sneak around the side of the farmhouse. There's no sign of anyone out here, so I hurry through the shadows until I reach the next corner. The smell of food is driving me crazy and forcing me to take risks I'd otherwise never even consider, but so far it seems as if these people haven't thrown a single scrap outside. Stopping under another window, I look up and see the flickering light of a fire cast against the stone, but I've learned to live without much warmth.

It's food I need. I'm already so weak and -

Suddenly I spot a scrap of meat on the floor, just inside the farmhouse's back door. It's nothing too juicy, just a strip of gristle, but I can't resist.

After checking to make sure that no-one is around, I creep through the doorway and edge closer to the chunk of meat.

"There he is!"

Startled, I turn and see the two children running toward me from the next room. After grabbing the piece of gristle, I set off in the other direction, running around the side of the house, but suddenly the adults come out through the front door and stop as soon as they see me.

"Kill it!" the woman shouts.

I bark at them, momentarily standing my ground before turning and racing out across the grass, away from the house. Too scared to look back, I run as fast as my aching legs can carry me, and I don't stop until I've made it all the way up the hill and over to the edge of the forest, at which point I stop and look back. My heart is pounding and my muscles are aching.

I can hear voices in the distances, but the humans' scents don't seem to be coming any closer. I made it. I chew the piece of gristle for a moment, before swallowing.

CHAPTER FORTY-ONE

"DOG! COME HERE, DOG! Where are you?"

The boy's voice suddenly interrupts the silence of the meadow, causing the rabbit to turn and run. I leap after it, landing in a patch of mud, and then I freeze as I hear footsteps in the distance.

I would have had that rabbit in my jaws by now, if it hadn't been startled.

"Dog! I want to be your friend! I've got something for you!"

Daring to look above the top of the long grass, I see that the boy is still quite a way off. The scent of meat reaches my nose, and I immediately feel a pang of hunger. A moment later, I'm able to see what looks like a small strip of meat in his left hand, and he's holding it up high as if he wants it to be seen. I know I should run and hide, but the prospect of food – even just a small scrap – keeps me rooted to the spot. I can't think of anything else.

"I saved this for you!" he shouts. "Technically I'm not allowed to give you food, but this is from my plate so no-one'll know! Are you still here?"

I wait.

Silence, followed a moment later by the sound of him heading toward the ridge.

"I won't hurt you!" he calls out. "I want to be your friend!"

I don't dare make a move, in case he spots me. I haven't been near a human since Melissa, Thomas and their friends, and they were mean enough to scare me for life. At the same time, the smell of meat is so strong and so appetizing, and I can't quite bring myself to turn and run. Without even thinking properly, I start edging forward while frantically sniffing the air.

"I'll put it here!" the boys shouts. "I hope you get it before one of the rabbits comes! You looked so thin last night, I don't want you to be hungry!"

I wait, and finally I hear his footsteps hurrying away. After a few more minutes, once his scent is much weaker, I finally dare come out from the long grass, and I immediately spot a small strip of meat resting on the grass. A rabbit is already edging closer, so I run forward and scare it away, before taking the meat and swallowing it whole.

"Dog!" the boy yells, suddenly breaking out from behind a bush. "Wait!"

Turning, I run, and I don't stop until I'm sure I've lost him. Still, the taste of meat was good, and I desperately want more. I need to find a way to get hold of the meat without letting the humans come too close.

CHAPTER FORTY-TWO

THE BOY COMES AGAIN the next day, and the next, and each time he brings a little more food. I don't dare approach while there's a chance that he might catch me, so both times I wait in the bushes, fighting the urge to snatch the meat from its spot out there on the grass. I always wait upwind of the food, though, so that my scent will warn rabbits away, and finally I take the meat late in the afternoon.

On the next day, the boy brings his sister, and now there's a little more meat. I don't know why they're doing this, but I figure I might as well stick around for now. So long as they keep feeding me and they don't get too close, I'd be a fool to leave the meadow. I can tolerate their presence if it means that I get some extra scraps.

The older humans are out in the fields every day, shouting at one another as they dig ditches. I don't know what they're doing, but they seem very busy.

CHAPTER FORTY-THREE

FINALLY, ON THE SEVENTH or eighth day, I decide to be a little braver.

Once the two children have left meat for me, I hurry out and gulp it down whole, and then I keep low as I run past the edge of the forest. Stopping at the ridge, I see that the children are racing across one of the fields, so I set off after them, keen to see where they go each day and whether they've found some hidden food source.

I follow them for a few hours, until they stop when they reach the long metal rails that run across the land. I've seen the rails before, but I've never dared spend too long near them since I have no idea what they are. They're definitely something from the human world, and they spread all the way through the meadow and off to the horizon, and the metal gets warm sometimes in the afternoon sun.

Staying low in the long grass, I edge toward to the spot where the children are hopping and skipping across the rails. Whatever they're doing out here, they don't seem to have noticed that I've followed. Once again, I'm lucky that the human sense of smell is so terrible.

"Mom says she saw a train once," the boy is saying as I get closer. "She was actually on one. Apparently we were, too, back when we were just babies. I wish I could remember what the world used to be like."

"Do you think they'll ever come back?" the girl asks. She seems a year or two younger than the boy, and something about her face reminds me a little of Julie. "I'd like to see a train. Even if I couldn't ride on one, I'd at least like to see what they look like."

"Dad says they can't," the boy explains. "He says they're rusting away somewhere and that no-one would be able to get them running again. But I know Mom thinks he's wrong. She thinks there might be trains again, and planes in the air too. I'd love to see a plane. Sometimes I think they can't be real, that everyone's lying when they say people used to fly, but Mom and Dad and Grandpa say they all flew once, before we were born. Apparently you used to have to get checked out before you were allowed on a plane."

"Why?"

"In case you were trying to hurt people."

The girl frowns. "But why?"

"I don't know, that's just what Mom told me. People sometimes tried to make planes crash. I guess people did weird things back then."

He reaches down and pulls a tuft of weeds out

from between the metal rails.

"Sometimes their stories make it sound like everything wasn't perfect. Like, I can't even imagine living with so many other people all around. Remember those photos Mom showed us, the ones of New York? How did people ever live like that? I think I'd go crazy, I'd end up -"

Suddenly he glances this way, and we make eye contact again.

I get to my feet, growling and ready to run.

Fumbling in his pocket, the boy pulls out another piece of meat and quickly throws it toward me.

"That's for you!" he stammers. "It's okay, we don't want to hurt you! We just want to be your friend!"

I know I should run, but the meat already smells irresistible, and after a moment I scamper forward. After swallowing it whole, I retreat into the grass.

"Give him yours!" the boy says, turning to the girl.

She takes some meat from her pocket and throws it toward me. I hesitate again, before crawling forward while keeping my eyes fixed on them. I don't growl this time, but I make sure to take the meat quickly and then I hurry into the grass again.

"What's your name?" the boy asks, taking a cautious step toward me. He taps his chest. "I'm Harry, and this is my sister Sophie."

He said my name again. My old name. But it's not my name now, I realize that, even if it brings back certain memories.

"Harry," the girl says, tugging at his arm. "Be

careful. He's wild."

"I know, but..."

"He's wild! Wild animals can be dangerous!"

"He doesn't look *that* wild. He's kinda small and cute."

He peers at me, as if something has caught his attention. After a moment he edges closer, and this time I stand my ground and wait to see what he'll do next. He seems friendly, but I've learned that humans can't be trusted.

"Can I pat you?" he asks, kneeling in front of me.

I know I should growl, to warn him away, but somewhere deep down I'm starting to remember those times in the past when I used to let strangers get close. Memories that I'd pushed aside during my years alone out here are now rushing back.

Reaching out, Harry finally places a hand on my side, and for the first time in many years I feel fingers gently running through my fur.

"It's okay," he says calmly. "You're cute. Little and cute. Can I take a look at your collar?"

I wait, tense in case he hurts me, but after a moment he turns my collar slightly and leans closer.

"Jon Anderson," he reads out loud, and then he turns to the girl. "He was someone's pet dog once. He must have been out here all alone ever since the bad things happened." He turns to me again. "Or is Jon Anderson still around? Are you with someone?"

I feel a faint shudder when I hear Jon's name again. Over the years, his scent has completely faded from my collar, but I still remember how he smelled. That's one thing I'll never forget.

"Come and pet him," Harry continues, stroking my shoulders. "Sophie, don't be scared."

The girl comes forward cautiously, but after a moment's hesitation she kneels next to me and starts patting my flank.

"See?" Harry says with a smile. "He's friendly. His tail's wagging. Maybe if we take him home, Daddy will say that -"

Suddenly Sophie's hand touches my injured leg. I let out a brief growl as a flash of pain runs through the bone, and the two children pull back.

"I told you he's wild!" Sophie hisses.

"I think he's just hurt," Harry replies, looking at my leg. "See there? The flesh is all knotted, like it's healed badly. He probably got hurt and there was no-one around to fix him up properly. It's okay, you just touched him in a bad place."

"He almost bit me!"

"Don't worry, dog," he continues, touching my shoulder again. "We're friendly. You look very thin, but maybe we can get you some more food. How long have you been all by yourself out here? Do you want to come home with us?"

I don't know what he's saying, but he seems gentle and I can't stop thinking about the meat he's been giving me. If there's even a slight chance that I might get more, then I guess I'm willing to stick close to him for a while. Even if I no longer like humans, they can be useful, and I'm still fast enough to get away if they try to hurt me.

"We should get back," he says as he stands. "You need a name, dog. I'm going to call you..."

He stares at me for a moment, as if he's lost in thought.

"Ben," he adds finally.

"Ben?" Sophie asks. "Why Ben?"

"That was our uncle's name, remember? And he was always nice to us. I think this dog is nice too, so I want to call him Ben. Unless you've got a better idea."

"I just want to get home," she replies, stepping past him and heading away from the rails, out into the field. "Keep that thing away from me, and don't blame me when he bites your hand off."

"You won't bite me, will you?" Harry asks, reaching down and stroking my head again. "Maybe you'll even be allowed to sleep inside, if I can talk Mom around. Dad'll be tricky, but if I can persuade Mom, then she'll get him to agree. Come on, Ben, this way."

He turns and heads off after Sophie.

For a moment, I'm not sure what I should do next. Part of me remembers what it was like to be around humans when Jon was still alive and things were good, and part of me remembers Melissa and Thomas. I've been fine by myself in the meadow, hunting for food and spending my time alone, but I can't deny that the pull of company is stronger than I ever would have guessed.

"Ben!" Harry shouts, turning and waving at me. "Come on!"

Ben.

That seems to mean me.

"Ben!" he yells. "Hurry, Ben! This way!"

I immediately set off after him, although I can't run too fast. My legs are old and painful, and my ribs still hurt even after all these years. I'm old now.

***

"Who do you think they are?" Sophie whispers a little while later, as the three of us sit next to the ridge and watch unfamiliar figures down at the farmhouse. "Do you think they're friendly?"

I thought we were going to go all the way to the house, but instead Harry and Sophie stopped and hid behind the ridge as soon as they saw a large black car ahead. Some new arrivals seem to have shown up, with two men having gone into the farmhouse with Harry's family, and now I can sense the children's fear.

"It's probably okay," Sophie continues, her voice filled with nerves. "It's probably just... It's just someone who came to say hello, that's all. They'll leave soon."

"Mom's always scared of new people showing up," Harry replies.

"Mom's scared of everything. I get it, but... Maybe these people are okay."

I look over at Harry and see the concern in his eyes. He hasn't said a word for the past few minutes, and he seems far more worried than Sophie.

Hearing voices down at the farmhouse, I turn and watch as the two black-suited figures head back to their car. Harry's parents watch from the doorway, and even from all the way up here I can tell that something isn't right. When the car's engine starts, I instinctively take a step back, reminded of the time I spent in cars with Thomas and his friends, and the scent of the new arrivals seems to be filling the area even as they drive away. Feeling nervous and scared, I turn to walk away, before stopping and looking back at the children.

"Well, *I'm* going down to see what's up," Sophie says, getting to her feet. "If you two cowards want to hide up here, that's your business."

As she heads down the slope, I wait for Harry to react, but he's still watching the black car as it disappears into the distance. After a moment, realizing that he's worried and that his heart is pounding, I step over to him and nudge his shoulder. He doesn't reply, so I wag my tail a little as I sit next to him.

"She's probably right," he whispers finally, turning to me with a faint, forced smile. "I mean... It's probably nothing. I just have a bad feeling, that's all."

With that, he gets up and heads down the slope.

"Come on, Ben," he mutters.

I want to go with him, but something about the men in that black car left a horrible stench in the air and I don't dare go any closer. As Harry gets further and further away, I let out a faint whimper, but he doesn't look back at me. I can't go with him, so I decide to wait here at the ridge until he returns.

I think I finally know what I didn't like about the scent of that black car, though. I think I could smell blood on its tires.

CHAPTER FORTY-FOUR

I USUALLY SPEND NIGHTS deep in the forest, preferring to gain a little shelter in case of bad weather. Tonight, despite a quickening wind that threatens rain from the far hills, I stay at the ridge after sunset, watching the lights in the farmhouse and listening to distant raised voices.

They're arguing.

Whoever was in the black car, they clearly brought bad news. The scent of blood might have faded, but my fear remains and I'm too scared to risk the journey down to the farmhouse's windows. Instead, I decide to wait here next to the ridge and keep an eye on things from up high, even as a cold wind ruffles my fur.

In the distance, beyond the farmhouse, the fields are starting to look very different. The humans have already begun to make changes to the land.

CHAPTER FORTY-FIVE

"I'M NOT SCARED!" Harry says firmly, as he balances on the gleaming metal railway lines. "Dad's got a rifle, hasn't he? If they come back, he can just shoot them!"

"Don't you think they've thought of that?" Sophie asks, sitting cross-legged near the grass, fiddling with weed-knots she's been working on for the past few minutes. "Dad's being stubborn. I think Mom's right, we should keep going and head further west, away from those people."

She turns to him.

"You were scared before," she adds.

"I was not!"

"Yes you were. Now you're just trying to act brave, but I can see the truth in your eyes."

It's been a few days now since I first came out here with Harry and Sophie. Although I still haven't dared approach the farmhouse again, I've fallen into a habit of following them to the old train-line, and in return they give me a few scraps of meat each day. My belly is still empty most of the time, but at least I don't have to spend all my time trying to hunt rabbits. Even if I don't like to admit the truth, my legs are hurting more and more, and I'm starting to get much slower. There's going to come a time when I'm too slow to catch rabbits.

"You want to run away?" Harry continues, before his foot slips and he has to step off the rail. "Is that it? That's cowardly!"

"It's realistic," she replies. "You know the stories. You know what people are like. And do you remember that burned-out farmhouse we passed a few days before we got here? It looked like -"

"That could've been anything."

"People are dangerous," she continues. "These wild gangs that roam the country are..."

Her voice trails off for a moment.

"I don't know exactly," she adds finally, "but I think they do bad things to people."

"Like what?"

"Like the worst things they could."

"Like what?"

She sighs. "Just use your imagination."

Harry pauses, and then he frowns. "Like what?"

"Oh, just -"

Letting out a grunt of frustration, Sophie tosses the weed-knots aside. She stares down at her fingers for a moment, and I can tell she's scared.

"Just think of the worst things possible," she continues finally, "and then assume that there are people who can think of things that are even more horrible. I heard Mom say the same thing one night, before we got here. She said there are these gangs roaming parts of the country, and she said they enjoy hurting people who refuse to pay them."

She sits in silence for a moment. Although I'm more cautious of Sophie, after she touched my painful leg when we first met, I decide to walk over to her. When I nudge her leg, however, she pulls away.

"Shoo!" she hisses. "Go play with Harry!"

Turning, I make my way to Harry, although after a moment one of my rear legs slips and I almost fall. Sometimes my old injuries seem to flare up, causing me to be a little less mobile, and today is one of those days. I can even feel another flash of pain as I limp over to the spot where Harry is once again balancing on one of the rails.

"Dad won't pay those men," he says after a moment, before losing his balance and having to step off the rail. "He shouldn't. They don't deserve anything."

"He has to," Sophie replies. "If we're going to stay here and try to run the farm, he has to pay them now they've found us."

"No!"

"They'll kill us!" she hisses.

"Don't say that!"

Getting to her feet, she comes over to him. "You're old enough to know things like that, Harry! Stop trying to act tough just because you want to be like Dad! Those men aren't just playing, they -"

"You're a liar!" he replies, interrupting her.

"They'll come back and they'll kill us all!" she

tells him, raising her voice. "We should leave! They said they'd be back in a few days' time, so we should be gone when they return. Mom was right, running is the only -"

"Shut up!" Harry shouts, turning and pushing her away.

Stumbling back, she trips on one of the rails and lands hard on the ground, letting out a gasp of pain.

"I didn't mean to do that!" Harry stammers. "I'm sorry!"

"You're an idiot," she mutters, getting to her feet and dusting herself down. "This isn't a game, Harry, and -"

"I know it's not a game!"

"They'll kill us!" she says again. "They have guns and knives! Don't you remember that other farmhouse? They'd hung the bodies up inside as a warning, to show people what happens to anyone who tries to make a stand! Mom and Dad tried to stop us from seeing, but we did anyway! Both of us!"

"We're not cowards!"

"Neither were those other people, and they still ended up burned and cut and swinging in the wind!"

There are tears in her eyes now, and after a moment she takes another step back.

"That'll be us soon," she continues. "We don't have anything to give to those men when they come back, so they'll take what they want, and eventually we'll all be hanging from the rafters. You, me, Mom and Dad, Grandpa... All hanging there with our bodies torn open and burned, to serve as warnings for the next people who come along." She wipes tears from her cheeks. "I'm not a coward, Harry, but I also know that you have to pick your battles. You don't fight when you're out-numbered and you only have one goddamn rifle against an army!"

"You're just scared of strangers," he replies.

"And you're scared of the truth!"

Turning, she hurries away, leaving Harry with a shocked expression as he stands between the rails.

"She doesn't know what she's talking about," he says finally, looking down at me. "Dad'll figure something out. He always does. And Mom too. They'll work out how to keep us all safe, and they'll make those men in the black car stay away."

He pauses, before reaching down and stroking my shoulder.

"They have to," he continues. "They won't let anyone hurt us or take our new farm."

CHAPTER FORTY-SIX

OVER THE NEXT FEW DAYS, I spend most of my time watching as the humans continue to work the land. Whereas the fields were overgrown with grass before, now they've been cut back and the ground has been disturbed, with thick ditches running through the soil. It's interesting to watch the changes, and each day I dare creep a little closer, until eventually I'm watching from the very edge of the largest field.

I'm still wary, especially of the adults, but I can outrun them if necessary. Even with injured legs.

"We can't afford to give food to a mangy dog," the woman says one morning, although she smiles slightly as she glances at me. "Harry, I thought we told you not to encourage it."

"I didn't encourage him!" he replies. "And his name is Ben!"

"He's not even useful," she continues. "I mean look at him, he's barely any bigger than a cat. What is he, a Jack Russell?" She sighs. "I suppose maybe he can catch mice."

"This is so stupid," Sophie mutters, reaching down and poking some seeds into the ground. "I can't believe Harry thinks this is the right time to get a pet."

"I didn't *think* anything," he tells her. "Ben chose us, not the other way round!"

"Whatever," the woman mutters, "can one of you go and fetch more water from the stream?"

"It's her turn," Harry says, pointing at his sister.

"I'm busy here," Sophie replies. "Besides, you can take your stupid dog, can't you?"

"I'm planting seeds too!" Harry protests.

"No, you're arguing about the dog," she continues. "I'm *actually* planting seeds, and you're just sort of hovering around, slowing everyone else down."

A few minutes later, Harry and I are heading away from the farmhouse. He's carrying two buckets, and we're soon past the ridge and walking around the edge of the forest. Harry isn't saying much now, but that's fine by me. I like coming with him when he has jobs to get done, and it's very important that I stay close and warn other animals to stay away. I've only seen rabbits and mice in the area lately, but something more dangerous could show up at any moment, so I have to stay alert. For the first time in many years, I actually have a job, and it feels good to know that I'm doing something important.

It takes a few hours for us to make the journey. Harry talks a lot during that time. I don't understand what he's saying, but I'm reminded of the times when

Jon used to take me out for long walks. He used to talk, too, and I liked the sound of his voice even if I never really knew what he was on about.

"Sophie thinks she's *so* smart," Harry mutters finally as we reach the stream and he crouches down, dipping one of the buckets into the water. "She's just bossy, that's all. When we're older, I'm gonna show her who's right."

I start drinking from the stream, and after a moment I look over and see Harry watching me. He smiles slightly, as if he's amused. After a few seconds, he leans down and tries to copy what I'm doing, although in the process he almost falls head-first into the water.

"How long were you alone for," he continues finally, "before you met me? Who was that Jon guy whose name is on your collar?"

I instinctively turn and look around, and for a fraction of a second I almost expect to see Jon coming this way. I know he's long gone, of course, but sometimes I get these little flashes where I think there might be a chance. Looking along toward the bend in the little stream, I imagine what it would be like to see Jon and Julie coming this way. One day, years and years ago, we were out near the cabin in a place a little like this. The three of us went for long walks every afternoon, and I thought those days would never have to end. I'd give anything now to go back to how things were.

"Holy crap!" Harry says suddenly, dropping the buckets and hurrying past me. "Ben! Look!"

Startled, I limp after him. After a moment,

however, I stop as I see a set of clean white ribs poking out from the long grass.

"It's a person!" he continues, his voice tinged with both excitement and fear. "I wonder how long it's been here!"

Stepping closer, I see that there's a human skeleton on the ground. Usually I'd have picked up the scent a while ago, but these bones look old, with all the meat having been eaten away. There are tattered scraps of clothing hanging from some of the ribs, but as I get closer and sniff the air, I can tell that this person clearly died at least eight or nine summers ago. Even the bugs and maggots have long since departed.

Crouching next to the bones, Harry seems mesmerized.

"Do you think this was one of those zombie things?" he asks after a moment, grabbing a stick and using it to poke the ribs. "Or was it just someone who starved out here?"

I take a step back, not wanting to get too close.

"I was too young back then," he continues, "so I don't remember life before everything went wrong. Sophie pretends she remembers, but I think she's lying. It's weird to think that there were once so many people around, though."

He leans even closer to the bones.

"I can see the skull," he whispers.

I bark, to warn him that he should stay away.

"It's okay," he says, reaching into the grass and taking hold of a piece of bone. After a moment, he carefully lifts the skull above the grass. "This was a person once," he continues, with a hint of awe in his voice now. "Just like you and me. Well..."

He smiles.

"Like me, anyway."

The smile fades as he stares at the skull and, for the first time since I met him, Harry appears to be genuinely lost for words.

"I wish you could tell me your story, Ben," he continues finally, turning to me. "It must be pretty unique for a dog to survive all of this. I bet you've seen some stuff, huh? We saw some wild dogs once, about six months ago, near a town. They were howling and hunting in a pack, they were pretty scary. How come you're not like that? Too domesticated?"

He pauses, still watching me carefully.

"Or did you just not bump into any other dogs? Have you been alone for a long time?"

I let out a faint whimper, hoping he'll set the skull down so we can leave.

"Dad says that more than 99% of everyone died ten years ago," he says after a moment. "Like, only 1% of 1% of 1% survived, maybe even less. I can't imagine that. I asked him once where they all went. He didn't seem like he wanted to talk about it, but then he muttered something about keeping away from the cities. I remember a few years ago, he and Grandpa went to a city, to check it out. When they came back, they didn't seem very happy." He pauses. "But one day *I* want to go to a city. Even if there's nothing left but bones in the streets, I want to see. And I want to -"

He stops suddenly, staring past me.

Realizing that I can smell something burning, I turn and see smoke rising high into the blue sky.

"That's coming from near the farm," he whispers, before staggering to his feet and rushing past me. In the process, he drops the skull, letting it smash to pieces as it hits the dry ground. "It's the farm!" he yells. "Ben, something's happening at the farm!"

I run after him. Even though my legs are hurting, I keep pace as we hurry past the buckets and make our way back past the forest.

***

"Mom!" Harry screams as he races down the hill. "Dad!"

Ahead, the farmhouse is burning, with flames roaring from the windows and already emerging through gaps in the roof. Thick black smoke fills the air, and as we get closer to the building I feel a wall of heat trying to push me back. Just as we reach the bottom of the hill, part of the roof suddenly breaks loose, sliding down and then crashing against the ground in a mass of burning wood. I don't slow my pace, though. Instead, I keep close to Harry as he stops in front of the building and stares at the fire.

"Mom!" he yells, his voice filled with panic. "Dad! Grandpa! Sophie!"

He turns and looks around, but there's no sign of anyone else.

The thick smoke smells so strong, I can barely pick up any other scents. The mud in front of the farmhouse has been disturbed recently, however, and after a moment I realize the black car must have been here. Not only are there tracks from its tires, but those tracks smell slightly of blood. I sniff the ground for a moment longer, and sure enough the tire tracks are only half an hour old, maybe an hour at most.

As Harry continues to call out to his family, I stay close to him. He makes his way around the side of the building, but it's as if everyone has suddenly vanished. I can see some of their tools and equipment, though, strewn across the ground, and the scent of blood is getting stronger and stronger.

And then I see them.

Three dead bodies, suspended on long wooden stakes that have been driven into the ground. The bodies are naked and bloody, and the stakes have been driven up through their bellies and then out through their gaping mouths. I stare for a moment, as the smell of blood fills my senses, but Harry has his back to the corpses and doesn't seem to have noticed them yet.

"Mom!" he yells, still watching the flames. "Dad! Grandpa! Where -"

He turns, and suddenly he stops in his tracks, staring at the dead bodies as they're silhouetted against the bright midday sky.

"No," he stammers, his voice trembling with shock. "No, please..."

He stumbles forward, almost slipping in the mud, until he's staring up at the bodies. Although I want to stay far away, I know I have to follow him, and finally I look up and see that his parents are up there on the

296

stakes, along with his grandfather. I glance around, but there's no sign of Sophie.

"Mom!" Harry whimpers, with tears streaming down his face. "Dad..."

He takes a couple more steps toward them, before his trembling legs give way and he drops down into the mud. He's muttering something under his breath now, but I can't make out the words. His whole body is shaking, and he can't seem to stop looking at the corpses of his family.

I start barking at the bodies, while taking a step back. If I keep barking, maybe they'll suddenly wake up and come down, and everything will be okay. Finally, however, I realize that the stench of blood and death is too strong, but I still can't stop barking, even though my throat is starting to hurt. Eventually I fall quiet, but Harry continues to cry and tremble for hours and hours, as if he might never stop.

Ahead of us, the three corpses stare in different directions, each with glassy dead eyes.

CHAPTER FORTY-SEVEN

FOR THE NEXT FEW HOURS, Harry simply sits on the ground and stares up at the bodies. His eyes are open wide and he barely even blinks.

The house is still burning, sending plumes of smoke drifting all around us, and carrying burned black ashes up to the corpses, resting them gently on patches of bloodied flesh.

CHAPTER FORTY-EIGHT

"SHE'S NOT HERE," Harry whispers, poking the rubble with a stick. "She can't be. There'd be bones or..."

His voice trails off for a moment. He's standing in the ruined farmhouse now that the flames have died down, and for a few seconds he seems lost in thought until, finally, he turns to me. In the space of just a few hours, his eyes seem darker somehow, with more shadows, and with sore red patches all around the edges. Since he stopped sobbing a few minutes ago, he's seemed to be in some kind of daze.

"That means they took her."

I watch from the doorway as he looks around at the charred stone walls. Everything inside the building has been burned, leaving a thick carpet of black ash all over the floor.

"Why would they take her?" he asks, his voice still trembling with shock. "Why would they want my sister? What would they want to do with her?"

He pauses, before coming back to the doorway and stepping past me, back out into the mud.

"There are tire tracks," he continues. "They were here in their car. They said they'd be back eventually, they said they'd want to be paid or... Dad said he could reason with them, but..."

Again, his voice trails off.

I wait for him to say something, but he seems to have stopped, as if he's in too much shock to know what he should do next. I can see the three bodies still impaled on the stakes, but Harry hasn't looked at them for a while now, as if he can't bring himself to face what was done to his family.

"Sophie said that I couldn't imagine the bad things these people might do," he stammers finally, still staring at the tire tracks in the mud. "Why would they take her? She's only a couple of years older than me, what would they want with..."

Again, he falls silent for a moment.

"When she said I couldn't imagine what they'd do..."

He stares at the ground.

"I have to get her back," he whispers. "I can't let them hurt her. I have to find her."

He turns to me.

"The tire tracks," he adds finally. "I have to follow the tire tracks and get my sister back, but first..."

He hesitates, and then finally he looks at the three corpses.

"First I have to get them down from there."

***

He works hard, first digging three separate holes in the ground and then one by one pulling the stakes down until the corpses are resting on the mud. For the first time since I met him, Harry looks less like a child and more like an adult. I can see that he's struggling, and there are tears in his eyes, and he lets out several pained grunts as he slips or falls.

Finally he gets his parents and his grandfather into the holes, and then he starts shoveling dirt back in to cover them up. He pushes on, even though I can tell he's close to collapse, and he doesn't stop until the graves have been filled. Only then, finally, does he drop the shovel and fall back, landing hard on the ground.

Stepping closer, I see something new in his eyes. A kind of anger.

"Now we go and find Sophie," he whispers breathlessly, before hauling himself to his feet. Almost tripping, he staggers toward the tire tracks. He needs to rest. "Come on, Ben. We have to go get my sister back. I don't care how far we have to walk, we're going to track her down."

I hurry after him, catching up just as he grabs an old dress from a pile in a wooden barrel. He examines it for a moment, before reaching down as if he wants me to smell the scent.

"That's Sophie's," he tells me, his voice trembling slightly. "Do you understand? That's what she smells like. Now let's go find her."

I sniff the dress, but I don't know what he wants

me to do.

"Sophie," he says firmly. "Come on, I know you can do this. You must have tracked someone before in your life. We have to find Sophie."

He presses the dress against my nose.

"Sophie! Do you get it now? Find Sophie!"

He pauses, before tossing the dress aside and setting off along the same path as the tire tracks. I follow, and after a moment I realize that we seem to be following the tracks away from the farmhouse. I start sniffing the ground as I hurry ahead of Harry. There's a strong small of blood mixed with the rubber, and I'm also picking up a very faint trace of his sister's scent.

"That's good," he calls after me. "Keep going, Harry. Find Sophie!"

CHAPTER FORTY-NINE

SO WE START WALKING, just the two of us, following the tracks across the wide, desolate landscape.

I'm exhausted, and I can tell from the way he stumbles occasionally that Harry is exhausted too, but neither of us stops, neither of us even slows our pace for a moment. The tire tracks are sometimes harder to see, but their scent remains strong and we manage to keep to them as they lead us for miles and miles. Occasionally we find spots where multiple sets of tracks pass one another, but I can tell from the scent which ones are the most recent and Harry seems to trust me.

Eventually, however, the sun starts to set up ahead, dipping down toward the horizon and casting long shadows across the land.

"We can't sleep," Harry says a short while later, his voice sounding harsh and ragged. "You can stop if you need to, Ben, but I have to keep going. You'll have to catch up."

Something seems different about him now. Even though he's walking, he sounds half asleep, almost delirious.

As night falls, we continue to walk, even as the temperature drops. There's a clear moon, which at least means we can just about see the tracks, although the scent is still strong. Harry almost wanders off in the wrong direction a couple of times, but I bark to let him know that he's made a mistake and each time he turns and follows me. Humans don't seem to have a great sense of smell, that's something I noticed all the way back when I was still living with Jon, but for me the tire tracks seem to be almost burning through the night, blazing a trail and showing us exactly which way to go.

And by the time morning comes and the sun rises behind us, we're still walking, still following the tracks.

CHAPTER FIFTY

LETTING OUT A SUDDEN GASP, Harry drops to the ground. His legs have seemed weak for a while now, and they finally seem to have buckled beneath his weight. He tries to get up, but the effort seems to be too much and he freezes for a moment before rolling onto his side and letting out a longer, slow groan.

We've been walking for two days and two nights now, and it has been clear for the past few hours that he's close to collapse. We haven't eaten since we left the farmhouse, and our only water has come from a bottle that has been hanging from Harry's waist, and now even that is starting to run low

Now Harry's on the ground, as if his legs can't carry him any further, and he doesn't seem able to get up.

Realizing that he seems to be on the verge of passing out, I step closer and start licking his face, hoping to somehow keep him going. His skin tastes

305

salty, but he's passing out so I start licking his ear and finally his eyes flicker open.

"I need to sleep," he whispers. "Ben, please... Leave me alone."

His eyes slip shut again.

Letting out a faint whimper, I nudge his cheek with my nose.

He mumbles something under his breath, before rolling over until he has his back to me.

I hurry around and immediately nudge his face again, and when that doesn't work I start licking his nose.

"Go away!" he stammers, pushing my face back. "I have to sleep."

I step closer, but he pushes me back again.

"Leave me alone, Ben," he whispers, with his eyes still shut. "I'm just going to..."

His voice trails off.

Whimpering again, I use my paw to scratch at his shoulder, but this time he doesn't respond at all. I try again, but he seems to have slipped into a deep sleep. Stepping back, I watch him for a few seconds before starting to bark, but even this doesn't seem to be enough.

I settle next to him, hoping that he'll wake soon. His breathing seems shallow after walking for two full days and nights, and I know that I have to stay alert in case any danger comes this way.

So even though I desperately want to sleep, I force myself to stay awake for hours and hours, guarding Harry and waiting for him to stir. Eventually I struggle to keep my eyes open, and my head feels as if it's starting to spin a little. My nose is getting sore, too, thanks to the relentless sun that beats down upon us, and my paws are cracked and bleeding.

But still I refuse to sleep.

If I sleep, something might happen to him, and I might not wake up again.

And then suddenly I feel the ground starting to shudder beneath my damaged paws.

I look both ways along the dusty road, but there's no sign of anyone coming this way. The vibrations suggest that a car is approaching, even though I can see for hundreds of meters in both directions and there's definitely no-one around. A moment later, I hear a high-pitched whistling sound, and I turn just in time to spot a plume of smoke in the distance, coming closer.

"What's that?" Harry whispers, his voice sounding slurred. "What..."

The whistling sound stops for a moment, but now I can also hear some kind of engine. The plume of smoke seems to be moving somehow, and finally I spot a car far away. Except it's bigger than a car, and much longer, and noisier too. Figuring that maybe it's someone who can help Harry, I step around him and hurry across the rocky ground, until I spot a set of familiar metal rails up ahead.

I edge closer, while taking care to hold back in case something tries to attack me.

The huge machine, whatever it is, has begun to slow as it reaches a point where the gleaming rails turn through a bend. I can hear voices, too, and suddenly I spot a figure waving at me from a window at the very front of the machine. I hurry forward, putting aside my fears for a moment, and then I see the figure tossing something out the window. He leans back inside, and then he tosses something else out. Still a little nervous, I watch as the machine grinds around the bend, and then slowly it starts to pick up speed again, releasing fresh plumes of smoke as it heads off into the distance.

Once it's gone, the rails continue to hum for a few minutes before falling still, and finally I dare step closer so I can see what was thrown out.

There are two small packages on the ground. They look like clumps of paper, but there's something inside and slowly I start to pick up the scent of meat. By the time I reach the nearest package, the scent is even stronger, and I realize that the men in the machine definitely threw some kind of food out toward me. My belly is so empty, it's starting to hurt, but I know I can't keep the food for myself so, instead, I take one of the packages in my mouth and then hurry back to the side of the road, where Harry is still unconscious.

Setting the first package down, I run my paw against his arm to wake him. When that doesn't work, I scratch him harder, finally making him stir.

"Leave me alone," he whispers, "I just..."

His voice trails off, and a moment later his eyes flicker open and he stares at the package. He pauses, before suddenly sitting up as if he's gripped by a fresh burst of energy. His trembling fingers tear the package apart until he finds a chunk of meat inside, slipped between two slices of bread.

"Was that a train I heard just now?" he

stammers, before taking a large mouthful.

Turning, I hurry back to the side of the rails and grab the second package, which I carry over to him. He's already finished the first sandwich, and he wastes no time in tearing the new package open and finding another. He slips a piece of meat out before starting to eat, and then he holds the meat out toward me.

"Go on," he says with his mouth still full. "Eat."

I wait, not daring to take food from him, but finally he holds it closer and I can't help myself. I gulp the meat down without even chewing, and my belly immediately lets out a faint rumbling noise.

"I thought I heard a train," Harry continues, turning and looking toward the distant tracks. "I opened my eyes and saw it, but I thought it had to be some kind of hallucination."

He pauses, before turning to me again.

"How can that happen? How can a train just appear from out of nowhere, unless..."

His eyes widen with shock.

"Unless someone repaired it and sent it out!" he continues. "But that would mean that someone, somewhere, is trying to get things back to normal!"

Getting to his feet, he looks toward the tracks again. The scrap of food, along with the brief appearance of that huge machine, seems to have given him a fresh burst of energy, and he takes a sip from his bottle of water before pouring some onto the ground for me.

"Did you see anything, Ben? Did you see anything at all that might help us figure out where it was going, or where it came from?"

Not understanding what he's saying, I simply wait as he stares in awe at the gleaming metal tracks.

"That means that if we follow them, in either direction, we might eventually end up somewhere. I mean, somewhere with people who are trying to put things right. I mean, it's been ten years since everyone got sick, so eventually there had to be signs of life again, right? At least we know people are trying!"

He pauses, before turning and setting off along the road again, still following the tire tracks but with a renewed sense of enthusiasm this time, as if those two sandwiches were enough to give him a vital boost of energy.

"It's a sign," he continues. "It has to be. Come on, Ben, we have to find Sophie."

With that, he quickens his pace. Despite the pain and aches in my body, I hurry to catch up. The trail is still strong, although the heat has baked the tire tracks into the mud. Ahead, the sky is darkening.

CHAPTER FIFTY-ONE

"IT'S THEM," HARRY WHISPERS several hours later, as the sun sets in the distance and casts long shadows across a set of small farm buildings. Outside one of the buildings, a familiar black car has been left in a patch of shade, while loud voices can be heard shouting in the distance.

Rain has begun to fall.

My heart is pounding, and the thought of going anywhere near the buildings fills me with fear.

I can smell blood in the air.

"What's that, over there?" Harry says, pointing to the side of one of the buildings, where a large wooden barn sits with rotting walls. "There's something moving inside."

Sniffing the wind, I realize I'm picking up more than blood. Everything about this entire area is telling me to back away and leave. There's raw sewage somewhere, from humans, as well as the lingering scent of fear. I think humans don't tend to pick up on these smells, but I can tell that a lot of people are scared here. Bad things have happened, and blood has been spilled on the ground. The entire barn seems to be leaking the scent of fear from every battered hole in its walls and roof.

Suddenly Harry takes a step forward.

I immediately let out a whimper and paw at his leg, to warn him that we can't go any closer.

"Can you smell her from here?" he asks cautiously. "Is Sophie close?"

As soon as I hear that name, I realize I *can* smell Sophie. Her scent is intertwined with several others, and it's clear that there are a lot of girls somewhere down in one of the buildings. They're scared, too, and their fear makes me take a few steps back while whimpering in the hope that Harry will understand. Rain is already falling faster and harder, which makes it harder for me to pick out too many scents.

"It's pretty dark," he says after a moment. "The rain's loud, too. I can hear it hitting the barn's roof. We have to down there and see if she's around, but..."

He turns to me.

"You can't bark, Ben. Do you understand? If you bark, you'll give us away. Maybe you should stay up here."

He pauses, before cautiously making his way down the slope.

"Stay!" he hisses. "Ben, you have to stay where you are!"

I wait, watching as he heads closer and closer to the buildings. Every fiber in my body is telling me that I should keep back, that the stench of death and blood is too powerful, but at the same time I know that I should stay close to Harry. Finally, even though my heart is pounding, I start scrambling down after him, following his scent through the darkness until we reach a flat patch of mud just a short way from the long wooden barn. The sound of rainwater hitting the barn's roof seems much louder now, hissing ahead of us.

Now that we're closer, I can smell Sophie even more clearly. She's definitely in that barn. I can hear groans and cries, too, from several other girls.

"Do you hear that?" Harry whispers. "What are they doing to them in there?"

Keeping low, he hurries across the muddy open ground until he gets to the barn. I follow, jumping from one muddy pool of water to another, and trying to stay as quiet as possible. I can still hear the girls crying out, but now I can also hear the voices of several men a little further away, laughing and arguing around at the other side of the building. From the way they're talking, it's clear that the men are drunk.

"I have to go and take a look," Harry tells me, keeping his voice low. "Please, Ben, don't bark. Whatever you do, stay quiet."

He starts making his way along the side of the building, although he stops when he gets close to the far corner. Leaning down, he peers through a hole in the wooden wall.

"It's hard to really see anything," he whispers, but when he turns to me I can see the fear in his eyes. "It stinks, though. If Sophie's in there, I have to get her out."

He makes his way around the corner until he reaches the barn's large, open door. We both peer inside, but the place is vast and unlit, leaving us staring into pitch darkness. I can hear a lot of rustling sounds, though, and sobbing coming from either side of the cavernous space, as if there are girls lined up against the walls. The whole place stinks of sweat and other bodily fluids, and it's clear that these people are living in filth.

There are still loud, drunk voices arguing in the distance, although they sound as if they're around the far side of the barn, maybe even beyond the main building.

Harry takes a step forward. I can tell that he's scared, but still he makes his way slowly into the darkness, and I have no choice but to follow. Rain is pouring down now, hitting the barn's high metal roof and echoing all around us.

"Sophie?" Harry whispers. "Sophie are -"

Suddenly there's the sound of footsteps outside, traipsing through the mud and getting closer to the barn. Fortunately Harry hears them too, and he picks me up before stepping back against the wall. I can feel his body shaking with fear, and he puts a hand around my jaw, as if to keep my mouth shut.

A moment later, a figure steps past us and then stops, and I see a faint orange glow in the darkness. There's a strong smell, too, and I realize he just lit a cigarette once he came in from the rain.

"Please let me go," a female voice begs from the far end of the barn. "I won't tell anyone, I just -"

Immediately, several other girls also call out, their voices rising to a crescendo as the dark figure laughs. I can just about make out his silhouette as he leans a rifle against the wall, and then he turns and starts heading deeper into the barn.

Reaching out with a trembling hand, Harry grabs the rifle and pulls it closer.

"Don't hurt me!" a familiar voice shouts suddenly. "Please, just let me go..."

A moment later, there's a flash of light as the figure switches a flashlight on, and the bright beam swings across the barn, picking out the horrified, bruised faces of several girls who have been chained to the walls in tattered rags.

Turning, the figure shines the light directly at one particular face, and I realize that I've seen her before.

"Sophie," Harry stammers, suddenly dropping me down onto the mud as he runs forward, holding the rifle up high.

The man turns at the last moment, startled, but Harry quickly slams the rifle's butt against his face, sending him crashing down into the mud. As the flashlight rolls away, Harry hits the man a couple more times, before stopping breathlessly and staring down at the prone body on the ground.

I step forward. My paws are already sinking slightly into the mud.

Grabbing the flashlight, Harry slips a set of keys from the unconscious man's belt and then hurries over to Sophie, who's trembling on the ground with a large chain attached to her ankle.

"Stay quiet!" Harry hisses, fumbling as he tries

to find the right key. "I'm gonna get you out of here!"

"And me!" another girl shouts. "Don't leave me here!"

"Me too!"

"Help me!"

"Quiet!" he says firmly, shining the flashlight around and picking out more and more of the terrified faces. "I'll get you all out, but you have to keep your voices down!"

He struggles with the chains for a moment longer, before finally managing to get Sophie free. She immediately grabs him, holding him tight as she starts gently sobbing.

"I thought I'd never see you again!" she whimpers. "Harry, thank God you found me!"

"I had help from Ben," he replies.

Sophie glances toward me, and I can see the shock in her eyes.

"We have to get everyone else out," she says after a moment, turning back to her brother. "Ben, these people are maniacs. I think they already killed one girl since I got here. After what they did to Mom and Dad and -"

"I saw what they did," he replies, turning and hurrying to the next girl. "Let's just get out of here as fast as we can!"

I watch as he makes his way along the barn, and he quickly gets better at unlocking the padlocks that are keeping the girls fastened to the walls. While some of the girls seem relatively fit and healthy, like Sophie, others are barely more than skin and bones, wasting away with cuts and bruises all over their emaciated bodies. A few of them can't even stand, and simply stay slumped in the mud once they're free. One of them in particular simply slips down face-first, as if getting out of the chains is enough for her and now she's ready to die.

Slowly, one by one, the freed girls start limping and staggering toward the exit, framed against the rain that continues to crash down.

"That's everyone," Harry stammers finally, hurrying back over to Sophie with the flashlight still in his hand. "We have to get the hell out of here before those assholes realize what's happening."

"They killed my family," one of the other girls says suddenly.

"Mine too," says another.

"I know," Harry replies, "but -"

"And ours," Sophie adds, grabbing his arm. "We can't just let them get away with it."

"There are too many of them," he stammers. "Sophie, please -"

"There are only four left," another girl says, interrupting him. "There were five, and with this one down..."

She pauses, staring at the unconscious man on the ground.

After a moment, Sophie crouches next to him. She fumbles with something around his belt, before pulling out another gun. This one is smaller, and she stares at it with a hint of shock before turning to the others.

I step back, horrified by the sight. The last time I saw a gun like that, it was in Melissa's hands and a lot of people died. Turning, I see that the girls in the doorway have stopped and are looking back at us, as if they're waiting for something.

In the distance, the drunken voices are still arguing.

"You can't," Harry says after a moment. "Sophie, you can't just go and shoot them."

"Someone has to," she says firmly.

She hesitates, still holding the gun, while Harry and the other girls watch.

"If you kill them," one of the other girls stammers, "then aren't we just as bad?"

Sophie pauses, before nodding.

"I want them to pay," another girl adds. "I don't want to be a killer, but I still want them to pay. How do we do that?"

They all stand in silence for a moment, as rain continues to come crashing down outside.

"It'd only need to be one of us," Sophie says finally.

"Whoever does it," a dark-haired girls says after a few seconds, "I mean... those guys are drunk right now. We all know what they're like, and what they did to us. They deserve to die, but still... Whoever goes and does it, it's still killing, isn't it? I don't know if I can pull the trigger, even when those assholes are..."

Her voice trails off.

"We don't have time for this!" Harry says, clearly running out of patience. "We have to get out of this place!"

"You weren't here with them," one of the girls tells him. "No offense, but you don't know what it's been like. They killed our parents -"

"They killed my parents too!" he hisses.

"And they kept us alive," the girl adds. "Just the girls, just the young ones." She limps toward him, with blood stains all over her tattered shirt and pants. "I don't need to tell you why, do I? I could show you where they split me open, if you need proof."

Harry stares at her, his eyes wide with shock, before slowly shaking his head.

"We have to kill them," Sophie says finally. "One of us has to..."

They all stand in silence for a moment.

"We could draw straws," another girl suggests. "Well, not straws but..."

She heads to the door and grabs some strands of grass. After fiddling with them for a moment, she holds them carefully in her right hand.

"Everyone take one piece," she says finally. "One of them has a yellow mark on the blade, near the bottom. Whoever gets that one, has to take the gun and... Those bastards will be passed out drunk by now, anyway. You can't even hear them singing. Come on, we have to do this so that they can't go and hurt anyone else."

"So... One of us has to basically sacrifice her soul?" Sophie asks, her voice trembling with fear.

"At least the others will be able to leave with a clear conscience," another girl suggests. "And we'll never tell anyone. Whoever does it... We'll keep it between us."

Silence returns, before one of the girls reaches out and takes a blade of grass. Slowly, one by one, they all do the same, until finally they're left standing in a small circle, each holding one blade.

"I don't know if I *can*," one of them says finally, staring down at her hand, where a discolored blade of grass rests in the palm.

"Oh Lily," a girl whispers. "Not you..."

"Does anyone want to volunteer to take her place?" Sophie asks.

Again, they all stand in silence for a moment.

"What did they do to your parents?" one of the others asks, turning to Lily. "Did you see?"

She nods.

"And do you want them to pay for it?"

She nods again, with tears in her eyes.

"If you really can't do this," Sophie says finally, "then maybe -"

"Give me the gun," Lily whispers, before stepping toward her and holding her hand out. "If they're all asleep, it'll be easy, right?"

"But -"

"Just give me the gun!" she snaps. "Before I change my mind!"

She takes the gun from Sophie, before turning and limping out into the rain. Despite the fact that she's obviously in pain, she manages to walk tall, silhouetted against the moonlit rain.

Everyone else stands in silence, glancing

nervously at one another, listening to the sound of rain beating down against the shed's roof.

"Are we really innocent?" one of them asks. "I mean, Lily's the one who's going to pull the trigger, but the rest of us... We still know."

"Poor Lily," Sophie whispers. "She's the last one who -"

Suddenly there's a loud shot outside, followed quickly by three more.

I turn and look at Harry, hoping that he'll tell me what to do, but he's just as ashen-faced as all the girls.

A moment later, Lily returns, soaked now from the rain but with the gun still in her trembling hand. Whereas before she was walking fairly steadily, now her legs seem somehow stiffer and her eyes are open wide with shock.

"They were..."

She pauses, staring down at the mud.

"They were asleep, like you said," she stammers finally, holding the gun out. "They were drunk. Only one of them had time to wake up, but he didn't manage to..."

Her voice trails off.

"It was pretty easy, actually," she continues, with tears in her eyes. "I just... did it."

"Thank you," Sophie says, before turning to the others. "Now we have to get out of here. We'll go somewhere else, but we can't stay here. They have partners, remember? Other people who'll come eventually and find out what's happened. We have to get far away from this place, and head west."

They start limping out into the rain. I turn to

follow Harry, but a moment later I sense movement nearby. Turning, I see that the other man, who was knocked unconscious earlier, is now stumbling to his feet, while trying to get a knife loose from his belt.

Barking, I race toward him and sink my teeth into his ankle, biting down as hard as I can manage. He screams as my fangs scrape against bone, but a moment later he rips me away and slashes me with the knife, causing me to cry out as I feel a sharp pain against my left leg. As I'm dropped down into the mud, I hear another gunshot ring out, and the man slumps down dead next to me.

"Ben!" Harry shouts, hurrying over to me.

I try to get up, but it takes a moment before I'm steady again. Glancing toward the exit, I see that Lily is still holding the gun as the other girls start stumbling outside.

"Where did he get you?" Harry asks, reaching down and picking me up. He holds me carefully and carries me out, but I struggle to get free and I can see blood pouring from the knife wound that runs all the way up my left leg from the ankle to the hip.

I can taste the man's blood, too, but at least I know I got him before he could hurt anyone else.

"Go up the hill!" Sophie shouts to the girls, as rain crashes down all around us. "We'll find shelter in the forest, but we can't stay here! We'll stop in the forest and come up with a better plan!"

Harry holds me tight, carrying me through the darkness, and finally I stop struggling. My leg hurts too much, and I know I'd find it hard to walk now. All I can manage is to curl against his chest and listen to the comforting sound of his heartbeat. My body is trembling and I don't want to show pain or weakness, so I just have to hope is that my leg will be better soon. If it doesn't heal, I won't be able to hunt anymore.

Closing my eyes, I realize I can feel my warm blood still running from the wound, pooling in my fur.

CHAPTER FIFTY-TWO

THE MORNING SUN BRINGS light and warmth, although the land is still wet all around us. Having walked all through the night, the girls have finally stopped at the edge of a field, and some have gone to look for food in the forest while others are too exhausted to do anything other than sit and hope.

Harry has carried me all the way, and although I can tell that he's tired, I feel safe in his arms. Finally, however, he gets down onto his knees and sets me on the damp grass.

I immediately get to my feet, although the pain in my injured leg is intense. I slip and have to get up again, and then the same thing happens.

"Easy, boy," Harry says. "Don't struggle."

I try yet again to get up, and this time I just about manage. I'm getting old now, and all the wounds I've picked up since leaving Jon's cabin have begun to take their toll, but this fresh injury to my leg is the worst yet.

"You'll be okay," Harry continues, forcing a faint smile. "You're a tough boy, Ben. Your leg's already stopped bleeding, so you'll just be left with a cool limp. One day we'll find you a lady dog, and you can impress her with all your war stories."

He reaches out and ruffles the hair on my flank, and I sit in an attempt to take the weight off my leg. After a moment, I start licking the wound, and I find that blood is dried in my damp, matted fur.

"We didn't find anything," Sophie says a short while later, as she and some other girls emerge from the forest. "No berries, nothing edible. No water, either."

She glances at Harry, and I can see the fear in her eyes.

"What do we do?" one of the other girls asks. "There are twelve of us. Where are we gonna go?"

"Eleven," someone else says.

Sophie turns and starts counting the girls.

"Where's Lily?" she asks finally.

"She was with us when we left the barn," another girl replies, before holding up the gun. "She asked me to carry this. I noticed she seemed to be drifting away from the rest of us, but I thought she still..."

Silence falls for a moment.

"Did she just go off by herself?" Sophie stammers. "Why would she do that?"

"She shot those men," another girl points out. "She basically executed them. Maybe she just... Maybe she didn't feel like she fit in with the rest of us anymore.

I'm kinda... I mean, I know this sounds bad, but after she did it, she seemed different. Maybe it's better that she's gone."

"We could just stay here," the girl next to her suggests. "It can't be completely beyond us to find something to eat, and then to grow more food. I saw some sheep not far away, maybe we can herd them together."

"And then what?" Sophie asks.

The girl hesitates for a moment. "Eat them?"

"That's gross," another girl says, scrunching her nose up. "I can't kill a sheep."

"We might not have a choice," Sophie mutters, before looking over at a few other girls who are resting on the grass. She seems lost in thought for a moment. "I could do it," she adds finally.

"Do what?" the girl next to her asks.

"Kill a sheep. I don't want to, but I could do it if it's the only way to eat."

"Me too," Harry adds, still stroking my flank as I continue to lick my injured leg.

"We can all take jobs," Sophie tells the others. "I'm sure everyone here has something they can contribute. We can learn to farm, and we can figure out the details later, but we're not idiots. We *can* do this. We just have to be patient."

"We need food *now*!" the girl behind her points out, her voice filled with fear. "Not in six months' time, not next week, not tomorrow... We need it now, and we need water too, or people are going to start dying."

"At least we were fed back in that barn,"

someone says quietly. "Even if we had to..."

Her voice trails off, and everyone sits in silence for a moment.

My leg is hurting more and more, but I know I can't whimper. I can't show them that I'm weak.

"What's that?" a girl asks suddenly, with a hint of concern in her voice. "Look! Over there!"

They all turn. When I follow their gazes, I see a plume of smoke in the distance, heading this way.

"It's a train," Harry stammers, getting to his feet. "I saw one yesterday. There's a train-line, and someone's got some steam trains running. I almost... I almost thought it was a hallucination."

"Where do they go?" Sophie asks. "Where do they come from?"

"I don't know," he continues, turning to her, "but someone threw some food out the window for me. That must mean they're friendly, right?"

"Do you think they'd take us with them?" another girl says, as she and all the others slowly start to stand.

Some are too injured to stay up unaided, but they're given help.

"There's a bend in the track over there," Harry continues, pointing past the trees. "The train has to slow there, we could jump on."

"And go where?" Sophie asks.

"Anywhere! Away from here! Somewhere better!"

She turns to him, her eyes filled with shock. "But what if -"

"It can't be worse than starving in a field!" he shouts. "I'm not saying the rest of the world is back on its feet, but someone somewhere has got things running, and all the evidence so far makes it seem like they're friendly! Come on, if we don't take this chance, we might not get another!"

"Sounds good to me," another girl says, as she helps a friend start limping toward the train-line.

"Me too."

Slowly the girls starts heading across the field, as the train gets closer and closer.

"We don't know what we're getting into," Sophie stammers. "Those trains could take us somewhere horrible!"

"They could," Harry replies, helping another girl up, "or they could take us somewhere we won't die of starvation. I'm willing to take that risk. Bring Ben. You'll need to carry him."

With that, he turns and starts struggling after the others, helping the limping girl. I try to follow, but my leg is too painful and I can't quite keep up with him.

"Bring the dog," Sophie tells one of the girls finally, before turning and helping one of the others.

Over the next few minutes, they all stagger toward the bend in the train-line. I hobble along with them, just about managing to keep pace with the slowest, but I'm starting to panic as I see Harry getting further and further ahead. My injured leg is starting to sting, and I feel as if it might buckle at any moment.

The fastest girls are at the bend now, waiting as the train races toward them, and a moment later I hear a screeching sound as the engine slows for the bend.

"Jump on!" a man shouts from a window at the front of the train. "We'll take you to the city!"

The train creaks and groans as it takes the bend, and the girls start running. One of the wagons has an open door on the side, and already a couple of the girls have managed to jump onboard. Turning, they lean out and start helping the others.

"Bring Ben!" Harry yells as he helps the injured girl onto the train and then climbs up.

"Bring the dog!" Sophie shouts.

Everyone's running now. Even the sick and wounded are being helped by the other girls, and I have to dart between their legs to avoid getting trampled. There was a time when I'd have been able to easily outrun them all, but my legs are hurting and I'm starting to feel old, so right now even the walking wounded are able to go faster. They're all so focused on the train, they haven't noticed that I'm struggling.

"Hurry!" Sophie yells. "It'll start speeding up soon!"

Ahead, the rest of the girls are finally managing to clamber up into the wagon.

I'm running as fast as I can manage, but I feel as if my chest is going to explode. One by one, the final couple of girls are helped up, and a moment later the train starts to accelerate as it passes the final part of the bend. Only one girl is still running now, and she's already way ahead of me.

"Ben!" Harry shouts suddenly, and I see him up ahead, leaning out of the train with his hand reaching toward me. "Hurry!"

The last girl is struggling slightly, but Sophie grabs her arm and drags her onto the train, leaving me half running, half limping as fast as I can manage. The wind is rippling through my fur, but my legs are spitting pain through the rest of my body and the train is getting faster and faster.

"Get Ben!" Harry yells. "Somebody get Ben!"

He reaches toward me and I start running faster, desperate to get closer so he can haul me up into the wagon.

At the same time, the train picks up more speed and starts to out-pace me, pulling ahead no matter how hard I try to keep up.

"Ben!" Harry shouts, his voice sounding much further away now.

I can see him up ahead, with his hand still reaching out, but the train's wagons are rushing past me. Finally the last part of the train pulls away and I'm left running next to an empty track. I keep going, but my tired, injured legs are already slowing me and finally I come to a halt. Desperately out of breath and panting, I watch as the train speeds away.

"Ben!" Harry carry calls out, but now his voice is mostly just lost on the wind.

The tracks next to me are still humming as I stand panting, watching the departing train. As the hum fades, however, I'm left all alone, and the only sound now is the rustling of nearby trees.

Everyone's gone.

Watching the train, I'm shocked that I wasn't

able to keep up. Then again, my legs are hurting so much, there's no way I could have run any faster. I remember when I used to run for miles and miles with Jon. I could easily outpace him, and I used to have to stop and wait for him to catch up. We'd go all around the lake near the cabin, running and walking for hours, and I swear I never once felt weak or tired.

Those days are long gone now.

And as the train races in the distance and disappears from view, I think of Harry in the wagon and I realize one more thing.

He'll be fine.

I don't know where he's going, but nothing about the train gave me reason to worry. There was no scent of blood, or fear, Wherever it takes him, and wherever it takes his sister and those other girls, they'll be safe.

I watch the horizon for a few more minutes, just in case the train comes back, but then finally I cross the tracks and limp out across the next field. After running alongside the train for so long, my body aches like never before, and I'm still out of breath as I make my way down the sloping hill. I stumble a couple of times, and my collar jangles slightly, reminding me of the times Jon used to put it around my neck whenever I'd had a bath. I used to hate baths, and once they were over I used to race around the apartment at full speed, trying to get dry. And Jon would laugh at me.

When I get to the bottom of the hill, I find myself at the edge of another field. I stop for a moment, but my leg is still throbbing with pain. Ahead, several sheep are grazing, and a couple of them glance at me as I step forward and start limping through the grass. My plan is to keep going, to cross this field and then find another, and maybe to discover a place where I can hunt rabbits, but my bones are aching and I have to sit down for a moment once I reach a patch of grass near the sheep.

I've been tired before, but never like this.

This feels different.

Finally I have no choice but to settle down and roll onto my side. I'm still panting, and my body is starting to feel so much heavier than ever before.

I should have got my breath back by now.

A sheep comes closer, clearly curious about me, although it doesn't seem threatened. It simply chews on some forbs and grass, while keeping its eyes fixed on me. A moment later, I hear another sheep nearby, but I don't have the energy to turn and look. They certainly stink, and for a few seconds my nose is filled with fresh scents, but slowly I realize that several other smells are tugging at my senses.

I can smell Jon.

Not just him, but his cabin.

And his old jacket.

And his car.

And my basket at his house in the city.

Even that old giraffe toy I had as a puppy, the one that I eventually tore to pieces.

And I can smell Julie too. Her perfume and her clothes.

The wind ripples through my fur.

I'm still out of breath.

I close my eyes. Not to sleep, just to rest. I just need to stay here for a few minutes and get my breath back, even if my eyes already feel so heavy. The memories of old scents now flood my senses, and I feel a wave of contentment as I realize that it's almost as if I've made it back home. Jon's scent is so strong now, and Julie's too, that with my eyes closed I can almost believe that I really *have* made it back to the place I want to be more than any other in the world.

My breathing is getting shallow, but that's okay. I don't even mind the sheep as they continue to chew grass next to me.

I'll open my eyes again soon.

For now, though, I just want to keep them closed while the scents of my old life wash over me. And as those scents become stronger, all the pain seems to lift from my body.

I can definitely smell Jon.

Somehow, I manage to get back up and start running again. I run past the sheep, picking up speed as I race across the field, and all the tiredness seems to fall away from my legs. I run and I run and I run, following a familiar scent that seems to be coming from just over the top of the next hill. I can't remember the last time I felt so strong and so powerful, and running feels easier with each bound.

I'm young again.

Also by Amy Cross

The Soul Auction

"I saw a woman on the beach. I watched her face a demon."

Thirty years after her mother's death, Alice Ashcroft is drawn back to the coastal English town of Curridge. Somebody in Curridge has been reviewing Alice's novels online, and in those reviews there have been tantalizing hints at a hidden truth. A truth that seems to be linked to her dead mother.

"Thirty years ago, there was a soul auction."

Once she reaches Curridge, Alice finds strange things happening all around her. Something attacks her car. A figure watches her on the beach at night. And when she tries to find the person who has been reviewing her books, she makes a horrific discovery.

What really happened to Alice's mother thirty years ago? Who was she talking to, just moments before dropping dead on the beach? What caused a huge rockfall that nearly tore a nearby cliff-face in half? And what sinister presence is lurking in the grounds of the local church?

Also by Amy Cross

American Coven

He kidnapped three women and held them in his basement. He thought they couldn't fight back. He was wrong...

Snatched from the street near her home, Holly Carter is taken to a rural house and thrown down into a stone basement. She meets two other women who have also been kidnapped, and soon Holly learns about the horrific rituals that take place in the house. Eventually, she's called upstairs to take her place in the ice bath.

As her nightmare continues, however, Holly learns about a mysterious power that exists in the basement, and which the three women might be able to harness. When they finally manage to get through the metal door, however, the women have no idea that their fight for freedom is going to stretch out for more than a decade, or that it will culminate in a final, devastating demonstration of their new-found powers.

Also by Amy Cross

The Ash House

Why would anyone ever return to a haunted house?

For Diane Mercer the answer is simple. She's dying of cancer, and she wants to know once and for all whether ghosts are real.

Heading home with her young son, Diane is determined to find out whether the stories are real. After all, everyone else claimed to see and hear strange things in the house over the years. Everyone except Diane had some kind of experience in the house, or in the little ash house in the yard.

As Diane explores the house where she grew up, however, her son is exploring the yard and the forest. And while his mother might be struggling to come to terms with her own impending death, Daniel Mercer is puzzled by fleeting appearances of a strange little girl who seems drawn to the ash house, and by strange, rasping coughs that he keeps hearing at night.

The Ash House is a horror novel about a woman who desperately wants to know what will happen to her when she dies, and about a boy who uncovers the shocking truth about a young girl's murder.

Also by Amy Cross

Haunted

Twenty years ago, the ghost of a dead little girl drove
Sheriff Michael Blaine to his death.

Now, that same ghost is coming for his daughter.

Returning to the small town where she grew up, Alex
Roberts is determined to live a normal, quiet life. For the
residents of Railham, however, she's an unwelcome
reminder of the town's darkest hour.

Twenty years ago, nine-year-old Mo Garvey was found
brutally murdered in a nearby forest. Everyone thinks
that Alex's father was responsible, but if the killer was
brought to justice, why is the ghost of Mo Garvey still
after revenge?

And how far will the real killer go to protect his secret,
when Alex starts getting closer to the truth?

Haunted is a horror novel about a woman who has to
face her past, about a town that would rather forget, and
about a little girl who refuses to let death stand in her
way.

Also by Amy Cross

The Curse of Wetherley House

"If you walk through that door, Evil Mary will get you."

When she agrees to visit a supposedly haunted house
with an old friend, Rosie assumes she'll encounter
nothing more scary than a few creaks and bumps in the
night. Even the legend of Evil Mary doesn't put her off.
After all, she knows ghosts aren't real. But when Mary
makes her first appearance, Rosie realizes she might
already be trapped.

For more than a century, Wetherley House has been
cursed. A horrific encounter on a remote road in the late
1800's has already caused a chain of misery and pain for
all those who live at the house. Wetherley House was
abandoned long ago, after a terrible discovery in the
basement, something has remained undetected within its
room. And even the local children know that Evil Mary
waits in the house for anyone foolish enough to walk
through the front door.

Before long, Rosie realizes that her entire life has been
defined by the spirit of a woman who died in agony. Can
she become the first person to escape Evil Mary, or will
she fall victim to the same fate as the house's other
occupants?

Also by Amy Cross

The Ghosts of Hexley Airport

Ten years ago, more than two hundred people died in a horrific plane crash at Hexley Airport.

Today, some say their ghosts still haunt the terminal building.

When she starts her new job at the airport, working a night shift as part of the security team, Casey assumes the stories about the place can't be true. Even when she has a strange encounter in a deserted part of the departure hall, she's certain that ghosts aren't real.

Soon, however, she's forced to face the truth. Not only is there something haunting the airport's buildings and tarmac, but a sinister force is working behind the scenes to replicate the circumstances of the original accident. And as a snowstorm moves in, Hexley Airport looks set to witness yet another disaster.

Also by Amy Cross

The Devil, the Witch and the Whore
(The Deal book 1)

"Leave the forest alone. Whatever's out there, just let it be. Don't make it angry."

When a horrific discovery is made at the edge of town, Sheriff James Kopperud realizes the answers he seeks might be waiting beyond in the vast forest. But everybody in the town of Deal knows that there's something out there in the forest, something that should never be disturbed. A deal was made long ago, a deal that was supposed to keep the town safe. And if he insists on investigating the murder of a local girl, James is going to have to break that deal and head out into the wilderness.

Meanwhile, James has no idea that his estranged daughter Ramsey has returned to town. Ramsey is running from something, and she thinks she can find safety in the vast tunnel system that runs beneath the forest. Before long, however, Ramsey finds herself coming face to face with creatures that hide in the shadows. One of these creatures is known as the devil, and another is known as the witch. They're both waiting for the whore to arrive, but for very different reasons. And soon Ramsey is offered a terrible deal, one that could save or destroy the entire town, and maybe even the world.

Also by Amy Cross

Asylum
(The Asylum Trilogy book 1)

"No-one ever leaves Lakehurst. The staff, the patients, the ghosts... Once you're here, you're stuck forever."

After shooting her little brother dead, Annie Radford is sent to Lakehurst psychiatric hospital for assessment. Hearing voices in her head, Annie is forced to undergo experimental new treatments devised by a mysterious old man who lives in the hospital's attic. It soon becomes clear that the hospital's staff, led by the vicious Nurse Winter, are hiding something horrific at Lakehurst.

As Annie struggles to survive the hospital, she learns more about Nurse Winter's own story. Once a promising young medical student, Kirsten Winter also heard voices in her head. Voices that traveled a long way to reach her. Voices that have a plan of their own. Voices that will stop at nothing to get what they want.

What kind of signals are being transmitted from the basement of the hospital? Who is the old man in the attic? Why are living human brains kept in jars? And what is the dark secret that lurks at the heart of the hospital?

Also by Amy Cross

The Ghost of Molly Holt

"Molly Holt is dead. There's nothing to fear in this house."

When three teenagers set out to explore an abandoned house in the middle of a forest, they think they've found the location where the infamous Molly Holt video was filmed.

They've found much more than that...

Tim doesn't believe in ghosts, but he has a crush on a girl who does. That's why he ends up taking her out to the house, and it's also why he lets her take his only flashlight. But as they explore the house together, Tim and Becky start to realize that something else might be lurking in the shadows.

Something that, ten years ago, suffered unimaginable pain.

Something that won't rest until a terrible wrong has been put right.

Printed in Great
Britain
by Amazon

32015097R00210